LIFE IS STRANGE

Heatwaves

Also available from Titan Books:

Life is Strange: Steph's Story

LIFE IS STRANGE™
Heatwaves

BRITTNEY MORRIS

TITAN BOOKS

Life is Strange: Heatwaves
Print edition ISBN: 9781789099645
E-book edition ISBN: 9781789099652

Published by Titan Books
A division of Titan Publishing Group Ltd
144 Southwark Street, London SE1 0UP
www.titanbooks.com

First edition: July 2024
10 9 8 7 6 5 4 3 2 1

A CIP catalogue record for this title is available from the British Library.

Printed and bound by CPI Group (UK) Ltd, Croydon CR0 4YY.

To the Life is Strange fan
community, for loving these
characters as I do.

Get in, losers, we're going
back to Colorado.

Yee... and I cannot stress
this enough... haw.

The Timeline – Author's Note

Life is Strange: Heatwaves occurs in a timeline where Steph and Alex hit the road out of Haven Springs to chase their rambling band fantasy together. Whether your game choices led to pg. 1 of this book or not, I hope you enjoy the ride and continue to add your own spin to Life Is Strange's world of infinite possibilities!

LIFE IS STRANGE™

Heatwaves

1: In the Wild

Steph cranks the volume.

"Drivin' to the middle of nowhere," she belts, arms thundering out an air drum solo, "with peaches on my plate."

The urge to add my air guitar to the mix is overwhelming, but I keep my hands on the wheel and find something else to focus on. The trees stand tall and still as we fly past, skies clear and air blowing hot through the window.

"You know what that song is about, right?" I ask.

Steph keeps the drums going and smirks at me. "Ass, obviously."

"Pretty sure the peach emoji didn't exist in 1985," I grin.

"Were you *there*?" she asks, jumping back into the lyrics with, "A plateful of peaches, and someone to share them with." And winks at me.

"Too much," I giggle. I can't help it. She's so goofy. "So, for real, do you know this song's origin story?"

This was one of the first songs my brother Gabe and I heard on our dad's record player. It sat in the living room for so many years before Gabe asked to dust it off and try it out.

I miss him so bad it hurts. Still.

Steph rolls her eyes. "Yes, I do. Some guy took too much of something, squeezed a bunch of peaches, and wrote a song about how horny he was. The source of all great songwriting."

I'm afraid to ask.

"Horniness? Or 'too much of something?' Or... peaches?"

"All three. When we get to Fort Collins, we need to find something to smoke, and squeeze some peaches."

"*Stop*," I laugh. "I will tuck and roll right out of this car." My cheeks feel hot. My whole head feels hot.

I glance at her again.

She's smiling at me, an aura of golden light glowing around her head.

"What?" she asks, knowing very well what. To know Steph is to be constantly embarrassed as hell, and also delighted. I can't believe I'm really here. With her.

I shake my head and turn back to the road.

"You're reading me again, aren't you?" she asks.

"You know I can't read you unless I reach my hand out to you."

"But you can see I'm happy. At least, I hope you can. And that I'm excited."

Of *course* I can. And I soak in every beautiful, tingly, warm ray of gold.

"For Fort Collins?" I ask, our first destination.

"For the *world*," she says, reaching over and squeezing my knee. "With you."

If she had my powers, she would see I'm glowing too. I'm not even sure with what. Gold for joy? Purple for the tidal wave of butterflies I'm feeling right now? I look down at her hand on my knee and quickly turn my attention back to the road.

"So," she says, turning down the music and nestling cozily into her seat, "when we get there, what are you going to do first?"

I breathe, and think.

"I, um..." What does one *do* there? Fort Collins is so... *big*. Compared to what I've gotten used to, anyway. Foster homes used to be my whole world, each one the size of a cardboard box. I caught glimpses of Portland on nights when I could sneak out for acoustic shows and underground raves. I never really got a sense of the whole city. And then there's Haven

Springs, which is no city at all, but a tiny community in a big wide world of mountains and open sky. I don't know how to calibrate anymore.

As if she can read my mind: "See a farmers market? Rent a bike? Smoke weed?"

"All three."

"At the same time? I like it."

I chuckle. But I have to agree. All three sounds nice.

"You glad we left?" she asks me.

"Of course! Haven Springs was great to both of us, but… it's time we moved on. Did what we want, you know?"

"Rockin' out on stage," she dreams aloud.

"Playing whatever." I'm surprised to hear the dreaminess in my own voice too. This feeling of the open road, literally and, I guess, metaphorically, feels… free.

She pulls something out of her pocket. From the corner of my eye, I can see that it's purple, and fits in her palm. She shakes it.

"Of *course* you brought a shaker egg."

"Can't go nowhere fast without rhythm," she sings, tapping her free hand on the dashboard, her occupied hand shaking the egg in tandem. "Can't go nowhere at all without time."

I join in, lending my vocals, my fingers itching to strum my guitar along with the *shik-shik-shik* of the egg.

"Can't go nowhere good without you, babe. You're the rhythm to my rhyme."

I study Steph, all aglow as she sings with me, like we don't have a care in the world. New city, new careers, new dream.

But, we've got each other.

My mind drifts back to the word *babe*, and I realize how effortlessly it rolled off my tongue. Off both our tongues. Could I… call her that one day? Would she let me? Or would she say it's cliché?

Then, suddenly, something deep and dark settles into my stomach, something that twists and coils. Something's… wrong.

What's the color of feeling like you've forgotten something?

"Holy shit, the oil!" I exclaim, just as a soft clicking sound starts *tick-tick-tick*ing away under the hood.

"The oil? Didn't you check it before we left?" exclaims Steph. She takes her feet down from the dash, so I know shit just got serious.

"I-I thought I did! I guess I forgot!" Ugh, I had literally one job. Steph had to load our instruments and backpacks in the car after buying this junker from her friend Hector. All I had to do was keep it on the road, keep all four tires on it, and check the oil.

"What do I do?" I panic, feeling my breathing spiral into something I don't recognize.

"Stop!" screams Steph.

I slam on the brake *way* harder than I needed to, and the car lurches. Everything in the back seat and trunk flies forward—our instruments and most things we own. My guitar case slams into the back of my seat, and falls back down and hits the center console sticking into the back seat, letting out a sour *twangggg*.

Steph and I sit frozen in this car for what seems like forever, just catching our breath.

I can't look at her.

How could I when this was her dream? *Our* dream. Taking our music on the road, performing for new people in new places, the Fort Collins Lamplighter Festival up first. We were finally starting the lives we'd dreamed of for months after getting a taste of the world. We were finally doing the thing.

And now we're stuck somewhere on the way…

Wait, where the hell even are we?

As if we're both thinking the same thing—and I'm sure we are—we look around. Down the road ahead of us, as far as we can see, there are zero street signs. Not even a speed limit.

I glance at the rearview mirror. No street signs back the way we came either.

"What's the last city sign you remember seeing?" I ask her, praying for something, anything.

"Um… something like… Barbell? Bar something."

"Had enough of bars lately, thanks."

And then she surprises me by *laughing*.

I look at her, confused.

"I'm laughing at how right you are," chuckles Steph, leaning back against her seat and pressing her hand to her forehead. "Anywhere is better than the Black Lantern, huh?"

She sighs, content. "Can you believe we made it all the way out here?" she asks.

I'm already feeling the effects of the A/C having been off for twenty seconds. But no, I can't believe it. It's only been weeks since I lost Gabe, since Steph and I lost a friend in Jed. No, more than a friend. A father.

It was right for us to leave. What else would we do? Stay in Haven Springs and put on shows for the few dozen people who live there?

I guess that wouldn't have been so bad… I look at Steph, and I realize all over again that I'd go anywhere in the world, as long as she's there with me. I've never had a best friend before. Not like this.

Not even the words "best friend" feel right.

I look around. The trees definitely look like they're turning their autumn hues. So why is it so hellishly hot out here?

"All by ourselves," she continues, swinging the door open. "Welp, time to find Barbarella. Maybe they have peaches."

We walk forever.

Well, not forever, but long enough that the gold aura around Steph's head has disappeared.

"Walkin' to the middle of nowhere," she reprises, panting as she slings her duffel over her other shoulder for the fiftieth time.

"With peaches on my plate," I jump in, my guitar heavy on my back. What can I do but lend my voice? She needs to know she's not alone out here in this sweltering heat. But I look back for only a second, anxiety welling up as I wipe away beads of sweat from my forehead.

I can feel my hair sticking to my face. Some is plastered to my glasses.

"Um, hey," I say, stopping and pulling off my guitar case for a moment of reprieve, setting it down on the pavement as gently as I can. I still feel the need to apologize to it. Putting it on the ground, even in these circumstances, seems… callous. I pat the top of the case to ease the guilt.

"Yeah?" she answers me, stopping and turning around. "Whoa, you trying to fry your case?"

She gestures to my instrument, and I quickly pick it up again. What's the color of guilt?

"That's… actually why I stopped," I say, unable to hide the exasperation in my voice. I gesture over my shoulder. "You don't think your drum kit might melt in the car? Shouldn't we, you know, stay close and open the doors for it? Maybe a car will drive by eventually."

A smile plays at the corner of Steph's mouth, and she drops her duffel full of both our clothes and rests her hands on her hips. I notice the sweat glistening on her neck. A droplet runs over her collarbone, and I swallow.

"You really want to turn around and walk twenty minutes back to the car?" she asks, her voice playful. "When we haven't seen a car all this time?"

She has a point, because of course she does.

I stay silent. There's not much else to say.

"Maybe… the sun will set soon?"

"You wanna be out here when night falls?" she asks.

Would it be such a wild suggestion?

"I mean, we have granola bars, and crackers."

"And coyotes?" she asks. "We had those in Seattle too. Trust me, they're scarier than you'd think. Creepy as hell, and they travel in packs."

That's enough to keep my ass walking. But she continues anyway.

"Besides, Alex, we came out here for an adventure!" she exclaims, fists in the air. "And dammit, we've found one! We've got three days before we have to be in Fort Collins. Let's, you know, see the sights. Even if it is just trees."

"And pavement."

"And pavement."

She turns and walks on, and I look ahead at the heatwaves shimmering in the middle of the road.

We walk until the car shrinks to a dot behind us, and a tiny green highway sign appears in the distance before us.

"Look!" exclaims Steph. "That has to be a sign for Barbarella."

"That has a Z in it," I say, squinting to read it. "Beelzebub?"

"Ah shit, we're walking into a demon cult," she jokes. "Or a demon *sex* cult." But I'm not fucking joking.

"Yo, what if B-town *is* a bad idea?" I ask. "A place with no cars coming in or out is… maybe not somewhere we want to be?"

Steph is looking past me.

"Prayers answered."

I follow her gaze and spot a car in the distance behind us, flickering with the heat of the road. I find myself hoping that even if this person doesn't stop for us, maybe they could spare some water?

"Hey!" calls Steph, jumping up and down and flailing her arms. The duffel drops to the ground beside her. "Hey, help, please!"

"Steph, we don't even know who this is!" I whisper. I don't know why I'm whispering. This person is still too far off to even see us, probably, let alone hear us. "What if they're a serial killer?"

"Then we have a chance to solve a murder," she says, without missing a beat.

What?!

"And what if they really do run a sex cult?"

Steph smiles at me, a laugh threatening to pour forth.

"Then let's hope they're hot."

"What the hell?!" I laugh.

"Hey, help!" hollers Steph, stepping dangerously close to the road. The vehicle is near enough now to make out that it's a little blue pickup. An old one. Probably older than me.

The truck pulls up, slows, crawls to a stop, and a guy leans out the window looking exactly how I imagined he would. Forties. Slightly disheveled. Checkered shirt with the sleeves rolled up to the elbows. He looks like one of those guys from the sun exposure experiments where half the subjects' faces are scarred from constant UV, and the other half is mostly pristine, because he's been driving the same sixty-mile stretch of road all his life.

"You ladies lost?" he asks. His voice doesn't match his face. It's… soft. Gentle.

I study him, but he's looking at Steph. Steph glances at me before turning back to him and stepping up to the truck.

"We could use a ride to… uh…" She looks down the road and squints at the street sign, in a last-ditch effort to say the actual name of the town.

"Barb-zal?"

"Yeah…" She hesitates, looking at me again. "Barb-zal."

The man smiles. I don't know if it's a friendly smile or a knowing smile, which is only contextually different from a sinister one. Maybe if I could read him…

A glistening golden aura grows around his head, warm like summer winds in Midwestern fields, soft like cotton balls. Nostalgia floods me, lifts my insides 'til I'm so light I feel like I could fly. This man *loves* the thought of Barbazal.

"That's my home. Born and raised. Name's Silas."

"How's it hanging, Silas?" asks Steph, picking up the duffel full of our few belongings, and—to my horror—heaving it into the back of the truck.

I catch her hand just as she lets go of the bag.

"What are you doing?!" I hiss.

At first, she looks startled, then her mouth curves into a grin as she glances down at my hand, still around her wrist.

"Do I look afraid?" she asks.

There's no gold halo around her, but I study her eyes, beaming with hope. All peace. No fear.

"No," I admit, "but maybe you should be? You wanna climb into a random truck with a random guy?"

Just because he's all warm and fuzzy about Barbazal doesn't mean he's warm and fuzzy.

"He's not a random guy. He's Silas."

But before I can jump in with just how unhelpful it is to know his name—if that's really his name at all—she continues.

"And besides," she says, breaking away from my grasp and reaching for the guitar strap slung over my shoulder, "the sooner we get to 'Barb-zal,' the sooner I can get us more oil. The sooner we get more oil, the sooner we get back on the road. And the sooner we get back on the road…"

She lifts my guitar up over the truck door and lays it in the bed as gently as a newborn baby.

"The sooner we can get to Fort Collins," I finish for her.

"And then onto the rest of the world," she smiles, her eyes sparkling.

She winks and walks up to the passenger door as casually and cozily as if this were Ryan's truck.

I sigh, because she's right. She's charging ahead into the Colorado wilderness to find motor oil and sustenance, because it's our *only* way forward. Maybe if I suck it up and pretend we're choosing to get into this strange car with this strange man and drive to a strange town we've never heard of, it'll feel like a choice. But as I stare at our duffel and my guitar case in the truck bed, and I rub my wrist to quell this unsettling wriggling I feel in my stomach, I can't help but think…

"You comin', Alex?"

…this doesn't feel like a choice.

And now Silas knows my real name. I take back what I said earlier. Knowing someone's name suddenly feels *very* personal.

I look up at the driver's side, where Silas's head turns and I hear him say something softly. Steph laughs, that gold aura glowing around her head again. Silas has one to match. He's still happy.

That means we should be safe, right?

2: Barbazal

The truck smells exactly how I expect it to.

Like ass.

But Silas is warm. A goofball. He's in the middle of an improv session right now, which he claims are world famous.

"Had my bacon, had my eggs, had my coffee today. Got my energy drink and I'm on my way."

Steph glances over her shoulder at me with a face that asks, *Where else could you find free entertainment like this?*

I smile at her optimism. I stare out the window, getting lost in the scenery, and notice the first sign we've seen in a while.

Jonah Macon for Senate, it reads.

I've heard of that guy, but I don't know much about him.

Jonah Macon will bring home the bacon!

I roll my eyes. Whoever he is, he's not afraid of doing the expected.

"Got my liquid sunshine and friendly faces," continues Silas, "Um…"

Silas goes quiet, and Steph jumps in for him. "We're all piled in this truck, and we're off to the races!"

"Woohoo!" whoops Silas. "You're a natural! Y'all musicians or something?"

"Actually, yeah!" replies Steph.

I glance over my shoulder through the back window of the cab at my guitar case, happily nestled in the bed of the truck. I wish I'd brought it in here with me. My fingers itch to pluck the strings, to sit cross-legged back here, shut my eyes, and let the music carry me away. I think of Gabe, whose arms would have been long enough to reach through the window and get it for me. He'd insist I play.

He'd insist I do what makes me happy.

I'm facing my fears, Gabe. Finding new spaces, I continue the song in my head.

I watch the trees go by as I let Silas's truck take me to wherever Silas decides. He doesn't *have* to stop in Barbazal. What if he does and Barbazal's not safe anyway?

You know how I feel about brand new places.

"Hey," comes Steph's voice. I'm yanked back into the conversation. "Alex, you okay?"

"Oh, yeah. I'm just, um…" I look around for a distraction and my eyes find the crate of water on the floor beside my feet. "Silas, mind if I have a bottle of water?"

His eyes find me in the rearview mirror, and they narrow so slightly that at first I wonder if I'm seeing things.

"Yeah, uh, sure! Go ahead," he says. But the aura around his head fades from brilliant gold into a sad, ever-bluing cobalt.

"Are you sure it's okay?" I ask. Steph cocks an eyebrow and looks from me to Silas.

His adjust his hands on the steering wheel and lets out a long, deep breath.

"I don't mean to be inhospitable," he apologizes. "We're just… short on water, is all. Mind keeping it to one bottle each?"

Steph nods. "Sure," she says, reaching into the back and finding one. I reach down and do the same. They're warm. Of course they are. It's approximately five hundred degrees out here, and if this truck has A/C, Silas isn't using it.

"So," I begin, too curious to let the question go unasked. "Why is Barbazal short on water?"

I take a swig, letting the clear liquid slake the thirst I didn't realize I'd been carrying. I immediately want three more bottles.

Silas lets out another sigh, and his eyes meet mine in the rearview mirror again. The blue aura around his head brings out the depth of them as he studies me.

"It's a long story, miss," he says, his voice heavy, "and we're already to Barbazal."

The truck slows, and I look around as we turn right down a dirt road. The trees are sparse here—tall and austere. Dry. Everything about them looks pained, bending like old war-weary soldiers.

"Woah," says Steph, probably thinking the same thing I am. Feels like we're driving through a graveyard.

"Just up this way to Elias's shop," says Silas.

Another sign.

Vote Jonah Macon, it reads, followed by *Beat Lazy Maisie*. Jonah vs. Maisie I guess? Never heard of the latter.

"Who's Jonah Macon?" I ask. Steph side-eyes me, probably because I just rocketed this conversation headlong into politics. But I couldn't help myself. My chest tightens, and I hope she intercepts the telepathic message I'm beaming to her—god, telepathy would be really convenient right now—*Sorry, Steph.*

"Little Jonie? He was born and raised here. Now he's a big-shot senator. Or, hopeful anyway. Long as he beats that snake woman Crazy Maisie."

I tense at that word. *Crazy*.

I rub my thumb along my wrist, a comforting motion my therapist taught me to do when I'm stressed. *Crazy*—I've heard that word so many times. From others. From myself until just months ago. So many adult faces staring me down with disdain, using synonyms they thought were kinder.

No, less legally incriminating.

Insane.

Unwell.

Unbalanced.

Disturbed.

Demented.

I haven't heard the word *crazy* in so long, and it's still too soon.

Steph brings me back to the present.

"Who's… Crazy Maisie?" she asks gingerly. Clearly she's not sure she wants to know the answer. Neither am I.

"Maisie Dorsey? She took my rain barrel away," Silas sighs. There's the faintest bite to his words, an edge he's suppressing, like he ate something that's turning his stomach. That blue wavering aura that had been pulsing since I brought up the water bottle fades from blue to indigo, to purple, to magenta, and heats up, searing and prickly, all the way to red.

Searing hot, blazing, *angry* red, that blares in my ears like a siren, sending shockwaves of pain through my head.

"Passed a piece-of-shit legislation s'posed to be about conserving water, when it's really all for show to get the swing votes in the middle. She's as right wing as they come. Don't give a damn about the environment or nothin'—" He stops himself, like a dinner host realizing he's upsetting his guests. "Sorry," he says, taking a hand off the wheel, picking up a cloth from the dashboard that looks like it was used as a dipstick cleaner in a past life, and dragging it across the back of his neck. "Got carried away there for a minute. I'm sure Maisie's a nice lady, but… she's just… so misguided. Could use some common sense. Know what I mean? She ain't been here, in Barbazal. She's in Denver, where there ain't no water shortage. How's she know what the hell Barbazal needs?"

Steph throws a look at me that I can't quite read. It's not quite fear. Apprehension? Is she nervous?

Not enough to warrant a purple aura, apparently. She looks back to Silas.

"So, I'm guessing Jonah has your vote?"

Smart. Get him back to a topic he enjoys. The truck wobbles slightly on the road as we approach town. Little buildings grow bigger, although sparsely placed. Looks almost like a ghost town.

"My vote and my sword," he jokes.

We make our way through the town square, where more signs for Jonah litter the streets. Every telephone pole, every stop sign, every lawn has a sign that boasts the owner loves Jonah Macon or hates Maisie Dorsey, or both.

We drive up to a building with a big, rusty sign: *Elias's Spark*.

"This here's the place!" declares Silas, swinging the door open and hopping out before the truck has just barely begun to idle. Steph gives me a comforting smile before turning and hopping out of the passenger side.

My door opens and Silas is there to greet me with a beaming smile, hand out to help me down.

"Thanks," I offer. Now that I can see him up close, his eyes look heavy, showing every bit of his age. Forties? Fifties? However old he is, he's clearly been through a lot.

And a lot of days without sunscreen.

He helps me down and adjusts his baseball cap on his head, marching to the back of the truck, where Steph is already heaving our duffel out.

"No, no, let me get that," he says. "My back might be older than yours, but my biceps lift more each day, I guarantee it."

"Careful with the assumptions," she says, chuckling, "I'm a drummer. My double-kit pedals alone are heavier than that thing."

"Too-shay!" he says, in the worst French accent I've ever heard. I have to smile at his heart, though.

I look around. Elias's Spark has seen better days, or at least I hope it has. From the looks of the place, it was once a gas station. There's an old, I assume broken-down, gas pump on the corner right by the front door stuck on the price ".79". I can't remember a point in my lifetime when gas was that cheap, so I'd guess this thing is way older than me. In fact, everything here screams that word: old.

Everything is dusty, rusted, worn down, or all three. I count six vehicles parked side-by-side in the gravel lot around the side of the building, and several stacks of tires sit baking in the sun. It smells like rubber, motor oil, and gasoline.

"Woah," says Steph, clearly in awe of the place. She steps up next to me, duffel bag in tow and eyes wide.

"Ain't much, but it's been here eighty years," says Silas. "Wish I could've seen this place back in its heyday in the Forties." He whistles his respect. "Every gleaming road rocket in a fifty-mile radius came through Elias's Spark."

"People don't anymore?" I have to ask.

"Not like they used to. Barbazal used to be a mandatory road-trippin' stop on I-70. Now people just drive on through for Denver. It's only six hours away now. Back when cars would max out at forty mph, you're talkin' near twelve hours without food, water, or gas. They *had* to stop somewhere."

I guess he makes a good point. Clearly he's thought long and hard about this. Silas walks around the front of the truck toward the gaping garage door.

"Elias!" he hollers, although with his accent, it just sounds like "Lias."

A voice replies from somewhere nearby, muffled, buried.

"Yup!"

Steph looks at me.

"You okay?"

"Yeah!" I answer too fast. I shrug to further sell the reply, because I know she's not buying it, but now she's looking at me like she flat-out doesn't believe me. "Yeah, I'm fine. Just tired."

"And super nervous about something," she says, reaching forward to take my hands. "Listen, Alex, if this place is really making you uncomfortable, we can get us a bottle of oil and get out. I'm sure Silas would take a fifty to drive us straight back to the car."

I think for a moment about what she's saying, and I look around.

How easy would it be for Silas and Elias to grab us, tie us up, throw us in the back of the truck, and take us out into the woods somewhere to kill us?

It would've been easy enough for Jed, even if I hadn't walked out there with him willingly first.

Who would come looking for us? Ryan? Sure. But would he ever find us? He's Mr. Park Ranger Man, yeah, but… a homicide investigator?

I had to get myself out of that mine shaft. No one would've found me. I'm *not* going through that again—

"Alex?"

"Huh?"

"Yeah, let's hurry and get out of here."

Steph can tell when I'm spiraling. Anxiety is like that for me. My brain starts locking up, I start dissociating, and information bounces off my ears instead of being processed like it's supposed to. The children's home attendants used to call it "spacing out," but now I know it by a better name.

Maladaptive daydreaming.

Maybe Steph is right. Maybe we should get out of here.

"You coming?" she asks. I look up and she's walking up the driveway to Elias's shop.

"Yeah."

I thought the outside smelled like motor oil and gasoline, but inside the aroma is almost unbearably strong. Broken equipment fills the garage. The space is twenty feet across, with only four feet of walking space. It looks like someone set up for a garage sale, and then never got around to selling anything.

Car parts I can't identify line the walls—belts and wheels, pipes and bottles of fluids I couldn't identify if I wanted to because their labels have fallen away.

Something crashes at the back of the store, making me jump. Steph glances over her shoulder at me to ask silently if I'm okay. I nod.

"Come on back, girls!" comes Silas's voice from somewhere in the back of the shop. Then I hear another voice follow that one. One less excited at the idea of company.

"Not up for visitors," it mumbles. "There's oil in the lobby."

"Come on, Elias, you want 'em to just leave the cash on the counter?"

"Yup."

"Don't be like this. You know that's why people don't come round here no more."

Steph and I exchange a glance at that last part. *That's why people don't come round here no more.*

Implying that, one, people don't "come round here no more" and, two, there's probably a reason for that. Could it be the unfriendliness Silas just mentioned? Or maybe that everyone here is as reclusive as Elias?

Or could it be something worse?

I narrow my eyes at Steph in a way that I hope says, *Let's just leave the cash on the counter and get out,* but she tears her gaze away and spies something that's clearly more important.

"Alex, look!" she exclaims, darting to the wall where a huge picture of a shiny red hot rod hangs, slightly crooked. "She's beautiful. 1965 Mustang." She whistles.

"Didn't know you were so into cars."

"I may drive a bag of screws, but I can dream."

She sighs as she looks up at it.

"When we get that record deal after Harson sees us perform in Fort Collins, I'm getting one of those."

I have to chuckle.

"What makes you think we're getting a record deal?"

She looks at me like, *How could you think anything else?*

"Dude. When Isaac Harson hears you romance those strings, he'll go weak at the knees. Like I do."

I feel heat creep into my cheeks in the best way.

"Oh my god, Steph," I say, smiling, tucking my hair behind my ear and glancing at the far side of the room, where I know Silas and Elias are waiting for us. "Let's just get a bottle of oil and get out."

"Sounds like a great idea. Pick a favorite." She's smiling and gesturing to the shelf behind her, where I see… nothing?

The shelf is empty.

And at the very bottom is a little yellow price tag that's partially covered in rust.

Motor Oil. $5.99.

I sigh.

"How can they be out of motor oil?"

"Guess Silas was right—this place isn't exactly a road-trippin' stop anymore," replies Steph, following it up with a mock-dramatic gasp. "Maybe we should go… oh, I don't know, ask the owner?"

I roll my eyes.

"If he's a cannibal," she says, taking my hand in hers, "he can eat me first."

"Yuck."

We round the corner, Steph first, and as I lean my head in, I half expect to find Silas and Elias crouched side by side with some unidentifiable piece of meat roasting over a campfire. But nope. They're standing. Looking perfectly normal. Silas is leaning on the workbench behind him, turned toward Elias, who's got his back turned to us. He's leaning over another workbench, working hard on something. I can't see it from here. But something else about him catches my attention. His shoulders are slumped, his posture hunched, and a huge blue aura glows brightly around his head, thick and suffocating like a humid fog. And cold. So, so cold. And I get the overwhelming feeling of something heavy. Like a lead sack resting on my chest.

Elias is deeply, crushingly sad.

About what, I wonder?

I clear my throat.

Silas looks up at me, but Elias stays where he is.

"Hey, ladies, welcome to the shop," he says with a warm smile, gesturing to the rest of the room.

"Silas," spits Elias. A single word, but it speaks volumes. Steph clocks the tone switch too, because she glances at me and then clears her throat.

"Mr. Elias? Sir? Uh, we're just here for motor oil, so… if you could find a bottle in the back, we'll just—"

"Don't have any in the back. Whatever we've got is out front."

Jesus, this guy is cranky. Why the attitude? We're paying customers after all. I feel my eyes narrow, involuntarily. Whoops. But I can still feel the anger welling up.

"There is no oil out front," I say, catching the snip in my voice. I soften. "You're all out."

Clearly, I've said something earth-shattering because everybody freezes. Everyone. Elias's hands stop working on whatever he's working on. Silas's eyes do a slow sweep from Elias to me, and then to Steph. And then something softens in Elias's face.

He sighs, like a teacher who was about to reprimand a student for talking out of turn and then realized they made a good point.

"I'll see if I have more in the back—"

"We might! I'll check," says Silas with one foot already out the door. "If we're out, maybe Jonah's caravan has a bottle we can use."

And Silas is out.

Whrrr, whrr. Elias immediately pours himself back into his mysterious project.

"Woah, Alex, look." Steph stands and wanders to the wall of shelves, where more photos of classic cars rest, all of them in black and white and dusty. Elias must be really into cars. Like, more than a hobby. It looks like cars are his whole life. They're to him what music is to me.

Steph leans forward to examine a little red box with gold trim, and I get up to join her, but my eyes remain on Elias's back.

It couldn't have been the oil, could it? Who gets that worked up over running out of motor oil? Maybe the simple act of Silas leaving? Leaving Elias alone with his thoughts? Or… wait, no…

It feels like something deeper.

I glance at Steph one more time before stepping forward, hand outstretched to Elias's back. Something about this man, about how a single sentence can send him into such deep sadness that I can see it around his head—feel its temperature, almost taste it—ignites a curiosity in me that I can't extinguish.

I can't just ignore his pain.

Cold seeps into my fingertips, trickling up my fingers and into my palm, my wrist, my forearm, like water defying gravity. I clench my teeth as the blue hue travels up into my chest, and I shut my eyes, sinking into Elias's feelings.

I step into the aura.

I'm still in Barbazal, but outside. Red, white, and blue flags flutter in the wind, strung along pennants weaving through the town square. There are people. *Everywhere.* Like, more people than I thought could live in a town as empty and off-the-map as Barbazal. I'd never even heard of this place before today.

And yet there are crowds, bunching up along the side of the main road we just drove through, eager to reach the barriers keeping them from throwing themselves into the street. I crane my neck and stand on my tiptoes to get a better look. I'm already short, and the arms in the air cheering on whoever's over there aren't making this any easier.

I can hear cars crawling past. Flashes of shiny red, glittering chrome bumpers, and brilliant white rims with white walls indicate that these are classic cars. Is it some kind of car show?

The crowd swells from cheering into straight-up shrieking in excitement, and soon I see why. A gigantic balloon float pulls up the rear of this... parade?—I don't know what else to call it—at least ten feet high. Two smiling women in white blouses and jeans with cowboy hats and red lipstick toss candy into the crowd. Only the youngest out here bend to find it. And when I look back up at the float, I see him—the subject of everyone's worship. A man in a navy-blue blazer with a lighter blue necktie, tied perfectly, dark jeans, white cowboy boots, and a matching white cowboy hat. His glistening smile is warm, charming. He must be at least in his forties. He's actually incredibly handsome, in a Ken doll sort of way? Like if Ken owned a farm and never had to actually farm anything a day in his life.

Jonah Macon will bring home the bacon, reads the banner along the side of the float as it passes. I look around at all the smiling faces, and I think back to Elias. Why would such a joyful scene make him so profoundly sad?

And then I look around for him. Wait… where *is* Elias?

I look over my shoulder and find Elias's shop across the way, just as worn down as it was today when Steph and I walked in. This must be a recent memory.

There he stands, wearing the same overalls, downing the last of a bottle of water which looks like it had only a few drops in it to begin with. He tenses—I feel the tightness in my shoulders with him—then crushes the empty bottle in his hand, and hurls it to the ground. Then he marches back inside.

I look back up at Jonah, expecting to see that movie-star smile, but instead I see something else.

His smile has fallen as he looks toward Elias's shop. He's… broken. Just a little. That political mask he's wearing—that all politicians have to wear at least sometimes—cracked for a moment. Did anyone else see it? Or are they all mesmerized by the banners and the free candy and the fact that he's already back to smiling and waving again?

Whatever's up with Elias, it has everything to do with Jonah Macon.

Whooooosh!

I'm back in the shop. I'm staring at the ground. I hear the faint tinkling of music, like the world's tiniest xylophone, playing a song I recognize. It's a song my mom used to hum all the time when I was little, a song that she kept in her back pocket her whole journey to America with my dad.

When all the world is darkest,
You're alone and feel forgotten,
Know the road ahead is there.

Even if the fog is thick,
You're lost and feel alone,
Know the road ahead is there.

The rain can make the journey slick,
You're insecure and unsure,
Know the road ahead is there.

And so am I.

I'm staring up at Elias's back. No, his *face! He's looking at me!*

"Uh," I say, lowering my hand and weaving my fingers together sheepishly behind my back. "Just… wondering what you're doing over there."

But he's peering *past* me, at Steph.

"Don't touch that," he growls, marching past me toward her.

Panic sets into my chest and creeps up my neck. My heart races as he nears her, marching, fists balled, red fireball erupting over his head, growing so huge it burns my eyes. Is he going to hurt her?

"Steph!" I yell. Steph looks up at me in alarm, and then to Elias, and jumps out of the way just before Elias slams his hand down on the now open red box. Just before it shuts, I catch a glimpse of a bright red classic car under the lid, rotating slowly.

The music stops as abruptly as it started.

Steph and I look at each other, and then I look at Elias.

"Sorry," offers Steph, "it just looked so pretty. I wanted to see—"

Elias's hands curl into fists on the table.

"I'm... really sorry," continues Steph.

That gets Elias to soften again. The red aura vanishes. I see my way in.

"Elias?" I ask. "Earlier, when Silas brought up Jonah Macon, you seemed upset. Who is he?"

He scoffs. Steph looks at me like, *Why the hell are you asking that?*

I know, Steph, get the oil, get the hell out. But I have questions! Important ones! Ones with answers that might only lie here, right now, in this room, with Elias.

"Jonah Macon—" says Elias. He speaks like the name burns on his tongue. "—is the lowest, vilest sellout I've ever met."

He turns and looks at me.

"He's all anyone talks about 'round here anymore, now that he's back from his fancy office in Denver, suckin' up to conservatives, callin' himself a 'centrist.' He's a damn liar."

"Why the fanfare then?" asks Steph.

"Because these people of Barbazal are too gullible to know what's good for 'em. They think ol' Jonah Macon will fix our drought, bring us our water supply back after they dammed up the river. Well, I tell you what." He takes a step closer, and I flinch before I realize he's walking past me. "Jonah Macon won't 'bring home the bacon' until he makes it rain."

A dam? They're in the middle of a drought and someone dammed the river?

I glance at Steph, who nods at me. We both catch that Elias may have meant "make it rain" literally and figuratively. But even with all the venom spewing from his words, Elias's aura still glows blue. There's more to this story. People who have it out for politicians often seethe with rage, boil with anger with no place to put it. Elias... something about Jonah makes him sad.

Not just sad.

Hopeless?

Silas bursts back into the room with a triangle-shaped yellow bottle in his hand and takes one glance at Elias before analyzing the whole situation.

"Aw, hell, you got him talkin' about Jonah, didn't you?" he asks me, setting the bottle on the table, shoving his hands in his pockets, and sighing.

"Actually, *you* did," chuckles Steph. "You said Jonah's entourage might have some oil with them."

"Well, luckily I don't have to ask," he says, nodding at the bottle. "Besides, his little club is impossible to get a minute in with anyway. Damn politicians are so hard to talk to."

"See?" hisses Elias. "Ain't got time for nobody, no common folk anymore. Jonah's too good for us now."

"Aw, Elias, don't say that," Silas encourages. "You know everything he does is spelled out for him—what he says, what he wears, hell, how he shapes his beard. They probably don't even let him wipe his own ass anymore."

I believe Silas on that one. People in positions of power, bought or not, are often highly curated. I once saw a TikTok from an ex-advisor to the White House talking about the rounds of analysis that go into choosing a politician's *socks*.

Who pays that much attention to socks?!

"Well," says Steph, bringing the conversation back around, "thanks for the oil." She holds out a ten-dollar bill, Elias takes it, and just like that, we have a precious bottle of oil in our possession.

I exchange a smile with her, and her face says it all. *We're getting out of here*.

"Thanks, Elias," nods Steph. "Thanks, Silas."

And we turn to leave.

But just before we reach the door, I hear Elias's voice behind us.

"Hey, uh, ladies, how'd you know to pull over for oil? Most cars don't give an indication that it's low."

I turn and feel my cheeks growing hot with embarrassment. I scratch the back of my neck and chuckle.

"I, uh… kind of let the engine die."

"What?" asks Elias.

Silas bursts into laughter. "Oh hell, you might need a whole new engine then!"

"What?!" cries Steph.

"What kinda car is it?" asks Elias, bringing the conversation back down from hysterics.

"2001 Saturn SL."

Elias whistles and shakes his head. "Yeah, I don't even know if they make parts for those anymore, girls. I wouldn't even know what I was lookin' at if I did take a look."

"Let's see," says Steph, pulling out her phone and showing it to Elias. "I took a picture of under the hood just in case I needed to… I don't know… compare… oils…? Or something."

Silas stifles another laugh, but Elias just furrows his brows and squints down at the phone.

"Hard to tell from just a photo, but… those pistons look scratched to hell."

"What are pistons?" asks Steph. "And 'scratched to hell' doesn't sound good."

"Long story short," Silas chimes in, "they keep the car runnin'. But again, you're not gonna find twenty-som'n-year-old pistons here. Maybe not even online."

"So," I begin, "we have more oil now, but if we can't get new pistons, then…"

I finish the sentence in my head, hoping against everything that the answer is no.

Are we stuck here?

"Prob'ly won't run."

I think back to Steph's drum kit in the sweltering heat, the skins warping, the pedals loosening. I hope it's okay. If it hasn't been stolen.

We covered it up well enough, but if people see an abandoned car and decide to poke around inside, they might find the drum kit anyway. Renewed vigor grips my heart, and this time I finish Steph's sentence out loud.

"There has to be somewhere else we haven't tried."

"I'm the only mechanic in a fifty-mile radius. I can see about ordering specialty pistons for ya, but that'll take at least two days."

"Two days?!" exclaims Steph. "But that's Saturday! We have a show in Fort Collins Friday night!"

"Silas," I ask, "what if we… I mean could we… could we borrow your truck? Just to get us to Fort Collins for the show, and then we'll bring it right back. Promise. You could even keep collateral. Um…"

Steph raises an eyebrow at me like, *What the hell do you mean by collateral?*

She's right, we don't own anything. A granola bar doesn't exactly scream *collateral*. We'd have to bring along all our instruments for the show, and even the most expensive thing we have—the car—is a piece of shit on four wheels.

Maybe fewer wheels than that by now.

Silas gives me the saddest smile I've seen in a long time.

"Sorry, ladies, no can do. I've got some sheetrock to haul up to the dam tomorrow night. Even if I did trust y'all—no offense, but we've only just met—"

"None taken," says Steph, but I can hear the disappointment in her voice.

"I can't." Silas holds his hands out and purses his lips apologetically. His head glows purple. He's nervous.

Probably at the fact that two complete strangers just asked to borrow his car.

But Elias's blue ring around his head has disappeared, and he chimes in.

"Y'all can stay at the Crown Inn for the night, since you're stranded. Ask for Jude, tell him I sent you. He'll give y'all a room. On the house."

"Really?" asks Steph eagerly. "That's amazing, thank you!"

37

She's right, that really is amazing. Elias must be super dialed into the neighborhood to be able to just whip up a hotel room like that, especially with all the huge crowds here to see Jonah.

"Thank you," I say, and I mean it. It's great to have a place to stay. Beats having to sleep in the car. Miles away. Alone. In the dark. In the middle of nowhere.

Steph has gone suddenly silent after that expressive thank you she uttered only moments ago, and she clasps her hands and stares at the ground, lost in thought. Her aura glows blue, and my heart sinks. I know exactly what's wrong.

"Oh, Silas?" I ask before he steps out the door. He turns to look at me.

"Would you… mind driving us back to our car tonight? We left something important in there."

I glance at Steph as her face lights up. That blue ring hovering around her beanie fades into the brilliant gold from earlier. I'm sure I'm smiling the biggest, dumbest smile right now, but I'd do anything for Steph.

We're getting that drum kit before it melts.

"Sure thing!" exclaims Silas. He keeps talking, but his words fade into the background for me as I notice Elias leaning on the worktable. Hands balled. Staring at that music box.

3: The Hotel

The motor oil is now in the car. And it still won't start. Elias was right. We need new pistons, and they don't make them anymore.

But at least now, Steph's drum kit is safely in the back of Silas's truck. Silas and Steph are standing here with me in line in the lobby...

...and the hotel is an absolute *zoo*.

Photographers, with cameras as big as my guitar, stand lingering around, keeping their eyes moving. Clearly, they're here to catch a glimpse of Jonah Macon, but who knows if he's even staying here? Silas said he has an "entourage"—you'd think he'd have his own trailer parked somewhere secretive in the woods. Rock stars have tour buses, don't they? Why not politicians?

"Hey," whispers Steph, "you really think Elias can get us a room here?"

She looks way more relaxed now that we've got her *other* best friend in tow. Her drum kit is in pristine condition. Well, at first glance anyway. It'll be impossible to tell until we can see it up close, and once it's cooled down from the heat.

The sunset outside the window just behind her is glowing a brilliant orange, and I smile up at her.

"He seemed pretty sure of himself," I reply, but I hope the answer is *yes*.

If not here, where else will we stay?

We're about to find out.

"Yes. Are you here for emergency water bottles or do you need a room. Because we don't have either right now," drones the weary young man at the counter, clicking through something on his keyboard faster than I've ever seen anyone type before. Clearly he's too busy to even make eye contact.

But I clock the mention of emergency water bottles. Silas wasn't kidding.

"Uh, hey there, Jude," Silas cuts in from behind us. "Busy night?"

Jude gives him a smirk that seems to half say, *Are you stupid?* and half say, "Ha ha, very funny."

"I reckon you don't need a room for tonight?" asks Jude, all formal politeness and non-Barbazalian accent gone from his voice. He's with a friend now, or at least a contact.

"I don't," says Silas, "but these two ladies do. Courtesy of Elias, if you please."

Something changes in Jude's face as he turns to me and Steph.

"Silas, I can't—"

"Elias says you have a spare room."

"Well, it's not really available—"

"He insisted."

"Silas," Jude is snapping now. "May I speak to you over here please?" He turns to us and dons that front-desk smile again. "Pardon, ladies, so sorry for the trouble."

"It's Steph and Alex, thanks," says Steph.

"Damn," I say to her as the two walk away.

"What?" she asks. "If I get referred to as one of two 'ladies' tonight again, I might scream. Might as well say, 'These two humans with tits would like to have a word with you.'"

If I was drinking water, it would be flying out my nose and all over the carpet.

"Oh my god," I snort.

"Besides," she continues, pulling her drumsticks out of her back pocket, "I have a feeling we'll get outta here a *lot* faster if we assert ourselves, you know?"

"Are you insinuating we start threatening people with drumsticks?"

"Hell, no. These are way too expensive to be used as weapons," she says. "Unless we're secretly in the middle of a LARP you forgot to tell me about, and these are actually magic wands."

I roll my eyes.

"That's what I need," I sigh wistfully. "Another LARP."

"Oh yeah, I forgot I still owe you my hand in marriage."

"Oh yeahhhh," I tease, "and all its associated benefits."

"At least wait 'til we *have* a room," she whispers, reaching over and intertwining her fingers in mine. I go warm all over.

We both look up at Silas and Jude, who are in the middle of a *quite* heated discussion, probably about the room in question.

I overhear a conversation right behind us, and I don't dare turn around.

"That Maisie miss is gonna get us all killed," says a woman.

Someone else lends their voice.

"Right? How can she support this?" they ask.

"Yes, *we* should get to decide what to do with our bodies," chimes another, reinforcing the first two. "This isn't a morality question, it's a question of healthcare." Damn. Zero regard for the environment *and* opposes the right to bodily autonomy. Yikes. I glance at Steph, who doesn't seem to notice the conversation happening behind us—she's still watching Silas and Jude.

"So," continues Steph, "what was up with Elias anyway, huh?"

"What do you mean?"

"He really freaked out at us. And you seemed really bothered by whatever you saw in his... uh... aura. Did you find out what his deal is?"

I grow quiet. I can only imagine. Clearly cars are Elias's thing, and... actually, they're Jonah's too. His whole procession was filled with them—classic ones, even that bright red one with the chrome rims and white walls. It looked just like the one in the music box.

"Uh, hello? Earth to Alex?"

"Ah, sorry, I was… thinking."

"Let me know if this is too personal a question but… since you saw his aura…"

She pulls her hand away and steps in front of me, all ears now.

"What was it like?"

"Blue, mostly," I say. "I can't figure out why. Something about Jonah Macon makes Elias *so* sad. Maybe they had a fight at some point?"

"Or *maybe* they fought over a lover."

Yuck. "Or *maybe*, given the fact that they look like they're thirty years apart, Jonah used to work for him?"

"You seem *really* invested in all of this," says Steph. She squeezes my hand and leans in. "Remember to protect yourself, alright? I know you feel for people. Deeply."

"Thanks, Steph. I promise, I'm looking out for me."

But, these people have a pretty dire situation on their hands. A drought? An election coming up? Isn't that happening this week?

I remember what the woman somewhere behind us said: *That Maisie miss is gonna get us all killed.*

"Or," I continue, "what if it has to do with Maisie Dorsey?"

Steph shrugs, just as Silas and Jude wrap up whatever they were discussing and walk toward us.

"Alright, ladies, here's what we can do for you," says Silas, hands out apologetically again.

Steph and I both know the answer we're about to get. *Nothing.* That's what they can do for us. Where the hell are we going to stay tonight?

"Shit," mutters Steph so only I can hear. I squeeze her hand back, letting her know that it'll be alright.

"I can call Darius. He's the town deputy. He can see if we have the resources to get y'all to Fort Collins. He's good friends with Henry, who leads the weekly convoy into the city for farming supplies. They might be able to get y'all there by Saturday—"

"Saturday?" asks Steph, shaking her head. "Our show is Friday night. We can't get anything sooner? Isn't there a bus out here or anything?"

Jude and Silas look at each other in humble disappointment.

"'Fraid not," admits Silas, lowering his voice to almost a whisper. "Oh, and uh, that room Elias promised you is being rented out to the man himself—"

Jude conducts the most aggressive throat-clearing I've ever heard in my life.

"Is *occupied*."

"The man himself" *has* to be Jonah Macon. Steph *has* to be thinking the same thing judging by how she's looking at me.

So he's already in his room, and all these paparazzi are standing around for nothing.

"Well, so much for that," says Steph, shrugging.

"Well, hold on now, I ain't finished yet. Y'all need somewhere to stay tonight, right? I don't have much space in my trailer as it is, but I got room in my backyard for a tent and a couple sleeping bags."

Steph and I exchange a smile. Camping doesn't sound so bad.

4. Camping

Silas owns a chicken coop. Chickens are *loud*.

"What if one of them shits on the tent?" I ask, staring up at the coop.

"Relax," chuckles Steph, engrossed in something on her phone. "We're not *in* the coop. When's the last time you saw a chicken projectile shit on anything?"

"Fair."

I watch Steph as she sits there, extremely focused. Her lips hang slightly open as she types, the light from her phone flickering in her eyes. She's sitting cross-legged on her sleeping bag. Both of the sleeping bags smell like animal, probably from Hector's dog, Chrissy. Poor Silas was so kind to let us stay in his yard, but his love for animals is quite... perceptible.

Steph sighs, and then notices me looking.

"What?"

"Does this count as a 'room'?" I ask, throwing in an eyebrow wiggle for good measure.

"Oh my god," she laughs. I love making her smile like that. I *live* for it. "Hold on, rowdy, I'm putting out an APB first."

"For what?"

"To see if anyone from Haven Springs knows anyone in Barbazal with a spare *actual* room."

"Wow, you must really love roughing it," I smile.

"I actually don't mind. It's beautiful out here. But the smell, and the… squawking—"

The rooster interrupts her just as she says the word *squawking*, sending us into an eruption of laughs.

"Exactly, buster," she gestures toward the coop. "Even the birds have started mansplaining."

I shake my head and look up at the sky. The stars are twinkling like diamonds, and here I am with the girl of my dreams, in a stranger's backyard with chickens and sleeping bags, our instruments safely covered under a tarp in the back of his truck. On our way to Fort Collins to start a new adventure, traveling the world, taking on everything, for real this time.

Hopefully.

And I think I must be the luckiest girl alive.

"You were right, Gabe," I mouth to the heavens, "I'm making my own way."

I'm facing my fears, Gabe. Finding new spaces, I hum, keeping the words to myself while Steph enjoys the scenery. I reach for my guitar case now, click it open, and pull out my friend, give her a quick tuning, and strum my fingers along her strings as I hum the next line.

You know how I feel about brand new places.

But under the stars, there's a world to explore,

I watch Steph as she stares up at the sky in wonder, smiling to herself.

With the girl of my dreams. How could I ask for more?

A summer breeze rolls through the yard, through the mesh of the tent, and makes the hair on my arms stand on end. And I realize why it feels weird. It's been so hot all day, sitting here outside feels like being in a refrigerator. It reminds me how cold that icy blue over Elias's head was—how it felt, how it weighed heavy on my chest.

I suddenly remember his words. *Jonah Macon won't bring home the bacon until he makes it rain.*

"What do you think Elias meant?" I'm asking Gabe, really, but this time I say it loud enough for Steph to hear.

"I think he meant business," says Steph absentmindedly as she scrolls.

"I mean about Jonah 'making it rain'?"

"Usually people mean strip clubs," she smiles.

"You think Barbazal has a strip club?"

"Horny people are *everywhere*."

She has a point.

Ugh, what am I saying? I'm letting her distract me again.

"I mean, this whole drought situation must be really serious. Silas couldn't even spare us more than a water bottle each. The hotel with the emergency water supply is now out of water too. The trees are dying. These people are desperate."

That gets her attention. She sets her phone down on her sleeping bag, curls her knees up to her chest, and stares at me.

"Yeah," she says, "I hope Jonah comes through for them."

Silence passes between us until Steph puts together what I'm thinking.

"You don't think Elias wants Jonah to play dirty, do you?"

"I don't know what else 'make it rain' could mean, with the way he said it. He pointed right at me with the Uncle Sam face like," I lower my voice and imitate exactly how he said it, like a grandpa, "make it rain."

Steph scoffs. "That could mean anything." But after a moment, she humors me. "But… with how much he hates Jonah, it could be why he's mad at him. Maybe Jonah won't ruffle feathers, and given the water situation, maybe Elias thinks it's high time they should?"

"'*High time*'?" I chuckle. "We've been in Barbazal too long."

"Anyway, again, don't get too invested," she says. "There's not much we can do anyway, you know? We've got a show to pull off in a couple of days and, for now, no way to get there."

I look out through the tent screen on the other side, where we can see half the town square. Up on this hillside, despite the noise of the chickens, Silas has a pretty sweet setup. The view is unbeatable. So many twinkling lights in the town. The Crown Inn has quieted down since we were there. Most of the guest room lights are off or dimly lit, everyone having given up on catching a glimpse of Jonah Macon. Then I notice something I never would have without a view like this.

Atop the inn, there's an extra block of building, like it was an afterthought when the engineers were designing the place. Windows on all sides, with curtains blocking the view in. The lights are all on one minute, and the next…

…they're off.

But before the last of the light dims, I'm sure I see, against the curtained window, a figure just inside.

Is… is that the penthouse suite? That's where penthouses usually are, right? On the very top floor? Surrounded by windows? Where no one can bother the super-important people inside?

Where else would Jonah Macon be staying but the penthouse suite?

Would Elias have access to it at all times like that? Confident enough to tell us to drop his name to Jude and guarantee it would be ours for the night? How does he have so many connections in this town?

I remember how easy it was for Jed to give me a room upstairs. He *owned* Haven Springs.

What if Elias "owns" Barbazal? How would he?

And then it clicks.

It's got to be Jonah.

Elias and Jonah have some kind of connection, after all. Who else would cause so much fanfare?

"Steph?"

"Oh no," she says, playfully. I look back at her. "You said my name like you're about to suggest something really crazy."

"Crazy? Or… brave?"

"Probably both, given how you're looking at me."

There's a hint of flirtation in her voice, a golden halo around her head, warm and bright and electric. I feel it zipping all over me like tiny shocks, and that glow in her eyes, as they travel down me and back up to my face… I shiver inside, and wish I didn't have to direct this conversation where I do.

"What if…" I begin. Steph's right, it's crazy.

And brave.

"What if I just… talked to Jonah?"

"You want to talk to Jonah Macon?" she asks. "You think he'll give us a ride to Fort Collins?"

"No, I mean," I say, scrambling for words. How do I make this sound like a *good* idea? "What if I talked him into helping these people with the drought?"

Steph does her absolute best, I can tell, to give my idea a chance.

"How would you do that?"

While I think of a way to answer that convincingly, she continues, "I mean, he's a politician, right? I'm sure he's heard every argument in the book about why he should help these people with their drought, and if he hasn't said yes yet, what can you do to convince him?"

"I just thought maybe if I just… tapped into his emotions?"

The longest pause in the history of pauses settles between us, and at exactly the most inopportune time…

Cockadoodle-doo!

"Not now, I heard what she said!" Steph exclaims vaguely in the direction of the rooster. I smile, and she smiles back at me, but her eyes are also huge with disbelief.

"You're kidding," she says, scooting closer. "You want to read Jonah?"

"No, just, I mean, not *invasively*, exactly? Just… if I could see past that smile… past the mask, past all the curated image that makes up Jonah Macon, maybe if I could see the real Jonah and make him realize what's important to these people, maybe I could explore his feelings about the dam?"

Her eyes are huge and hopeful, but then her smile falters slightly.

"Think you can do that before we get to Fort Collins?" she asks.

And I know what she's really asking.

It's Wednesday night.

Our gig is in two days.

"You want me to tap into a politician's subconscious, find out what makes him tick, *and* convince him to change his political position days before an election, in forty-eight hours?"

"I saw you take down the seven-year farce that was Jed Lucan's legacy in just a week. If anyone can do this, it's you. I just… our gig. What if we don't make it?"

I lean forward and take her hand in mine.

"It's *us*, Steph," I say, with more confidence than I feel. "We always make it."

Besides, I have to try. I saw the sadness in Elias, *felt* the sadness in Elias. "I know I can't fix everyone's sadness. I can't fix *one* person's sadness. Not even a licensed therapist can do that. But, if I can alleviate just a bit of the suffering I've seen here…"

I saw the pain in Elias's eyes as he watched Jonah's procession, and I saw Jonah's shell start to crack when he returned Elias's gaze. Whatever's going on with this drought, and that dam, and Elias, and Jonah, it all has to be connected. And if Jonah Macon the politician has a canned answer for any crowd question—and I just know he does—I have to get to Jonah Macon the *man*.

And given my powers, I might be the only person who can.

"I have to try, Steph. I can't just… do nothing. I can't leave these people like this."

I feel her squeeze my hand.

"I know," she says. "And… I meant what I said in Haven Springs. Wherever we go, whatever we do, as long as I'm with you, I'm in."

"Come on, Steph, I'm not giving up on Fort Collins, or the rest of the world with you," I say. And that's a goddamn promise.

Steph wouldn't say it to me. She knows how much this means to me—helping these people. But I know how much Fort Collins means to her. Another shot at the big time—a chance to perform in front of Isaac Harson and play music for anyone we want, wherever we want. A chance at a record deal and seeing the world with someone again. After all, that was Steph's goal before Haven Springs. Before me. She was on her way too.

And now?

This is our chance to do it *and* make a living. Together.

Who could pass that up?

"I promise," I say.

And I mean it.

And then I realize I've forgotten something. Something extremely important. Something I should have said this morning, and probably would have if I hadn't been so frazzled.

"I'm sorry I didn't check the oil," I say. "If it weren't for me, we'd already be in the city, taking it all in, playing together on some rooftop somewhere—"

"Gazing into my eyes," she says, leaning in dramatically close.

"Not having to ask your forgiveness like this—"

"Which you already have," she finishes, squeezing both my hands.

Her phone buzzes on the ground beside us and neither of us can resist looking down at it. A new message from Ethan Lambert.

> I can help! My uncle lives in Barbazal. He might let you sleep in the room I sleep in when I'm there!

I look at Steph in shock. "What did you put in that APB?"

She shrugs. "I just asked if anyone in the Haven Springs group chat knew anyone in Barbazal who might have an extra couch to crash on."

"Small world," I grin, and I hope she sees the pride in my eyes. "Thanks, Steph."

"Don't mention it," she shrugs, pushing herself to her knees.

"You sure, uh… you don't want to stay out here and enjoy the stars with me?"

…*and maybe each other?* I want to say it… I want *so* badly to say it. I lean forward, toward Steph.

But then…

Pffffft! All down the side of the tent, a thin white liquid drips, and one of the chickens *bawks* and flaps away from the side of the coop.

Steph jumps back from the wall, scrambles to grab for me.

"*Eww, is that—?!*"

I'm not ready for the weight of her, or her tripping over the blanket between us, and the tent goes tumbling. After we untangle a tentful of screams, tent poles, zippers, and projectile chicken shit—thank god this tent is waterproof—we escape, and twenty minutes later, we're knocking on the front door of Owen Lambert.

The first thing I notice about Owen's house is how clean everything looks. Sure, it's small. Tiny, even. Definitely a trailer for a single person. But it's pristine. The whole thing is a sharp white—like, hospital white. So sterile, it hurts my eyes. There's not a scrape of rust or dirt anywhere, which, compared to the rest of Barbazal, makes it look brand new.

You'd think the mayor lived here.

I suddenly feel out of place standing here next to Steph, with our duffel containing all our belongings, and my guitar, armed with only a message from Ethan to prove we're safe to harbor for a night.

"What do you think Owen is like?" asks Steph.

"Clean," I say. And that's all I really have to go on. She nods and looks around the place, probably noticing the same things I have.

"Nice statue," she says, looking down at the one thing keeping us company out here on this front porch: a clay figurine of a knight holding a sword to the sky. It's not well done—looks homemade. Could it be Ethan's?

I smile, remembering his comics. I'd kill to have a copy out here with me, something to pore through, something to distract me from the timer counting down the hours 'til our show.

If we just had Isaac Harson's number! But all we've got is a memory of a nod from him, and a promise that "I'll be there." In Fort Collins. Waiting to hear us.

I feel something well up in me—persistence? Defiance? We'll make it to Fort Collins, even if I have to walk our instruments there myself. We have to.

Steph leans forward and knocks again, harder this time.

"Think he's home?"

The door flies open, and Steph and I jump. Guess there's our answer.

A man more than a foot taller than us leans out, glances at the outside of the front door nervously, and then looks up at both of us.

"Yes?" he asks.

Everything about his stature—his hunched-over posture, the way his eyes shift between my face and Steph's…

His head glows purple.

Yup. He's afraid of something.

"Uh," she begins, sensing that there's *something* weird going on here. "I'm Steph Gingrich. This is Alex Chen. We're from Haven Springs."

His eyes widen and that purple glow retreats just a bit.

"Haven Springs," he repeats.

"We know your nephew, Ethan," I say.

The purple flares up again.

"What's going on? Is he okay?" His voice is totally panicked. "Did something happen to Charlotte?!"

Oh god, I'm handling this horribly.

"No, no," I reply, "I mean, *yes*, Ethan's fine! And no, nothing happened to Charlotte. We're not here about Ethan. We're here to talk to you."

"About what?" he asks, recoiling just a bit back inside the house. "If you're here with the press…"

"We're not the press," says Steph, her voice sharply turning this conversation back to the relevant topic. "We're here to ask if we can stay in the… guest room for the night. Ethan said it would be okay."

He raises an eyebrow.

"Look, we know it's late. But we're supposed to play a show in Fort Collins on Friday night and our car is stranded up the road with busted pistons, and no one's available to drive us, there's no bus and—"

"Crown Inn is booked with Jonah Macon's fan club," I cut in.

I hate to interrupt Steph like this, but I can feel her spiraling next to me, and I have to ground us. Someone has to. That's the real problem anyway—if this hadn't happened the week that Jonah Macon was running for office out here in the middle of nowhere, we'd be cozied up in that hotel and figuring out a way to get to Fort Collins.

Hell, somebody out here would probably be able to drive us.

I unclench my fists and shut my eyes, willing the patience to manifest in me.

It doesn't.

"So you're with Maisie's people?" asks Owen, visibly stiffening.

"We're not with *anybody*," insists Steph.

"Least of all a state senator," I say. *Least of all a right-wing politician*, I want to add. "We're just looking for a place to crash, and then we'll be out of here. Promise."

His shoulders relax. That purple halo shrinks just a bit. Clearly he's more comfortable with us now that he has the idea we're *not* cool with politicians, but honestly? I don't know how to feel about Jonah *or* Maisie. I still haven't heard a single detail about their political positions. Just that people around here feel very strongly about both of them.

"All we know is there's a dam and a drought and Jonah and Maisie," Steph replies better than I can, "and a lot of *really* strong opinions one way or the other."

"You've been talking to Elias," he says, a smile playing on his mouth. He glances over his shoulder as if he's going to find some guidance on a final decision here, before turning back to us and nodding.

"Come in," he says. "Just… please don't touch anything."

5. Owen

Steph and I sit at Owen's table as he stares down at his mug of coffee. I can tell it's coffee because I can smell it, and not because we have cups of coffee in front of us.

Because we don't. We have nothing in front of us.

I feel my stomach turn over with hunger, and I look around to keep myself busy so I don't ask what kinds of snacks Owen has and come across rude.

We really did just knock on his front door and ask for a place to stay, after all. I don't expect this single man to have enough food to feed three adults.

"So, uh…" he begins, breaking the silence. "How is Ethan, anyway?"

Steph and I nod silently until I venture a reply.

"He's great," I say, although it's been several days since I saw him. "Last we checked."

I spot a picture on the small console table behind us that looks worn down for decades based on the state of the wood. Inside the picture frame is a shot of Ethan. A much, *much* younger Ethan. It's a professionally shot picture—looks like it might have been taken at a department store. He's grinning between his chubby little cheeks, arms outstretched to the camera. I smile. He looks so damn happy, so bubbly, I wonder if even back then, people could tell he saw the world as a mecca of adventure, ripe for the taking. His parents, Liam and Charlotte, had to see it even then, right?

BRITTNEY MORRIS

He looks so out of place in such a formal photo studio. I might not even have recognized him as the LARPer who bravely defended Haven Springs from evil with me.

I look back at Owen, who hasn't taken his eyes off the table, gripping the coffee mug like something *serious* is on his mind. His head looks like an iris with that deep purple aura. He's scared again, the fear creeping bigger and bigger above him, like a looming, swelling giant threatening to swallow the whole room, like a balloon. It feels light and floaty, gossamer like a spider-web. He's absolutely terrified.

Of what?

His index finger traces his coffee-mug handle. Up and down. Up and down. Up and down.

Then he taps three times. *Tap tap tap.*

Then up and down. Up and down. Up and down.

I glance at Steph to see if she notices, but she's engrossed in her phone. I glance over her shoulder to see she's texting Ethan.

Thanks, man

Yeah! Have fun. I hid chocolate under the guest room mattress. If it's still there, you can have it.

I smile. Sick. Thanks, Ethan.

Up and down. *Tap tap tap.*

Does he have OCD?

That purple aura glowing around his head morphs into something that feels… prickly. Almost… like pins and needles. Uncomfortable. Like I would do anything to get away from it. An itch I can't scratch.

I want to scratch it.

"Hey, um," says Steph, setting the phone in her lap and looking up at him. "Why'd you think Ethan might not be okay?"

He sighs, almost in defeat.

"Yeah, uh," he starts, but then he shakes his head: *no*. "I know he's okay. I keep up on MyBlock and sometimes he texts. But his mom, she hasn't been herself for a couple of weeks now. Just completely shut down after she lost Gabe. Barely speaks anymore. Turned into a total zombie. Ethan shouldn't have to deal with that."

Oh.

I try not to squirm in my seat, but I feel like I might be sick.

"Has she tried therapy, or—" I cut myself off at the look he's giving me, like, *You think we haven't tried that?*

And then he goes back to tapping on the table and staring at nothing.

The purple aura remains.

"Mr. Lambert," I venture, leaning forward and resting my elbows on the table.

"N—" he starts, his hand flying out like the table is going to burn me. I flinch back. "I mean… I'm sorry. I, uh…"

"Clearly something else is bothering you. What is it?"

Steph looks first at me and then at Owen.

"Yeah, we're here to listen," she says, putting her phone away. "We've got all night while we figure out how to get to Fort Collins."

Owen lets out a huge sigh, and then glances over at the TV, which has been aimlessly broadcasting whatever's been on. He picks up the remote and shuffles through the channels until we land on a woman standing behind a podium.

Short, dark hair, dark eyes, faint pink lipstick, with a sign in front of her.

Maisie Dorsey.

"*That* woman is bothering me."

"Maisie Dorsey?" asks Steph. "Why?"

The hell is up with this town hanging their lives on a national election?

"It's about the dam, isn't it?" I ask.

That gets Owen's attention. He turns from the TV to me, and narrows his eyes.

"Who told you about the dam?" he asks, his voice darker than I expected.

"Uh… Elias? At his shop?"

"Oh right, Elias," he sighs with an eye roll. "He probably told you all of Jonah's business, tried to dissuade you from voting for him, huh?"

Of course, that's not how it went down at all, but Steph and I look at each other and exchange the same idea: *No need to tell him exactly how it happened, lest we feed this fire.*

That purple fireball above his head has warmed into red.

"Owen, we don't know anything about either candidate," I assure him, trying to calm him down. "We're just trying to get to Fort Collins."

He looks from me to Steph and seems to decide we're still trustworthy.

"I'll make it real easy for you, then," he says, leaning back in his chair and pulling out a cigarette. The red inferno cools down and dissipates into nothing as he clicks the lighter a few times and inhales, deeply.

"Lazy Maisie Dorsey wants to hold back even *more* water with that dam. At least Jonah would open the levels a little more so we could have enough water to live. Lesser of two evils if you ask me."

There's that dam again.

"Why?" asks Steph.

"Why?" laughs Owen, heaving back into a huge guffaw. "Don't you know what the hell dams do?"

"Uh…" begins Steph.

Now that I think about it, I don't really know either. Besides, you know, hydropower? "Don't they generate sustainable power?"

"Some of 'em," he spits. "Not ours. It's just your regular run-of-the-mill, water-limitin', ecosystem-disregulatin' corporate erection.

Maisie's in the pockets of *all* the big-wigs on Capitol Hill. She wants the dam because they want the dam, and not because she cares if Barbazal needs water."

Steph and I exchange a glance, and I hope she's not as confused as I am.

Turns out, she is.

"Mr. Lambert," she starts, "no offense, but… why does Maisie Dorsey care about this particular dam, if she's after a Senate seat?"

"Because the Colorado River feeds right into the Barbazal River. If they divert the water back into the Colorado River, there's more water for other parts of the state—more 'important' parts. Parts with *lawns*, and *sprawling estates*."

I let him talk, but I'm not so sure that's how dams work.

He hisses those last two words and takes another drag of his cigarette.

"I don't want to come across bitter, but… she's so easy to hate, you know? We've been doing what they ask—conserving water, doing our part. We're a farming community, goddammit. How are we supposed to conserve any more than we have without it affecting our livelihood? This is what Barbazal does!"

I see.

But then I realize there's a piece missing—a connector in this network of cause-and-effect.

"Why is Maisie campaigning here though? In Barbazal? With so few voters? No offense, but why isn't she campaigning in Denver if she wants to win the whole state?"

"Because her biggest competition, Jonah Macon, is campaigning to come up with some kind of agreement on both sides, on the basis of protecting the environment. In a blue state? She'd better have her ass down here campaigning on his home turf."

I glance at Steph again.

"You mark my words," says Owen, huffing out another plume of smoke. "Much as I hate politicians, Jonah Macon is our only way out of this."

＊

The extra bedroom—the guest room Ethan promised us—is small, but cozy. In fact, it looks *too* cozy. My eyes find a picture of Ethan on the dresser, dressed in head-to-toe LARPing gear as the noble knight Thaynor. The only evidence of Ethan in the room. He must not spend much time here. I wonder how often he visits his uncle.

A huge Nordic patterned blanket covers the queen-size bed, which takes up most of the room. The space between it and the dresser is barely squeeze-through-able, but I manage. While Steph explores the room and unzips her duffel, I plop down on the bed, find my pocket journal, and do what most of the therapists I've ever known have told me to do: I write down my thoughts. As disjointed and shattered as they are, it feels better to get them out. They don't have to be well-written or even coherent. They just have to be out of my brain.

Poor Elias, I write. *Something's weighing heavy on him. He seems to feel so strongly about so many things. Jonah Macon. Cars. His shop. Silas. The dam. His sadness felt deep, like the sting of frostbite, something he can't get rid of, craving warmth to melt it away. I have a feeling that this situation with the dam goes a lot deeper than Jonah Macon.* I sigh, clutching the pen tighter— How the hell am I supposed to untangle this in two days?—press it down again. *I have to do something. I can't just leave this place to burn itself…*

Steph finds her way around the other side, and without hesitation, she climbs on beside me and sighs.

…alive.

I look up at the ceiling, at the little green stars speckled all over it, and some even trickling down the walls, and I remember lying in the woods with Ryan that day we found a sliver of joy after Gabe's passing. It was… so weird.

So surreal.

It felt strange to laugh after having been through so much pain and shock, but we found a way.

Gabe, I think quietly, *I'm doing it. I'm on my way to Fort Collins, the first stop on our tour of the world.*

If we ever get there.

If only we had Harson's number. I guess we could DM him, but he's got over a million followers. His DMs are probably...

I pull out my phone to check.

Yup, closed.

Thunder cracks outside, rumbling across the sky like a hungry stomach, and I shut my eyes, thankful that Barbazal is about to get some rain. Who the hell would divert the Colorado River away from a farming community? Do rich people not understand that their locally grown organic produce requires water? Would they rather have a lush green lawn than food?

Why is the world so twisted and backwards?

Ugh, and why am I back to thinking so hard about other people's problems? This isn't even my issue. There's not much I can do but talk to Jonah Macon, if I can even get close enough to him, and even that's a long shot.

I should just bury the Barbazal water problem in my brain, file it away somewhere in its deep recesses, and focus on getting to Fort Collins.

But I can't.

What if Jonah doesn't listen and Barbazal dries up, and all these people who have spent their whole lives here—Ethan's dad, and Silas, and Elias—have to pack up everything and leave the only home they've ever known?

As far as I know, nobody else here has the kind of power that would let them tap into what makes someone tick, what makes someone *really* afraid, and use it to remind them what's really important.

So the fate of Barbazal might rest in my hands.

I sigh.

Our car breaks down in the middle of nowhere and suddenly I'm responsible for thousands of livelihoods.

I roll to my side and look at Steph, who I'm startled to find is lying on her side staring at me.

Those piercing brown eyes…

"What's up?" I ask.

"I could ask you the same thing."

I sigh.

"Just thinking," I say, which isn't a lie but isn't the truth either.

"Thinking or spiraling?" she asks.

I smirk. She continues.

"We're going to make it to Fort Collins, I can feel it. And Barbazal is going to be fine. Out here in the wilderness, I'm sure they've had droughts before, right?"

I shake my head.

"I get the feeling they haven't," I say. "Not like this. Maybe a natural one, but not a manmade one."

Steph sighs, conceding that I'm right.

"I wish I had telekinetic powers," she says, "so I could just divert the river myself. Let the politicians sort it out later."

"You'd really do that?" I ask, teasing.

"Hell yeah! If Owen is right and they're really rerouting the Colorado River to serve a bunch of rich-asses with lawns? They can choke."

I snort. This girl is too much.

I stare into her eyes, dark and deep, and find her hands under the blanket.

"I told you," she says, "I'm here for *you*. Whatever happens. I know you care about people. Like, a lot. So, if you need to talk to Jonah Macon, we'll talk to Jonah Macon."

"But how?" I ask. "He's a celebrity politician. Apparently."

"At least to these people," says Steph. "But he has to be alone sometimes, right? Everybody shits."

"I am *not* talking to Jonah while he's taking a shit."

"You won't have to. We'll figure it out tomorrow. For *now*," she says, rolling over and unzipping her duffel on the nightstand. I hear the crinkle of cellophane and my stomach folds over and growls.

"Corn chips anyone?" she asks, tossing a bag over her shoulder so it hits me square in the chest.

"Oh, hell yeah," I say, sitting up and tearing open the bag like a wild animal.

I chonk 'em all down so fast I barely have time to taste them. I look up and see Steph turning up her bag and pouring the crumbs into her mouth.

We look at each other. Still hungry.

"Let's find a diner tomorrow. First thing in the morning."

I nod, and then I remember Ethan's text.

I turn and reach down under the mattress we're both on.

"What are you—"

I pull out a bar of chocolate. A *huge* bar. Like, Ethan mentioned he had chocolate stashed. He didn't say he had a chocolate stash the size of my face.

"Jackpot."

6: The Diner

Pretty much every small town I've ever been to has a diner. Usually it's retro, the kitchen grease hasn't been replaced since the Nineties, the coffee tastes like dog shit, and the food is exactly what you need at 4 am on a cold morning when you wake up for no reason because you're in a new place in a new bed and you're hungry and the guy you're staying with has only enough food for one.

This is the Plate and Skate Diner.

Steph takes a sip of her coffee.

"This tastes like dog shit."

I grin and stare down at my cup. She's right. But sometimes bad coffee just hits the spot.

She smiles up at me, and the sight of her holding back a laugh sends my sides into orbit. We both burst into laughter, and I hear the bell ring behind me announcing the arrival of a new customer.

I hear hushed voices behind me. From over the rim of her coffee mug, Steph stifles her laughter to look just past my head, and I can't help it—I turn around to look.

A woman in a navy pant suit has stepped up to the front counter, where Anita—that's the name of our waitress—runs up to meet her.

"Mornin'," she smiles, but the woman in the suit is clearly not here to be seated.

"What do you suppose she's here for?" Steph's voice intrudes. I hear her take another sip behind me, but I don't turn.

"I don't know," I reply absentmindedly, watching as our waitress turns and walks back toward the kitchen. The woman in the suit spots me, and I turn around *way* too fast.

"Wow," says Steph. I tuck my hair behind my ear and pick up my coffee mug so I can look busy.

"What?"

"You're *really* bad at spying on people."

I roll my eyes and Steph leans over the table, shoulders hunched, smile huge and mischievous like she's stalking prey.

"Who do you think she is?"

"Gotta be Maisie Dorsey."

"You think Maisie Dorsey would be slinking around the Plate and Skate at…" she taps her phone screen and it lights up with life, "four in the morning? No."

She has a point.

"I mean, I don't know many people who would be slinking around a Barbazal diner in a business suit like that."

"Yeah, that thing probably costs more than my car. Not a wrinkle in sight either. Reminds me of Diane from Typhon Mining."

My entire spine prickles with how obviously Steph is leaning to look past me.

"Uh, hello? She'll *see* you?"

"So?" she grins. "We don't even know who she is."

I hear footsteps behind me, and then I hear our waitress's voice.

"Coming right out for you," she says, before those same footsteps grow closer. Anita appears next to our table.

"Have you two decided what you'd like?"

"Um, yeah," says Steph, "I'll take the California benedict, please. Side of fruit?"

"Uh, sorry, the California's unavailable."

"What?" asks Steph, glancing down at the menu again just to make sure she read it right.

"Anything with poached eggs is off the docket," sighs Anita apologetically. "Sorry, hun. Dishes like that use up too much water.

We've been over our quota lately and had to make some tough choices. I could do scrambled on the side if you like?"

Steph shrugs. "Sounds good."

"Uh-huh," Anita says, jotting it down in her notepad. "And for you?"

Aw shit, I haven't even had a chance to look.

"I'll just have… uh…" and then I panic and stare straight at Steph, as though she would have any idea what to order for me? Steph shrugs and glances at Anita and I blurt out the first thing that comes to mind.

"I'll have… toast?"

"Toast?" they both exclaim in unison. Steph and Anita look at me with so much judgement, I wonder if I've spoken English.

"Uh, French toast," I correct. "With bacon." Okay, now that I'm talking, my stomach reminds me of just how hungry I really am. "And two eggs over medium, please."

Satisfied, Steph gathers up both of our menus and hands them to Anita, but she doesn't let her go just yet.

"So," asks Steph, "who's fancy suit lady?"

"Name's Daphne Brinkley," Anita says, "but I know who this order is for."

I steal another glance behind me, where I find Daphne twisting her hands and looking around nervously.

"I've worked here for thirty-five years and only one person has ever ordered a short stack of chocolate-chip smiley-face pancakes, a tomahawk steak, medium rare, a side of home fries with ketchup on the side, and a bowl of bread-n-butter pickles."

"What the—?" I blurt out. Steph snorts in my direction, but I couldn't help it. That order is weird as hell. "I mean, I'd remember that order too."

"Jonah's been orderin' it since he was a kid. Well, minus the tomahawk steak. That started when his doctor told him he was low on iron. Must've made up for it by now eatin' like that."

"Woah, you know Jonah Macon?" asks Steph, glancing at me with the most suggestive smile. Who's the worst at snooping again? She might as well do a full-blown eyebrow wiggle at me.

"'Course," she says, refilling Steph's coffee mug. "Y'know he was born and raised here?"

"What was he like as a kid?"

Damn, Steph isn't holding back.

"Oh, you know, shy. Quiet. Used to come in with his dad all the time. Never gave me any trouble. Sweet kid. I'm sure he'll do right by us with this drought mess. Hope so anyway. Hard to run a diner on limited water."

Steph glances down at her mug, and I glance down at mine. Maybe that explains the state of the coffee.

Anita turns to leave.

"I'll be back with y'all's order."

I try to picture a tiny Jonah walking into this diner, hand in hand with his father. Did he have that million-dollar politician smile even then? Or did that only develop after the cameras and the interviews and the speculation that must come with having such a publicly available face?

I think of his diner order. Chocolate-chip smiley-face pancakes. Tomahawk steak, medium rare. Side of fries. Bowl of pickles. I can picture the news people covering the story.

I just can't see how someone who claims to be environmentally responsible can order a tomahawk steak, something that's not only hostile to animals but requires gallons and gallons of water to produce. Did he even take care to ask if that steak was grass fed and sustainably raised?

I'm all for eating sustainably, but if Jonah Macon has to order such a bizarre breakfast from his hotel room because of the paparazzi, that's... kinda sad.

"Hey," says Steph, "you're thinking again."

"I was just thinking about Jonah."

Steph's smile doesn't fall, but it doesn't rise either.

"Y'know, I meant what I said about being here for you and helping you do whatever makes you happy. But I'm also here to ask you questions like: Yo, Alex, are you doing what makes you happy or are you ruminating on something that might make you sad until you fix it?"

I put my mug down, unable to look at her.

"Just," she says, resting her hand over my fingers, "be careful, okay?"

I nod.

And our food arrives.

The French toast distracts me for a while, because, hey, it's French toast, and a boatload of calories ends up being exactly what I need. Steph's phone lights up just as she pops a couple of fresh berries into her mouth. She leans and peers over the street before muttering, "Dammit."

"What?" I say, wedging another piece of French toast into my mouth.

"I asked the group chat if anyone knows anyone with a Saturn that doesn't need pistons. Or, you know, can drive us."

"Let me guess," I say. "We're too far away?"

"Can no one spare a six-hour drive on a weekend? I even offered to pay!"

"Not even Ryan?" I ask around another mouthful.

"Not even Ryan," she sighs. "Apparently, he's gone off to Appalachia to explore some exotic bird calls or something."

I chuckle. "Sounds like Ryan." A thought hits me. "Are there exotic birds in Appalachia?"

"Who knows?" she chuckles, taking a bite of her eggs. "So anyway, what's the plan?"

"What plan?"

"To get close to Jonah?"

A plan? I don't really have a plan. I was just going to wait around and see if we ran into him?

I need a plan.

"What if," Steph says, "we wait until he goes to the bathroom—?"

"No," I say immediately. I've already played that idea out in my head, and I'd rather not pick up a stalking charge before we get to the big city.

"I know, I know," she says, "but just hear me out. We wait for him to go to the bathroom, and then you reach over the stall and read his emotions."

"Steph, there's no way I'm doing that in the bathroom! What emotions would he have in there anyway?"

"You've never taken a joyous shit before?" she asks.

The laughter bubbles forth so quick, I feel coffee spray from my nose and I scramble for a napkin, trying not to choke on more laughs. Steph is trying so hard to stifle her laughs, she has to turn away from me and cover her face completely.

I look around, heat flooding my entire face, and when I can finally get a breath in, and Steph's composed herself too, she continues. "Think about it, though. Where else will we catch him alone?"

"What if we do this the right way and just ask his assistant for some one-on-one time with him? I'm sure he could spare a five-minute interview."

"His schedule is probably *packed*," she says. "And that's probably with press engagements only. We've gotta be sneaky."

I look over my shoulder where Daphne is still standing there, wringing her hands, waiting on Jonah's ridiculous order. Maybe tomahawk steaks take a long time to sear to perfection. Before I have time to talk myself out of it, I'm up and out of the booth and walking toward her.

"No! Wait! Alex, what are you doing?" come Steph's frantic whispers behind me. But I press on toward Daphne, who's staring back at me like she's unsure if I'm going to ask her a question or walk right by.

"Hey," I say, *way* too eagerly. I give her a generous distance, because a huge purple aura flares up around her head like one of those lizards with the fans that pop out when they're startled.

"Good morning," she grins, that same plastic, glazed-over look that Jonah was wearing in Elias's memory. She's all smiles, but clearly nervous about something, probably wondering whether I'm paparazzi or not.

"You look like you know your way around this place," I say, having no idea where the hell I'm going with this. "Is the food good?"

She smirks and nods past me. "You tell me."

Oh. Right. I've been sitting eating with a friend. She's the one who hasn't eaten yet. *Stupid, so stupid! Come on, Alex.*

"Can I help you with something?" she asks. I look at her again, sheepish this time.

"Look," I begin, pressing all my fingers against each other. "I know Jonah must be super busy this week, but… could he spare ten minutes with me?"

It's gonna be a no, I just know it. Steph was right, this was a bad idea. I'm so embarrassed, I want to curl up into a little ball and disappear.

But that "no" doesn't come.

"Are you a student?"

Am I a what?

"Uh, yes! I mean, I'm always down to learn…" *Alex, get it together.* "What I mean is… I'm not a student at an accredited institution, but I really care about the people of Barbazal, and I know Jonah does too. I want to know what his plan is for the drought situation."

Daphne's purple aura vanishes suddenly, and hope wells in my chest. Maybe I'm getting somewhere with her?

"Mr. Macon is dedicated to ensuring a better life for all Coloradans," she smiles comfortably, "Climate change is of the utmost importance to him, and with the recent heatwave affecting several farming communities in the area, the drought is at the top of his list of priorities."

She just spent several dozen words not answering my question. And then I realize why that purple aura disappeared—Daphne is in her element now. Catch Jonah Macon's assistant sneaking around a diner stealth-ordering a steak and pickles, and she's frazzled as shit. Ask Jonah Macon's assistant a political question, and it's all cupcakes and roses for her.

I'm going to have to take a different approach.

"What does that mean?" I ask.

Her face is unwavering as I continue.

"What does 'at the top of his list of priorities' mean? Is he doing anything to stop it? Anything to help Barbazal and the people who make their living farming? Or does it mean he's ready to tell people that it's at the top of his list of priorities?"

I come off harsher than I intended to. Daphne forces a smile, but her narrowed eyes tell me she's prepared to do battle.

"It means that I'll forward your concerns to Jonah, and I'm sure he'll be delighted to hear such passion from a supporter."

I keep my eyes trained on her, silently studying her, wondering what I can say to throw her off her game.

"Jonah didn't always order the tomahawk steak, you know," I say. "He started with just the pancakes."

And I turn to leave. But when I glance over my shoulder, I see her standing there with the blankest expression. When Anita practically jogs up to her with the stack of three Styrofoam to-go clamshells, Daphne doesn't flinch. A new color blend blooms above Daphne's head, mixing together like watercolors in the air. It reminds me of the hospital, sitting with Gabe and Dad in a way-too-white waiting room, in a chair so high my feet dangled above the floor.

She came in with a clipboard—they always had clipboards—and she shut the door behind her and sighed.

"Well?" asked Dad. But he didn't have to. He knew. Gabe knew. I knew.

"We got the results back."

I slam myself back down into the booth across from Steph, who stops mid-chew to stare at me wide-eyed.

"Are you okay?"

We cried that day at the doctor's office, auras oscillating between purple, deep blue, and red.

Purple, for fear of losing Mom.

Blue, for the deep, aching sadness we felt.

I wonder if I would've seen this new watercolor magenta blend over us all if I were this familiar with my powers back then.

"Alex?"

I don't look at Steph—I can't. If I do, the tears will come, and if the tears come, Steph will call the whole plan off.

I focus on my plate, shoving a huge forkful of French toast into my mouth.

And then I offer a sliver of an explanation.

"She's confused."

7: The Car

"Confused, huh?" asks Steph.

"Yup."

I hate to give a one-word answer, but my brain is busy. We're lying side by side on the grass in Owen's backyard, if you can call it a backyard. It's about the size of a queen-sized bed, but it's the only chill spot we have in this town. So, here I lie, and I take a deep breath of the fresh and hot Barbazal air. I can feel how dry it is in my nostrils. Feels like the moisture here is just… gone.

I'll forward your concerns to Jonah, and I'm sure he'll be delighted to hear such passion from a supporter.

Daphne, that… that…

No, I won't call her names. She's just doing her job. And doing it well, frankly.

"You know what you need?" asks Steph.

I need a lot of things. A hug. A nap. A drink.

"What do I need?" I ask, humoring her.

"A walk," she says, peeling herself from the ground. "A long, boring walk in the hot sun."

"In a town with no water? Pass."

She glances up at Owen's trailer.

"Owen's got water," she says.

That gets my attention.

I sit up and look at her.

"You can't mean to imply that we should really go steal from Ethan's uncle, right?"

"I mean, is it stealing if we're staying there? What kind of host doesn't offer their guests water? And then tell them they can have as much as they want? It's *water*, for god's sake."

I mean, she has a point. But also…

"The kind of host that also doesn't offer their guests anything to eat?" I remind her.

"Good point," she says. "Alright, time to find a garden hose in a public park then."

"The hell?" I chuckle. There's no way I'm drinking from a public park hose. Do they even have hoses in public parks?

After way too much debate, we end up asking Silas for two more water bottles and walking ourselves down the main thoroughfare of Barbazal. It's cooler today than it was yesterday, and there's a welcome breeze rolling through, rustling my hair, making my skin prickle.

"Ever noticed how it smells here?" asks Steph.

"Smells? Like what?"

"I don't know. Farm stuff?"

"The hell does farm stuff smell like, Miss Seattle?"

"Hey, I was in the city."

"Then how do you know what farm stuff smells like?"

"It smells kinda like a combination of… daisies…" she begins, sniffing at the air goofily like a basset hound, "dirt… and rust."

I sniff the air, much less theatrically, and realize she's right.

"It smells dry."

"Yeah, I guess it kinda does," she says. "Speaking of, since you're determined to get back to the subject, no matter what extracurricular activities I suggest, what's the new plan to talk to Jonah? Daphne didn't seem too keen on us. What did you say to her anyway?"

"I…" Where do I even start with recalling what happened?

"That bad? Did you tell her she needs a lint roller or something?"

That gets a laugh out of me.

"Uh, no. But I uh… kind of told her I knew Jonah's diner order?"

"You what?" she asks, mock outrage playing on that last word. "Why? Like as a threat?"

She drops her voice down a whole octave lower than I even thought her voice could go.

"I'm Alex Chen. Give me ten minutes with Jonah Macon, or I'll tell everyone Mr. King-of-climate-change likes his tomahawk steak medium rare and his pickles *extra* sweet!"

"Yes, Steph," I grin, my voice dripping with sarcasm, "as a threat. *No.* I don't know, I just wanted her to know that I knew information she didn't want me to know."

"Wait, wait, wait. You wanted her to know that you know something she doesn't want you to know? What if she knows you know that something she doesn't want you to know, *because* she knows you know how to see things you shouldn't know, but you know, you know?"

"You think she can tell I have powers?" I ask.

"I mean, no, but just be careful, okay? Have you told anyone about them? Besides me, and Ryan?"

I shake my head.

Not even Gabe knew.

I kept it all to myself.

Until I met her. This girl.

"Nope," I say, "just you and Ryan. You're both… kinda special to me, you know?"

"Couldn't tell," she says, playfully elbowing me in the arm. "Anyway, I've got your back. Always. But also, be careful."

I have to smile, because Steph cares. But also, I've had these powers ever since my dad left us. Like, straight-up grabbed his car keys and walked out the front door forever.

When I learned that he died, I learned to control it. Make it work for me. Help me instead of hurt me. I know how to use my powers now. I've been hiding them for half my life. I know Steph cares, so why is something tightening in my chest at the thought of her trying to tell me how to manage my ability to take on the emotions of others?

I stuff those feelings down. *Deep* down. And smile.

"Be careful?"

"You just… seem *really* confident messing with people's feelings, you know?"

I remember what Owen said about Charlotte, how I turned her into a zombie. I *know* not to take on the emotions of others without considering that the consequences could be dire, and permanent. I don't do that anymore.

But that doesn't mean I can't use my powers to my advantage. I know what I'm doing.

"Steph, I've been doing this for over a decade. I know what I'm doing."

Her eyes are trained on me, her face even, and I can't tell what she's thinking. No auras glow around her, no sensations reach me. She just… studies me. And then she shrugs, and moves on.

"So, you told her his diner order. Now what?"

Oh shit. I hadn't really thought that far ahead yet. "I mean, we could try to find her again."

"Should we wait until Daphne goes to the bathroom?"

"What is it with you and stalking people in the bathroom?"

"What, should I try to ask her out like I did with Diane? Remember how well that worked?"

"Actually, it *did* work, remember? Maybe Daphne will fall to your charms like Diane did. Or, like I did."

She looks down at her shoes, but her smile brings out the red in the apples of her cheeks. She scratches the back of her neck in thought.

"Something tells me it'll be hard to get her *or* Jonah alone."

She's right.

*

The walk into town is on a slight decline. I look down at Steph's hand, swinging next to mine, wondering—hoping—she'll bump into mine and invite me to hold hers, but she doesn't. Instead she rattles my thoughts back into the present with a single word.

"Woah."

I look up at what we're about to walk into. The town square. Shop after shop lines the stone path, which looks carefully preserved through the years. Decades. Maybe even centuries. Some of the stones are cracked and brittle-looking, sharp scores in the earth here and there. I wonder if it's from the incessant heat that's sure to settle over this place in just a few hours.

Or the lack of water.

"Morning!" chimes a slender middle-aged man in a pub cap, which somehow feels *very* out of place among all this central American farmland. He hops down the front steps of his shop, a huge sign dangling overhead that says *Bobby's Books n' Things*.

"I don't recognize you two," he says, cocking an eyebrow, "and you're not dressed like reporters, unless…" He steps forward with a pointer finger and thumb on his chin. "Are you from some alternative publication outta Boulder?"

Steph grins, and I do too.

"Good guess," she says. "Alternative, yes. Publication, no. We're musicians."

Warmth pours over his face.

"Ah," he coos, "music is the spice of life. I can't get any work done without it." He gestures up at his bookstore and lets out a heavy sign. "Been in the business sixty years, my family."

I look to Steph, who also seems to have clocked the weight of his words. He said it so sadly. More melancholy than nostalgia.

"Has… business slowed down?" she asks.

He gives a sad chuckle.

"You could say that. You wouldn't think a drought would hit a bookstore so hard, but… we used to have a café attached. Right over there."

I follow his gaze to a tattered awning off the side of Bobby's Books n' Things. Totally empty underneath. No chairs, no tables, no other sign that a café had ever been part of the business. I imagine what this place must have looked like just a few years ago. Did kids gather here after school to do their homework? Did parents use this as a pickup spot once they were off work? How many first dates happened here that led to deeper connections? How many business deals happened here, starting new ventures that may not have otherwise existed?

Did little Jonie Macon come here when he was little?

"You can't run a café on no water," he shrugs, "so there that went. Anyway, I'm Bobby."

Steph shakes his hand.

"Did your parents name you after the place?"

Bobby and I both look at Steph in total confusion.

"I, uh… You just said it had been around for sixty years, so… it's older than you, right?"

His face goes blank for a minute before he absolutely *erupts* in laughter.

A woman across the street, straining under the weight of an enormous potted plant, emerges from her flower shop.

"The hell are you laughing about, Robert?"

"These two," he chuckles as he slowly regains his composure. "These lovely ladies, bless 'em, asked if I'm named after this place."

"Oh, don't flatter him," she grunts, setting the plant down on the porch and brushing the potting soil from her apron. "That's Robert William Dalliday, the *fifth*. He won't let me forget it. And I'm Paisley Anne Galloway, the first. Still Galloway Flowers though," she says, gesturing to her own business's sign. "So I overheard you two are musicians! Are we getting a performance here in Barbazal for the election?"

"Jonie musta covered it," grins Robert proudly, and then he levels his eyes at me. "He did pay y'all, right? I like Jonie, but I don't trust politicians, and he's, well…"

His voice trails off, but the look he and Paisley exchange says it all: *one of them now.*

There's a story there, but I don't press. I get back to the topic I want to know more about.

"You have a beautiful floral shop," I say. "But how do you run this place with the drought?"

Her eyes narrow slightly, and I wonder if I've said something wrong.

"You two here with the government?" she asks, her voice bitter. "I'm not skimming extra off the city's supply if that's what you're wondering."

"No, of course not," Steph jumps in quickly.

"I just," I say, trying to save this conversation, "wanted to know if you're doing okay. If this place is… doing okay."

Paisley and Bobby both soften, still staring at me.

"Sorry," says Paisley, her shoulders relaxing. "It's just… been a long summer."

"I apologize too," admits Bobby. "But if you want to know all 'bout Barbazal, how we got here, our journey to where we are today? Go look at that statue."

He points into the distance, through the shops, where the path continues to the town square. A huge white stone statue sits mounted on a pillar in the middle, and I look to Steph, who's looking back at me with a nod.

To the statue.

We make it to the center of the town, where that huge stone carving is waiting for us. It's clearly a man on a horse, but I find the little bronze plaque around the other side and read it aloud, curiosity taking a firm hold on me.

Augustus Jeremiah Oscar Rhett Barbazal, II

Commemorated here for his God-like love
and compassion in planting this town on a
foundation of love, where <u>all are welcome</u>.

1928

"Wow," says Steph, stepping up next to me and inspecting the plaque herself. She reaches down and traces the letters. Then she looks up at Mr. Barbazal. "That's… impressively progressive."

"1928?" I ask, following her gaze up to the horse and its rider. "I have a feeling love and compassion might have meant something totally different back then."

"What, letting their workers use the same bathrooms as them?"

"Maybe."

"Or maybe he was nicer than that. It says right there, underlined, *all are welcome*. Although, I guess, welcome doesn't necessarily mean accepted."

I study his face, turned up toward the sky, arm outstretched, holding his hat like he's about to fling it into the air. His other hand is, strangely, reaching behind him. Like, all five fingers outstretched, as if he's reaching for someone not pictured.

As if he's prepared to help those behind him.

I grin.

"I'm gonna believe he was awesome."

I feel Steph look over at me, but I keep my gaze on his face.

"In fact," I continue, beginning to walk, folding my arms and reaching into the deepest recesses of my brain's vats of creativity, "Mr. Augustus Jeremiah Oscar Rhett Barbazal, the second, began his life as a humble shoe-shiner—"

"What are you doing?"

I glance over my shoulder with a grin. "LARPing."

I catch her grin before I turn back to pacing.

"He began as a shoe-shiner in Denver, Colorado. Mr. Barbazal would shine the shoes of the *best* of men. Bankers. Venture capitalists. Hedge fund managers. Stockbrokers—"

"Do you know the difference between all of those, or—"

"Shh," I chuckle. "Do you wanna hear the story or not?" Steph folds her arms and rolls her eyes.

"Stockbrokers," I continue. "But he was unhappy. He was lonely. He was shining shoes… but his life wasn't so shiny."

"Oh my god."

"*But*," I continue over Steph's playful muttering, leaning around the statue for dramatic effect, "he had a vision. He had a dream. He knew he was going somewhere special, somewhere his heart could sing into the sky and the wind would rise up behind him, spurring him onward into the great unknown."

"Isn't that a Lord Huron lyric?"

"Sounds like it, huh? But no. Anyway, Mr. Augustus Jeremiah Oscar Rhett Barbazal, the second, packed up everything he owned, and he walked off into the night with nothing to his name except his shoe-shining briefcase and a granola bar."

"Had granola bars been invented yet?"

"Okay, then jerky or… hardtack or some shit," I laugh. "*Anyway*, he walked for days. He was so, so tired. So, so hungry. He dreamt of tomahawk steak and pickles."

That gets a *pffft* out of Steph.

"And then, just when he thought he couldn't go on, just as the hunger threatened to consume him, he found a clearing. Or what he thought was a clearing. He found a community of campers. Only three of them. But they all had the same dream: walking into the wilderness with only a briefcase and a snack, to create a place where love thrives, and compassion commands the law."

Steph's face has gone from *Oh holy hell this is the goofiest story I've ever heard* to *Oh shit, you've got my attention*.

"Turns out, he was devastatingly gay."

"Devastatingly, you say?" she laughs. "I'm using that from now on. 'Hi, name's Steph Gingrich. Expert drummer, impeccable radio host, devastatingly gay.'"

"I like it. And I guess that makes me Alex Chen, professional guitarist, expert emotion-reader, devastatingly gay."

"Lucky for both of us," she says, stepping around the statue to join me. Before I can realize what's even happening, she leans forward, slips her arm around my waist, tips my chin up with her free hand and plants a kiss next to my mouth.

"Hi," I whisper, slipping both my hands around her waist and pulling her into me. I kiss her back, square on the lips this time, wanting to drink her in and assure her we're going to make it out here in the middle of fucking nowhere, because we have each other.

She pulls back.

"Hey," she says, tucking her hair behind her ear. "Thanks for being out here with me. For this adventure. It's… pretty cool. Even if Fort Collins is… maybe not happening."

"It's happening," I promise, although I'm still not sure how we're going to fix this stupid car, and drive six hours to the show by tomorrow night. "Anyone in the group chat have an old Saturn for us?"

I immediately wish I hadn't asked. Steph's smile vanishes. She reaches into her pocket to pull out her phone and check. I take the moment to look back up at the statue, wondering what the original Mr. Barbazal was *really* like. He supposedly founded this place on compassion and love, but… would he have tried to fix the car of two strangers who'd wandered into his home?

I can feel my forehead wrinkling as determination wells in me.

"Someone in this town *has* to have the means to help, and I intend to find out who. Even if I have to start busting down some doors."

"Okay, woah," she says, hands up like she's calming a racehorse. "No need to get violent on these people."

"Violent on who?" comes a voice from nearby, so close it startles both of us into oblivion. As I focus on slowing my heart rate back down to a survivable pace, a figure emerges from around the other side of the statue—a tall man, white cowboy hat, grey T-shirt, dark jeans. He has a big gray handlebar mustache. Looks like a country singer from, like, the Eighties maybe?

"Morning!" He grins, warmly.

Warmth radiates from him. His smile is genuine, like the kind of smile you see on a parent's face at their kid's wedding. Is he always this bubbly? In a way… he reminds me of Gabe.

I somehow trust him immediately.

"Morning," I reply.

"Nice to meet both of you. I'm Mayor Griffin Biggs. I heard you two broke down just down the road. Hope you don't mind that I arranged a tow for ya."

"Mayor?" asks Steph.

"A tow?" I ask.

"'Course!" he says, as if the idea of just leaving the car out there was absolutely preposterous. "Can't have vehicles broken down on the highway. It's a hazard to drivers, not to mention who knows what could happen to it out there. You can find it at Elias's shop. It's just up the road that way. Walkable distance. Maybe half a mile. Get yer exercise."

I smile at him, then look at Steph.

"Sounds like the car will be safer now."

That gets her to crack a smile.

"Thanks, Mayor Biggs," she says.

"Don't mention it. City's covering the cost of the tow. Can't rightfully tow a car and then charge the owners, seein' as y'all are so young. How'd you end up here anyway?"

"We're supposed to play a show in Fort Collins tomorrow night," Steph explains. I nod.

"Oh, you're musicians?" He grins hugely. "That's delightful! I used to play the banjo myself years ago—don't tell anyone you heard that. Had to let it go after the missus passed."

"Oh, I'm… sorry to hear that." And I really am. "Why, uh, why did you give it up when she passed?"

A blue aura glows over his head, and Steph looks at me like *Why the hell are you asking this poor man such invasive questions?!*

He answers though.

"She loved the banjo. She's the one who taught me to play. My Wisteria Avileen. We used to be a whole family of musicians, me, Wisteria, and our twelve."

"Your twelve?" asks Steph.

"Children. Most are grown now."

Holy shit, this man has twelve kids.

"Clover, Ethel, Heather, Clementine, Blossom, Rosemary, Primrose, Juniper, Opal, Daisy, Laurel, and Iris. All girls." His aura fades from blue to a brilliant gold at the mention of his daughters, and my heart lifts. I feel a warmth come over me, a cloud-soft tickle against my skin like I'm neck-deep in a bowl of feathers, or like fish are gently swimming all around me in a sea of gold. It makes me wonder when, if ever, I would have seen Dad glowing gold. It's hard to imagine. If I'd had my powers then, I can only dream of what he would have looked like. Definitely purple. All the time. Especially right before he walked out.

When we visited Mom in the hospital, he might have been blue, perpetually. Until Gabe couldn't understand what Mom was asking for enough to get her a cup of water. Then he would have been red. But mostly, when all was quiet, when nothing was happening, when Gabe wasn't pissing him off and I didn't have to jump into the middle to mediate, he would have been purple.

Worried.

Anxious.

Terrified.

That was Dad.

"And what, may I ask, are your names?" he asks, adjusting his weight to one foot and looking from Steph, to me, and then back.

"I'm Steph," she offers, although I sense hesitation in her voice. "And this is Alex. Our car broke down because we ran out of oil and blew out the engine. Do you… happen to know anyone with an open afternoon tomorrow? Or… a Saturn with pistons they don't need?"

"Well, I might!" replies Mayor Biggs with a beaming smile.

"Know someone?" Steph and I both ask in unison, as all attempts to hide our desperation fade quickly at the prospect of some kind of rescue.

"*Have* a Saturn with pistons I don't need," he elaborates. Steph and I look at each other, and her smile matches mine. *Finally. Finally* we're getting somewhere! "My daughter Clover has been fixin' up a Saturn *way* in the back of our barn. I'm sure she's given up on the project. Maybe it's a match! I live right up there," he says, looking behind him and pointing up to the hill just beyond the town, where there's a clear view through the trees of a house—not a large one, or at least not a house the size you'd expect from someone named Mayor Griffin Biggs. A white house, average size, looks like a rancher—single story. Modest.

"I won't be able to join you, unfortunately. Too much election business to handle in town." His voice drops a bit at that last part, and I get the feeling this whole election is weighing him down. I mean, it's to be expected, right? It's a lot of pressure for a mayor of thousands of people. Dealing with the paparazzi and political entourages and fancy cars and parades and welcome processions. I can't imagine Mayor Biggs has ever dealt with anything of this magnitude before.

Although, I guess Mayor Biggs is a politician himself, so… maybe he has.

A thought crosses my mind that tightens my chest like little else has lately.

Gabe would have made a great, *great* mayor for Haven Springs. I could totally see it. Mayor Gabriel Chen. Although he would've insisted on "just Gabe," because that's the kind of guy he was. The kind of guy to risk his life—to *give* his life, to save someone.

85

"Hey," comes Steph's voice, and I feel her arm around mine, snapping me back into the moment. "I think that sounds like a great idea, don't you?"

"Uh, yeah!" I reply, assuming whatever part of the conversation I missed was related to Mayor Biggs inviting us over to his house.

"Hey, before we go…" I pause, resting my hands on Steph's, which is still resting on my arm, "how's uh… how are things with the drought? I heard Barbazal is really going through it."

"Yes," sighs Mayor Biggs, shoving his hands in his pockets and gazing up at the statue. "We, the people of Barbazal, have weathered storm after storm through the years. You don't get to be a hundred-year-old town of twenty thousand and fifty three—" I smirk inside because I was damn close with my population guess. "—without a fair share of hardships. But we'll figure it out. We've got resources in the meantime, you know. Water bottles were flown in from Denver just last week so we can save Barbazalians the drive. You know, most stores don't deliver out here."

"But," I have to ask, "is there a long-term solution?"

"Alex," whispers Steph.

"No, it's a fair question!" acknowledges Mayor Biggs. "Long-term solutions are for long-term problems. We're in a bit of a dry spell because of a recent heatwave, but now that it's over, our climate should return to symbiosis as quickly as it left."

"No offense, but… have you had experts out here to confirm that, or are you hoping that's the case?"

"We have made assessments," Mayor Biggs nods, even though that's not what I asked. "And our assessments have concluded that this was a temporary event, a fluke in the weather, if you will. We've had lower temperatures here than we've had in weeks, you know."

Oh god, it's the old "global warming can't be happening because it's cold where I live" argument. I like Mayor Biggs and all, I like his smile, I trust his heart, but if he believes climate change isn't a problem, if he thinks this recent heatwave that ripped through Barbazal isn't indicative of a larger problem, I *have* to side-eye his politics.

"Do you believe climate change is a real problem?" I ask.

"Of course!" he replies, to my *great* surprise. "Of course we do, but we can't uproot our lives and move out of Barbazal just because of a little weather shift, you know? We have to adapt, we have to bring our people resources so we can adjust, you know?"

He's throwing in a lot of "you knows" for someone who's not trying to give political answers. And sure enough, seconds later, a purple aura flares up around his head, and then it fades into blue.

If only I could get inside that head of his…

And then, as if the universe heard my silent wish, Mayor Biggs turns around and stares up at the statue again.

"As sure as Augustus Jeremiah Oscar Rhett Barbazal the second founded this place on love and compassion, we will continue this place—our home—on adaptation and resilience."

I glance at Steph, who's looking up at me with questioning eyes like *What the hell are you up to?* and I wink at her to let her know that I'm definitely up to something, and that I know exactly what I'm doing. I've had these powers for so long now, it feels like I'm holding a painter's palette in my hands. Just call me the Michelangelo of emotions. I'm a professional, and I know *exactly* what Biggs needs. I pull away from Steph and step right up behind Mayor Biggs, my hand outstretched so I can tap into that purple haze around him.

Voom! I'm sucked into his world, hazy and sickly plum, like the color of a bruise, and a dull pain creeps down my arms. Those golden goldfish are back, but when I look down at them, I realize they're not fish at all—they're leaves. My arms are covered in vines, coiling up over my fingers and wrists, anchoring me to the floor.

I'm standing in a living room filled with white, green, and light brown rattan. I'm not the only thing in here covered in plant life. Huge bursting ferns and monsteras line the baseboards, vines hang down from the ceiling like hair, a hazy mist covers the room. I'm in a literal jungle, which I guess is what living in a house with twelve kids must feel like. By the vintage design of the furniture and the realization that the carpet itself is green, I guess I must be looking at a place that's been in the family for generations. And then I get my answer.

"Girls!" coos a man's voice from the doorway.

A young man—maybe in his thirties?—stands there in jeans and a white T-shirt.

"Your mother and I have a surprise for you!" He pulls his white cowboy hat—exactly like the one Mayor Biggs was just wearing, just far, far crisper looking, brand new. His big blue eyes go even huger, and he squats down, arms outstretched at the sight of about a dozen—no… I count *exactly* a dozen girls, ranging in age from two to teens who sprint in from the kitchen, squealing for their father. A couple are dressed identically, which makes me think they might be twins, but they all run in with unbridled enthusiasm. They rush him right there in the living room, tackling him and covering his face in kisses, and I'm sure I've never seen so much love in one room.

"What is it, Daddy?" screams one.

"Are we getting a puppy?"

"Are we going to the park?"

"Is a storm rolling in, and can we watch it on the veranda?"

"No no no," he laughs, cuddling them all in close.

"Well, what *is* it, Dad? Don't leave us wondering!"

"Yeah, tell us!"

"Is it about the baby?"

I gasp.

A baby?

"Why, yes," he grins. "It *is* about the baby."

I hold my breath and wonder if I really want to be here. That aura I saw—an aching purple blotch—does *not* look like a father running in to meet his twelve daughters and talk to them about the thirteenth.

Oh no.

"You're getting a little sister!"

All of them erupt in squeals and cheering, throwing their arms around their father.

"Yay, another girl!"

"What should we name her?"

"I think we should name her Petunia."

"Petunia's an ugly name. What about Peony?"

"Peony isn't a name at all!"

"Your mother and I have chosen a name already, actually," assures Mayor Biggs, squeezing them all again tight. Suddenly another dogpile befalls him, all of the girls ready with more questions, rapid-firing at him so fast. I wonder how he copes with all this attention *all* of the time. But I guess that's how his job is too, as mayor and all.

"What is it, Papa?"

"Is it Tulip, Daddy? Is it Tulip?"

"Petal?"

"Orchid?"

He throws his head back in laughter at their curiosity. They seem like delightful kids.

"Magnolia May Biggs."

The silence is palpable, and then the questions start anew.

"Magnolia?" asks one with utter confusion.

"But that's not even a flower name."

"Neither is Laurel, Blossom!"

"Or Opal!"

"But Opal's at least a gemstone. Rosemary's just a plant!"

"A *yummy* and *useful* plant, thank you, *Daisy*."

"Girls, girls," coos Mayor Biggs, "there's a very good reason behind the name Magnolia, and do you know what that is?"

He looks up at the oldest, who can't be more than fifteen years old, with long curly red hair. She leans in close, a few of the ceiling vines bending with her.

"Is it because magnolias are strong?"

His smile beams so brilliant, I would expect a golden aura, but instead, those little purple flickers dance through the air like tiny tetra fish do. A thin haze of anxious purple all over, with flecks of absolute terror sprinkled across it. His bottom lip trembles so subtly, I almost miss it.

"That's exactly right, Clover," he nods. "Magnolias are strong. Resilient. They'll weather the driest earth and the cruelest of storms, and right now, your sister needs to be *strong*. Like a Magnolia. And she needs us to be strong for her, okay?"

I try to swallow but can't, and all twelve girls nod together, the oldest few exchanging glances like they know something's wrong. Horribly, horribly wrong.

Vines shoot up from the ground, racing up my legs and torso and over my arms, yanking me down, threatening to swallow me whole. I shut my eyes, but before I can scream, the vines vanish, disintegrating against my skin like dandruff and flaking into the wind. I open my eyes again.

I'm in a hospital. Mayor Biggs is holding a woman with long red curly hair, who is sobbing into his shoulder. Her knee-length floral dress looks like a hospital gown—it *is* a hospital gown—and he holds her so close, so tight, as she cries, that I feel tears spring to my own eyes at the realization of what's happened.

The thirteenth daughter of Griffin and Wisteria Biggs is…

… gone.

Grass sprouts up through the tile and up around my shoes. I'm standing on lush green grass, and when I look up, I find Mayor Biggs standing to my right, and exactly a dozen women, many of them around my age, some in floral dresses, some in shorts, standing in a circle across the yard. It's blazing hot out here, and some of them fan their faces against the scorching sun. But all of them—every single one—is staring up. Up at a tree as tall as the single-story ranch house behind them. A tree with big green leaves, bursting with pillowy white flowers as big as my head. One of the women reaches up and dabs at her eye with a napkin, and the next woman pulls her close against her.

I leave Biggs' side and approach, the sounds growing fainter as I walk.

I look up at the tree. A magnolia.

One of the girls, the tallest, with long curly red hair pulled back in a braid halfway down her back, breaks from the group and steps forward.

Slowly.

Her face is tear-stained, but she's not crying now, almost like she's cried every tear she has to cry. Her brows are knit together determinedly as she cradles something in her arms. I strain to see what it is, but soon I get my answer. She kneels at the foot of the tree and gently nestles a big glass fishbowl in the grass, as carefully as if it were a newborn baby.

In the fishbowl, a *huge* orange goldfish flits from wall to wall, sucking at the water as it swishes its fins around playfully.

She—I'm guessing this is the oldest, Clover, based on her hair—stands back up and rests her hand on the tree.

"Before you were born," she says, her accent sharp like her father's, "Daddy said I could get a pet goldfish, and if I took real good care of him, I could hold you when you joined us earthside, feed you bottles, and even roll you around in our little red wagon."

I feel my cheeks burning with more tears, and I glance down at my feet and take a deep breath before Clover continues.

"Well," she says, looking down at the fish, "I took care of him. He's an old man now. His tank uses too much water to keep him. We're in a drought, you know. We've all gotta do our part."

She glances around at her sisters, all of whom nod before turning back to the Magnolia.

"So," sighs Clover, shoving her hands in her pockets, "I thought he'd make a good friend for ya. 'Til his time is up too. He'll keep you company out here." Her voice cracks now, and I hear her sniff. "His name's Boy. Since he's the only boy among us. I'm not creative."

Several sad laughs ring through the group, and even I can't help but crack a smile.

"You take good care of him out here for me," she says, wincing in pain. "We… we won't forget you." She turns to leave suddenly. Right toward me. A moment of panic grips me, and then I remember she can't see me.

She steps right into me, walking through me like a cloud of smoke, and I feel a wave of cold come over my entire body. I begin to shiver, shutting my eyes and embracing the darkness until I hear a familiar voice.

Steph's voice. "Ha! Totally."

I look up at the back of Mayor Biggs' head. At the statue before him. And then I look over at Steph, who's mid-sentence.

"You'd think those people up in Denver wouldn't mind not watering their lawn for a few weeks, am I ri—"

Steph sees my face, and a breeze rolls through and I realize my face is wet. Just as Mayor Biggs begins to turn around to look at me, I wipe away my tears ferociously before he can see. But he does.

"That statue," I explain, my voice cracking, "something about it just… it's beautiful."

Fuck, that's probably the most unbelievable thing I've ever said, and from the look on Steph's face, she knows it too.

"Isn't it lovely?" asks the Mayor, sighing up at it. "I had it commissioned from an artist out of Denver. Over thirty years ago now." He whistles. "Man, does time fly."

"That water shortage," I say, wanting to cut to the point so Steph and I can get out of here. "Is it really because people in Denver don't want to stop watering their lawns? Is that why you're diverting the river?"

Mayor Biggs turns to look at me, his face just a shade or two paler.

"Actually, we're diverting the river to produce hydropower for Barbazal. I know the dam isn't exactly what folks around here wanted, but we're devoting funds to more sustainable power harvesting practices, and we're supporting farmers in their mission to switch to farming practices that use less water."

He steps closer to me; it reminds me of my dad—when he used to come forward, menacing as hell, and tell me to go to my room, or demand that I "stay out of this." But something about Mayor Biggs' posture, and the warmth in his blue eyes, assures me he's only being earnest.

"Don't believe everything you hear, Alex." He sounds almost like he's pleading. "Or even everything you read. We're in the middle of an election, and people will slant stories and twist facts into anything shaped like what they're trying to push. That's how politics go, I'm afraid. Everyone here has an opinion on your vote. Hell, *I* have an opinion on your vote. We here in Barbazal just want to do the right thing. I want to do the right thing. And I want *you* to do the right thing too."

Steph steps forward now to rescue me, her shoulders just slightly higher than they usually are.

"Thanks, Mayor Biggs," she says, resting both her hands gently on my shoulders and coaxing me to move. "We'll stop by your place later and talk to Clover like you said. Appreciate you letting us have a look around."

But I can't just let this end here. I can't just… let him get away with these platitudes about staying neutral. Where is the emotion about all of this? Why isn't he *furious*?

He chuckles.

"Yeah, I'm sure she can help you get the pistons out. Girl knows her way around a car," he says. "Got enough friends with tractors, you know?"

Steph's laugh is the most exaggerated, fakest, throatiest laugh, and she shuffles me away and down the road back toward town so quick I nearly lose my footing.

He's just so… *neutral*. So painfully, unnaturally *neutral* about what this drought is doing to Barbazal, to his town, to his family. I remember Charlotte's face weeks ago, as she looked at me and said, "I felt… horrible this afternoon. I didn't know if I could survive that feeling. But now… It's like when your leg falls asleep. And even though it's still attached, it's become something other than 'you.' My whole life, I've always felt so deeply. But… maybe this is better?" and the guilt hits me right in the chest. I shut my eyes against it.

"There's no shame in needing to feel numb for however long it lasts," I'd said, "if it gets you through another day."

I did that. I saw the rage she felt toward her own child, and I heaped confusion and ambiguity right on top. I wiped Charlotte's slate of emotion clean, took it all on myself, left her blank and empty.

I won't let Biggs numb himself to this.

Mayor Biggs turns to leave, and Steph is pulling me away, but what if I just…

I reach forward into that purple aura over his head, and a rush of emotion comes over me. I clench my hand tighter, almost into a fist.

If some stronger emotion would make Biggs see just what a serious situation this is, then maybe I'm the only one who can make that happen.

Mom said Grandmother used to tell her, "The tapestry of anger is woven with fear."

It's not hard to translate.

The cloud around him turns blood red and radiates like a supernova in all directions as I clamp my hand shut and fall to one knee in exhaustion.

"Alex!" exclaims Steph, running behind to help me back up.

I open my eyes and I see Mayor Biggs turning to look at us. "Y'all alright?"

"Yes!" I say, so fast that my voice cracks. I clear my throat and stand again, ignoring the wobbling in my knees. "Yup, just uh… a little dehydrated."

"Convenience store's open," he says tersely, nodding just up the road. I caught that tone switch. His steps are heavy as he turns to leave again, and I breathe a sigh of relief that I got away with that.

As soon as Mayor Biggs is out of earshot, Steph is all up in my ear, hanging onto my arm so tight I feel like it might fall off.

"What'd you see?!" she whisper-demands at me. "And are you okay?"

That last question settles deep in my chest like a cooling salve, and I feel my shoulders relax a little. I reach up and squeeze her right back, grateful for her care.

And then I try to think of how to answer that...

What *did* I see?

It takes me a moment to remember. And then her name.

"Magnolia," I say, so softly Steph doesn't quite hear me.

"Huh?" she asks.

This time, the full weight of the name catches in my throat, and my voice comes out like a croak.

"Magnolia," I say. "Mayor Biggs' daughter."

Steph gets quiet and relaxes her grip a little.

"I... don't remember him naming a Magnolia."

"She died," I say, the word biting through the air just as the wind picks up a little. "She was the thirteenth."

"Oh," replies Steph, pulling away. I can almost feel her thinking next to me in the silence, thinking of what to say maybe? What to do? She steps in front of me and wraps her arms around me.

"We don't have to do this," she says. "You know you can back out anytime."

I shake my head and embrace her back. No. This means even *more* that I have to do this. I can't just walk away from so many hurting people whose lives are being threatened over a water shortage. Barbazal citizens who have been here for decades are looking at uprooting their whole lives over this. I *have* to do something. For all of Barbazal.

For Magnolia.

I can't take away their emotions, I know that now. But maybe *rearranging* them a bit would help, starting with making Biggs care.

I look back up at Mayor Biggs' home, and Steph follows my gaze.

"Look, Alex," says Steph, "I hate to insist on it, but… this is really wearing on you. Let's just get the pistons and go, okay? I'm really worried about you."

I keep staring at the house.

"Alex?"

"Huh?" I ask, snapped out of it. Steph is looking down at me with eyes narrowed in worry.

"I'm fine!" I say, way too quickly. "I'm good, really. I just want to talk to Jonah and—" I pull away, wipe my eyes again and clear my throat. "—talk some sense into him about this climate situation."

"Before, you said you wanted to find out what he really thought about climate change. Now you're hoping to 'talk some sense into him'? What changed?"

"Nothing," I say. "I mean—"

"You didn't just see Magnolia, did you?" she asks. "There's more to it, isn't there?"

I sigh, unable to hide from Steph any longer.

"I saw all of Mayor Biggs' daughters. They were standing around a magnolia tree. And the oldest, Clover…"

I tell her everything. About Clover, about the sisters, about the tree.

"The water situation is so bad, Clover couldn't even keep her *goldfish*. We *have* to do something, Steph. I have to talk to Jonah."

And finally, I tell her about dialing up Mayor Biggs' anger.

"You… *what?!*"

"Shh!"

"Ugh!" She paces in front of me. "You… I just… This is *such* a bad idea. You just gave him a lit torch!"

I put it together.

"When… we're in a drought?"

"That's exactly what I'm saying," she sighs. "Look, Alex, I just… hope you know what you're doing."

"I promise, I've got this," I assure her. "I've had these powers for how long?"

She looks me up and down.

"Long enough to get comfortable with them."

"I've *mastered* them, okay?" I retort, surprised to hear the snip in my own voice. I soften. "Look, Steph, I appreciate the concern, but you have to trust me on this. I've learned from my mistakes. I know what I'm doing."

She's standing with her arms cradled around herself, staring at her sneakers with her forehead wrinkled in deep thought.

"I just," she starts, sighing deeply and shrugging, "I also want to make sure your mental health is okay? These are… *big* emotions to be experiencing with these people. I know it takes a lot out of you. I know what it's like."

It's a punch in the gut, remembering Steph's own struggle with depression.

She's been through so much.

And yet, here she is, worried for me.

I smile and reach forward to cup her chin, even though she's just an inch taller than me. "It will be, once I help these people."

Her eyes flicker with something.

"Helping these people won't undo what happened with Charlotte."

Another punch straight to the gut.

"I know," I swallow. "But, even if this isn't a do-over, I have to do something. I made the mistake of taking away her emotion. But, turning things up can't hurt. I can always turn that around if things go sideways, right?"

"You don't, you know," she says. "Have to do anything. You could just… leave people alone."

Ouch.

"Steph—"

"You're not just playing with emotions, Alex," she snaps. "You're playing with people's lives."

After a long moment looking at me, she walks ahead of me down the path back toward town, the Mayor's house sitting atop the hill just behind it. I watch her go, wondering what kind of monster she must think I am. Playing with people's lives?

"Steph—"

"Let's go get those pistons and figure out how we're gonna get your ass in front of Jonah."

I cringe.

"Please don't say that again."

"Regretted it as soon as I said it."

8: The House

If Owen's trailer is an average Barbazalian home, Mayor Biggs' rancher, which looked so small from the middle of the town square, is a *palace*.

I didn't realize it from where we were standing earlier by the statue, but the two double front doors are white just like the rest of the house, so we couldn't see just how tall they were.

And they're *tall*.

"Holy shit," marvels Steph. "Mayor Biggs is *loaded*."

"I mean, he's the mayor."

"He's the mayor of *Barbazal*," she scoffs. "No offense to this place, but they don't exactly scream that they're rolling in dough. How's this guy getting paid so much?"

"Taxes?" I shrug. She shrugs in return, and we both turn back to the door.

"Think we should knock again?"

"I don't know," I reply. "I wasn't counting."

"You *count* when you knock on someone's door?"

I feel my cheeks grow hot at how weird she clearly thinks that is.

"Uh… I mean, in my head?"

Her mouth curves into a smile, and any lingering tension from our conversation dissolves like sugar in water.

"You're pretty cute, Alex Chen."

And just as she's about to step forward, fist raised, to rap at the door again, saying, "One—" the huge white door flies open inward and Steph jumps back to attention next to me.

A tiny round face emerges in the doorway, a pointed chin, a button nose, long dark hair twisted into a messy braid over the shoulder, and big—huge, in fact—green eyes.

"Can I help you?" she asks, her voice soft, sweet, and… drawl-y?

"Um," I begin, surprised to hear the crack in my voice, "Hi. I'm Alex, and this is my friend Steph."

From the corner of my eye, I see Steph shoot me a look, but I can't make out the details in her face. I know I've said something off.

"Can we come in?" I ask.

"Opal," she says, pulling the door open further and stepping into the light. She folds her arms across her chest, her V-neck dark green sundress revealing just enough cleavage for me to have to physically concentrate on keeping my eyes on hers, but not so much that it wouldn't be church-worthy. "And that depends. Who is 'we'?"

"We're from out of town," I explain. *Eyes on her eyes. Eyes on her eyes. Eyes on her eyes.* "O-our car broke down a few miles down the road and we ran into your dad… Mayor Biggs?"

To my surprise and disappointment, she rolls her eyes.

"I've heard that one before. My daddy doesn't go outside of town, and we don't talk to paparazzi—"

She steps back into the house and just before she can shut the door, Steph reaches her hand forward to stop it.

Wham!

The girl gasps, and I guess I do too, because my hands fly to my mouth in shock as Steph fights for us.

For me.

"We didn't run into your dad on the road," she explains. "We ran into Silas, who took us to Elias, who told us to find Jude, who essentially kicked us out of the hotel, which is when we found

Owen, who recommended we eat at Plate and Skate, which is where we met Anita, and while we were out for a walk this morning by the statue of Augustus Jeremiah Oscar Rhett Barbazal the second, we ran into your father, Mayor Biggs. That enough of an alibi for you? We're not paparazzi. We're stranded musicians looking *everywhere* in this town for some goddamn help and *maybe* a chance to talk to Jonah about the water crisis so we can help *you* all!"

My heart is thundering in my chest. *What the hell are you doing, Steph?*

This could be our only chance to get some help with the car, and get some intel on Jonah. And she's ruining it!

Her mouth is going to get us banished from Barbazal altogether.

But then I remember what Mayor Biggs said to us back at the statue. Or, what *Steph* repeated that Mayor Biggs said. I was too busy at the time combing through his memories…

"Your dad," I offer, "said to ask for… Clover? He said she might be able to help us with our Saturn? Since she also has one?"

Opal's one green eye that I can see through the crack in the door widens, blinks a couple of times, looks from me to Steph, and then from Steph to me, and then softens its gaze.

"Well, why didn't y'all say anything in the first place? Daddy never mentions the Saturn, he's so damned ashamed of that piece of shit."

She swings open the door and welcomes us into the foyer, which is the size of Owen's whole trailer. I instinctively, politely, reach down and remove my sneakers, setting them neatly to the side as I try not to trip over myself while gawking at the deer-antler chandelier over us. What if that thing falls? How are the light bulbs wired through them if they're real? Are they taxidermized? Did Mayor Biggs hunt and kill those deer himself, or is this one of those synthetic five-thousand-dollar pieces of "art" that's been so overly processed you can't even tell if it once grew on an animal?

"Y'all drink sweet tea?" comes Opal's sing-song voice from the next room over.

Soon, we're sitting on huge plush sofa cushions, our socked feet kicked up onto leather ottomans—I don't have to wonder if they're real. This whole room smells of leather and wood polish, in the *best* way. It smells like an old library, or a cozy little bookstore that's ancient as it is beautiful, meticulously maintained. I look down at my glass of sweet tea and realize even as I sip it down, it doesn't feel like it's getting much lighter—that's just how heavy the glass is.

Everything in this house is unaffordable for me.

"Now," begins Opal. She sits across from us in a leather lounge chair, legs folded up to one side underneath her, her green floral dress falling over the edge of the chair. That dark braid sits over her shoulder just so. Every tendril looks like it was put there on purpose. Is this how rich people look just lounging around their house? Social media-worthy all the time? "Where'd you say y'all were from?"

She takes a sip of her sweet tea while Steph answers.

"Uh," she begins. I know exactly what her struggle is. That "Where are you from?" could be asking a million things. My mind cycles back through all the foster homes and centers I went through. Okay, maybe not every single one, because there were a *lot*, but several come to mind.

And whenever anyone used to ask me, "Where are you from?" for a while I'd answer with Portland, Oregon. Then when I moved to foster home number two, I realized the caretakers were asking me which center I was from, not where I was born and raised and called home, or even the age-old "Where are you *really* from?"

They didn't care about any of that.

Helping Hands Group Home, I'd answer. Great, they'd say,

confident in their choice to classify me as a promising addition, a charity case, or a lost cause. Or two of those, or all three.

Either way, I was another mouth to feed.

"Haven Springs," finishes Steph. And those two words pull me out of the spiral session I definitely didn't welcome and definitely didn't want to continue.

"Yup, Haven Springs," I echo, saying it aloud and helping my anxiety even more.

Opal looks from me to Steph, and back to me, her green eyes piercing and studying. But then her mouth curves into a smile.

"My sister Clover likes to visit Haven Springs. Says they have the most darling little flower shop there."

I smile inside, warmth radiating through me at the memory of Eleanor and Riley.

"Yeah," I smile, "yeah, they do."

"So, you drove up here to Barbazal?" she asks. "What for?" And she takes another sip.

This time I step in.

"We were supposed to be passing through to Fort Collins—"

Opal rolls her eyes at that, which makes me pause. What is it about Fort Collins that has her so irritated?

"Oh, it's nothing," she quickly recovers, holding out a hand in midair between us for reassurance, as if she would rest her hand on my knee if I were sitting closer. "It's not you, it's just that everyone's just *passing through*. S'what cost Barbazal all its tourist attractions."

"Tourist attractions?" Steph asks, the skepticism in her voice unmistakable. "Like what?"

I'm sure I can guess what Steph is thinking. Hayrides. Petting zoo. Corn maze. Maybe a community garden in the spring or a watering hole to swim in in the summer?

Opal must clock Steph's tone, because she lowers the glass from her lips before she's taken another sip, and stares at Steph, studying her.

"Theme park," she says, relishing our responses, which are, of course, audible gasps.

"You had a *theme park* here?" asks Steph, and then, probably to cushion against an accusation of being super gullible, "Was it a *real* theme park?"

"Real as the nose on my face," she beams, "Daddy used to take us all there. Used to be a lake park and all, with a water slide and everything."

She finishes the sentence, but the way she delivered that last word didn't *sound* like she was finished. It sounded like there was more she wanted to say. Much, much more.

"What happened to it?" I ask.

She blows a raspberry and sets her drink down on the huge metal side table next to her chair — seriously, how heavy is that thing? — and pulls her legs to the other side of her, leaning on the arm of the chair and sighing again as she prepares to jump head-first into… something.

"Like everything else around here," she hisses, "it dried up. The water first, and then all the tourism. People stopped comin', and so we stopped goin'. My family used to be there every Saturday morning at eight o'clock like… well… clockwork. Until we just… weren't. I was only six then. I'd been a few times, but every Saturday I'd ask Daddy to let me jump off the high-dive. I used to look up at that thing every time and wonder what it would feel like if I could jump and, for a moment, feel like I was flyin'."

Opal's staring at the wall behind Steph and me, and I follow her gaze up to a family photo of Mayor Biggs sitting in the very armchair in which Opal now lounges, a tall, blonde woman standing behind him who I can only assume is his wife, Wisteria, and all twelve of their little girls, gathered around their parents and sitting on the ground in front of them, all in beautiful little Sunday dresses, maybe even Easter, since all of the hair in the picture looks professionally curled.

The sound of Opal sighing brings me back to reality, and when

I turn back to her, she is now gazing toward the window at the far end of the room. I follow it and notice just how big this property is. The lush, sprawling grass keeps going for what seems like all the way up the hill behind it. Of course, I can't see all the way to the top. Far down the way, it turns into thick, verdant trees. But until then, it looks like a golf course.

Just the backyard.

Not the front.

Where people can see.

"Wow," I marvel as I survey the property, which seems to have completely—suspiciously—escaped this drought, and then realize I've whispered it out loud.

Steph glances at me and then back at Opal, just as Opal sniffs, and I realize she's crying.

There's a brilliant blue aura over her head.

"Beautiful tree, isn't it?"

I look back out the window and spot a huge magnolia tree along the edge of the yard, with huge green leaves.

But no white flowers.

I stare at it, strong and towering, the blue of Opal's aura reflecting off the window in front of me. And then…

That's not a reflection.

That's the tree! Blue light wanders over the leaves, flickering like flames, red and purple dancing among them. I suppress the urge to gasp at its beauty. How… how is this happening? Trees can't feel emotions… can they?

"Is that the magnolia?" I ask.

Opal looks like my words were a knife.

"What do you mean *the* magnolia?" she asks.

Oh shit, she's right. I wouldn't know there was a "the" in front of the magnolia unless I'd been here before. Or… I'd been poking around in her father's memories.

"I-I…" I start. Opal's eyes narrow in suspicion, and I realize I have to make some shit up. *Quick.* "I heard your father mention it."

"He doesn't talk about the magnolia," she says, pushing herself up out of the chair and looming over the two of us like she wishes she'd poisoned our tea.

Shit.

Shit. Shit. Shit.

"He said Wisteria!" exclaims Steph, leaning closer to me. "Not a Magnolia." She dons what is—to me—the fakest smile of all time. Even throws in a "pfft" for good measure.

Opal softens. Her shoulders lower. Her forehead relaxes, and she lets out a deep breath.

"Sorry," she offers, her voice suddenly mousy and fragile. She sits—no, collapses—back down into the chair. "That was rude of me. I know y'all don't mean no harm."

The silence passes between the three of us, tight and agonizing. That blue aura lingers around Opal's head as she focuses her gaze on the rug beneath our chairs—swirling browns and greens and ivories, and I realize there are fish swimming around in the pattern.

Steph ventures forward, gingerly.

"So," she begins, "what… what *is* the significance of the magnolia tree?"

Thank god for Steph. I *have* to find out more about that tree… I have to see it. Touch it. Find out what it feels.

Opal picks up her tea and looks at it, then pushes herself out of her chair and makes for the kitchen.

"We're going to need something stronger," we hear her say.

Steph and I look at each other. She shrugs, like *why not?*

I smile.

Just a couple hours later, Opal, Steph, and I have each had enough wine to tell our life stories, or at least the parts suitable for public consumption, and spill a little wine on the rug, only for Opal to reassure Steph that, "Daddy has the house deep cleaned once a month, and you needn't worry about it because it's old anyway."

I look down at it, the fish looking like they're *literally* swimming around the rug now. I look at the wine glass in my hand, at the Moscato sloshing around inside no matter how still I try to keep my hands.

Opal and Steph erupt in laughter over something I haven't really been paying attention to, sounding hollow and muffled in my ears.

"Alex, Alex!" calls Steph. I look up at her. Her own glass of Moscato is almost empty, and she tips back the last sip into her mouth and leans closer to me. Too close in fact. Actually—what the hell? Steph!

"Wha-what are you—"

"Let me look at you," she says, smiling *comically* huge. "Sooo prettyyy."

"What the hell?" I laugh. "Get off me."

"So you two are, like, *together* together?" slurs Opal, taking another sip.

"I mean, you tell me, Alex," Steph grins. It takes me way too long to realize what's going on here. "You used a word for me earlier. At the door. What was it? Oh yeah… *friend.*"

Friend.

That's what that look earlier was about.

I have to change the subject.

"Opal," I say, clearing my throat and sitting up straighter. I set my wine glass down on the side table next to me. That's quite enough of *that* shit. "Uh, so, would Clover mind if we took a look at that Saturn? So we can get to Fort Collins by tomorrow night?"

"Oh sure," she says, her "sure" swinging into the stratosphere with how high and squeaky it is. "It's out back. I'll show you."

She gets up, takes a step, and drops to her knee, then both.

"Opal?" I ask.

Opal falls forward and I lunge to reach her, but not fast enough. Opal's face meets the rug, and her feet swing up behind her before falling flat on the floor.

"Oh my god!" screams Steph. "Opal! What the—"

I race to meet her on the floor, finding her wrist and jamming my index and middle finger against a vein. I feel the *bump-bump-bump-bump-bump* and assure Steph, "She's alive. Just unconscious. Probably stood up too fast."

Steph says nothing, so I look up at her to make sure she's okay.

A crackling red corona flares around her forehead, then spits into a jagged crown of tight royal-purple spines.

She's not okay.

"Steph?"

She's glaring at me, eyes full of tears, her cheeks wet.

"What the hell are we going to do, Alex?" she demands. "We're stranded out here in fucking Barbazal in this fucking house with fucking—" She gestures wildly at Opal- "We've killed the mayor's daughter!"

"We didn't kill her!" I bite back. I feel the irritation welling up in me. Yeah, I don't want to be here in this mansion with an elected official's unconscious daughter, full of wine and likely no cell reception...

We need to call for help.

Or at least try.

My drunken hands scramble for my phone and dial 9-1-1.

Barbazal may be small, but they *have* to have a hospital, right?

"9-1-1, what's your emergency?" asks the operator. She sounds completely flat. Even. Like she's prepared for anything. In the city, they usually sound bored out of their minds—probably because they're getting calls about inconsequential injuries that could be handled in an urgent care center. Out here in farm land, I can't imagine people would call 9-1-1 for small things. With such heavy machinery everywhere, I'm sure this lady hears all kinds of calls about life-threatening injuries.

"Hi, um, I'm calling because my friend here is unconscious."

There's that word again. Friend. The same word I used for

Steph. My chest blooms with pain at the sound of it. I get it now. "Friend" is so… basic. Even *girlfriend* doesn't sound like it has enough weight. It's so much less than what Steph and I have.

She's so much more.

Especially when I can use the word "friend" for someone we only met hours ago.

I turn away from Steph so I can concentrate on the call, and the operator replies with all sorts of basic medical questions.

"Does your friend have any medical conditions?"

"Does she take any medications?"

"Has she had any intoxicants?"

I can answer that last one. But as for the first two…?

"Actually, I uh…I only met her a few hours ago—"

Just then, I hear Steph behind me, her voice soft but urgent. "She's awake! Opal?"

I turn and sure enough, Opal's eyes are fluttering, a huge purple aura of fear blooming above her head.

"Wh-wha—" she squeaks, before her eyes close again.

No! I have to see what's making that aura purple. Maybe if I can find out what she's so afraid of—someone who drinks must know their limits enough to not be terrified if they passed out suddenly—I can find out what's really going on with her.

I reach my hand out just as I hear the operator ask, "Is she responsive?"

But I'm already in Opal's world, watching as she tips back a couple of pills from an orange prescription bottle. I lean in closer to read it.

Cyclobenzaprine.

I'm back with Steph and Opal, whose purple aura is fading as she drifts into unconsciousness again.

"What's your friend's name?" comes the operator's voice.

"Her name is Opal Biggs," I say, my heart racing as I tell the operator, "and she's had cyclobenzaprine and… Moscato. A lot of Moscato."

The operator grows quiet for a long moment, so long that I wonder in panic if she's still on the line.

"Hello?" I ask.

"Opal Biggs?" she asks, her voice pointed and even. "I'm sending an ambulance right now."

9: Clover

The operator didn't just send *one* ambulance.

Everywhere I look, red lights flash angrily along the driveway. There are no fewer than five emergency vehicles here to transport Opal out of the house and onto a stretcher.

I turn to Steph and breathe a huge sigh of relief that Opal's in great hands now—better hands than ours. And to my surprise, she throws her arms around me, pulling me close.

"I'm sorry," she says.

"No," I reply, "*I'm* sorry. I shouldn't have—"

"Me first," she laughs, pulling back and looking up at me, her hazel eyes flickering. "I got mad at you for calling me a friend, which is… stupid. We *are* friends. Best friends. And it's great."

There's so much I want to tell her. *Need* to tell her. But as I search for the words…

I want to be even more!

Do you want to be more?

Is there already something more?

I mean, we've been making out on the regular, so I just assumed.

But at this point, even friend-with-benefits sounds too light.

Thank god, she continues.

"But—"

New words cut through all the noise around us.

"What the hell happened up here?" snaps a woman as she

climbs out of a big blue pickup truck, slamming the door behind her. Her curly red hair swings behind her in a braid—it's so long I can see it swaying past her hips on either side of her. She marches past every ambulance, all the lights, all the workers, and right up to the stretcher, which is only ten feet or so away from Steph and me.

"Ma'am, if you could—" begins an EMT with gentle hands outstretched to her.

"Don't you 'ma'am' me, Curtis, I live here. Now you tell me what the hell happened to Opal."

"Clover, I can't—"

"You can, and you *will*."

So this is Clover Biggs. Damn, is she a totally different person than the woman I saw resting that fishbowl on the ground in front of that magnolia tree, with the kind words about the goldfish keeping her sister company.

"And who the hell are you?" she snaps, staring Steph and me down like this is clearly our fault. "Some *friends* of Opal's from the city?"

"N-no!" says Steph. "We're from Haven Springs. We came up here to ask Opal for help with our car—"

"There are plenty of folks in town without you comin' all the way up here about car trouble. I know you're paparazzi. If you really needed help with a car, you'd go see Elias. He'll help you out. In the meantime, you leave me and my family alone."

"Clover," I begin gently, "your father sent us up here."

"Oh, like I believe that," she scoffs. "Did he tell you to get Opal hopelessly drunk and send her to the hospital too?"

"Opal got up to show us a car your dad says you keep in the garage that we could search for parts," Steph says. "If you can just get us the engine pistons, we'll be out of your hair."

She looks skeptically between Steph and me.

"Honest to god?" she asks.

We nod in unison. And I really mean it. There's absolutely nothing here that's going to get me closer to talking to Jonah Macon, so we might as well get what we really need.

Pistons.

"No questions," huffs Clover, marching between us and past the house. "Come on. I don't tolerate slow walkers."

I smile at Steph, who smiles back at me, grabs my hand, and leads me to follow Clover around the side of the house.

Guess I'll ask "But *what*?" later.

This backyard is *way* bigger than it looked from inside the house.

Clover is dead silent as we walk across the grass.

Questions swirl in my head. Why didn't Opal warn us she'd taken cyclobenzaprine? Why the hell was she drinking when she was taking muscle relaxants?

Clearly, Steph has questions too, because she ventures us all into conversation.

"Clover?"

"No questions," hisses Clover over her shoulder, marching onward.

Steph and I exchange an awkward glance, and then Steph begins to grin.

She has a plan.

Oh no.

"What happened back there with Opal?" she continues. "Is she okay?"

"She'll be *fine*," Clover spits. "Long as she can find herself better friends than you."

Now wait a goddamn minute. I feel my veins pumping with rage.

"She drank that Moscato on her own," I argue. "You'd think she'd know better than to mix it with muscle relaxants."

A huge red aura like a brilliant poppy flower blooms around Clover's head.

"If you want these parts, I suggest you shut the hell up."

Bingo.

I reach forward, into that aura, and make a fist, sucking me into her world.

It's daylight again. I'm standing by the tree. Clover is standing in front of me staring up at it, her red braid shining in the sunlight. She's wearing shorts and a simple T-shirt, and her arms are brushed here and there with white splotches.

Paint?

"Hey," comes a man's voice from behind me. Clover and I both turn, and at first I expect to see the face of Mayor Biggs, since we're on his property and he's the only man in the household.

But when I look, I see a much younger man, with dark jeans and a short-sleeved white collared shirt, lanky arms and neck, and a movie-star smile that I immediately recognize.

"Jonah?" I ask.

No way. This man, this... *kid*, can't be the same puff-chested politician I saw riding around on top of that flashy classic car in the parade in Elias's memory. No way. He looks so... my age!

Then, as if seeing Jonah on Mayor Biggs' property wasn't jolting enough, he walks right up behind Clover, who beams up at him proudly, and slips his arms around her waist, planting kisses up her neck.

I feel my cheeks warm with embarrassment, and I look away. Feels like I shouldn't be seeing this. After all, they think they're alone out here. Well, I mean, they *were* alone. Until I looked into their past and saw them.

Whatever. Point is, this feels like an invasion of privacy.

Actually... why is this scene such a happy one? I stepped into an angry memory. Where is that anger?

"Stop," giggles Clover. "What if Daddy hears us?"

"He won't," whispers Jonah.

"Where's Opal?" she asks, her voice suddenly tense with worry.

"She's fine," he scoffs. "She has the TV. Choo-choo and whoever the whoo-whoo will keep her busy for hours."

Clover giggles again, and even though I've only known her for a few minutes, it feels weird to hear her laugh, like that laughter belongs to someone else.

"Lou Lou and Benny the Choo-Choo," she corrects. "And… yeah, you're right."

They both breathe a looooong sigh, as if they've had a looooong day, and they turn their gaze up to the tree.

"It's as beautiful as ever," marvels Jonah. "Your mom and Magnolia are smilin' down on it, I just know it."

"Yeah," she says, her voice sinking with sadness. "You think they're together?"

"Wherever they are," he says, planting a kiss on her cheek, "I *know* they're together. I don't know if I believe in God, Clover, but if he's out there, he wouldn't separate those two for anything."

I can't help but smile, and I feel tears welling in my eyes.

My own memories creep in, one at the forefront, before all others.

Mom.

"Alex?" she asks, reaching up to find my face. "Alex, my darling, why are you crying?"

"Can I go with you, Mom? I… I don't have anyone else."

"You have your brother," she smiles, although I can see the pain in her face, the way her cheeks look more caved in than they ever have. The way her eyelids droop. The way her lips are tight. She coughs once, then again, and I reach for her water cup on the nightstand. Or, rather, the hospital cart.

She takes a couple of sips—the doctors always seem to want her to drink more—and breathes a deep, deep breath, as if she's just finished a marathon.

"Thank you," she whispers, smiling up at me again. "You have your brother. You have your father. And for now," she reaches over and takes my hands in hers, "you have me."

"*I want to go with you,*" I say, *catching my own voice splitting into a million pieces.*

"*You'll see me again,*" she says, *reaching up to brush some of my short, dark hair away from my eyes. It falls right back down, since I'm looking down at her in the bed.* "*Promise.*"

I shut my eyes tight and feel a sob escape.

Then, in the darkness, a sharp, ear-splitting scream bubbles forth from the ether. A long, droning holler that no one should ever have to hear. My eyes fly open to see Clover and Jonah looking back toward the house, eyes huge. They exchange a panicked glance before sprinting inside, and I follow close behind.

"Opal?!" shrieks Clover. "Opal, where are you?!"

"*Cloooooverrrrr!!!!*" comes Opal's voice, terrified and jagged. I race behind Jonah and Clover, who dart down the long green hallway and up the stairwell where Clover explodes into a bathroom to find Opal crumpled up on the floor in a heap, and…

…blood…

…*so* much blood.

Her face is pale, her eyes lifeless as she looks up at Clover and admits, "I'm sorry."

"Opal!" sobs Clover, kneeling and taking Opal's arms in hers. She lifts them, against Opal's whimpering protests, and I see a slash mark across each, deep red gashes bubbling forth with blood.

"I'll make a tourniquet," she announces to Jonah. "You call 9-1-1."

I'm frozen to the ground, rooted to the spot. My legs are jelly, disobedient even as I will them to move. My stomach turns over, and I feel like I might throw up.

There's blood everywhere—splattered across the bowl of the bath tub and smeared across the faucets, dripping down the side and smudged and dragged across the floor to underneath Opal, her once vibrant green eyes fading, her limbs going limp.

She's wilting in Clover's arms.

"Opal?" come Clover's pleas. "Opal! Please, God, no! Stay with me!"

Memories flood me, bubbling forth so fast I can't control them.

A white body bag being carried out of the front door of the second children's center I called home. All the interior door handles were replaced with grabbable indentations instead—things you couldn't tie a bed sheet to.

A supervisor I hadn't met before, running with a child much younger than I, cradled in her arms, graying skin, dripping wet, and screaming for someone to call 9-1-1. The next day, the pool was closed.

Several news crews with flashing camera lights and microphones waved in the faces of our teachers, demanding to know how a teenage boy was able to escape and make it to the highway, and what drove him to such lengths to take his own life.

I'm back in the bathroom.

Then, I'm back in the yard.

"Alex?" comes Steph's voice. "What do you think?"

I blink myself back into the moment. Yanking my hand back from the memory and clutching my wrist as if it burned me.

I can still see those... deep... gashes.

I look at Steph, having no idea what the hell she and Clover have been talking about.

Clover walks onward as if Steph hasn't said a thing, but Steph sees me—like, *really* sees me, again—and I feel tears about to burst forth from me, like I'm about to explode.

I want to disappear, I want to scream.

She snatches my hand as desperately as if I were stranded in the middle of the ocean and bleeding strength.

"Steph, I... I can't do this—"

"Let's just get the pistons and go," she whispers.

"The hell are you two jabbering about back there?" snaps Clover, turning suddenly toward the building to our left and reaching up to take hold of a huge barn door clasp. "I said no questions."

"We weren't asking questions," protests Steph, clearly annoyed now. "Just give us the pistons and we'll leave you alone forever."

That last word "forever" feels like it stabs me in the chest.

Forever?

We're just going to leave Clover and Opal here? Like this? Opal almost died, for god's sake! I can still see the blood. I can smell it.

"I," I whisper to Steph, but before I can say more, Clover yanks the clasp up, sending an eerie and piercing *SQUEEEEEEAK* ringing out through the yard. Steph jumps like I do, but Clover seems unbothered.

"It's right in here," she says, sounding more exhausted than anything.

"We'll wait out here," says Steph.

Clover looks between the two of us and rolls her eyes. She doesn't say it, but the word is implied.

Babies.

And I can't blame her. Who looks this calm as their own sister is being carted away in an ambulance after another possible suicide attempt?

I guess someone who can suppress all the rage I just stepped into. Someone who would be in that question with the word "another."

Opal has had at least two.

Maybe she's suppressed her *own* emotions, like I used to, before I learned to control them. I know what it's like to feel rage like a fireball, fear like an icy storm, and joy like heavenly sunlight, and still have to carry on with life as if nothing happened, because practicality demands it.

I'm no stranger to death. To suicide. To self harm. Not my own, but just as painful.

I take a deep, desperate breath of the cool evening air. I look up at the horizon line, at the sun slowly sinking beyond the horizon through the sparse trees, and I remember the sunset from Haven

Springs, wedging itself between the mountains in the distance.

And suddenly, sharply, deeply, I miss home.

We never should have left for good.

I cradle my arms around myself.

"Hey," begins Steph gently, now that Clover is deep within the barn. "You saw something."

I shut my eyes and let the tears fall, my jaw burning from holding them back.

"Doesn't matter," I croak. "I'm no closer to meeting Jonah. I just want to leave."

I shut my eyes tighter than I ever have and allow myself a single, biting sob. Then I feel something warm and hard against my forehead. I peek and see Steph's eyes inches from mine, the tip of her nose touching the tip of mine, and I drink in her company.

"We can go if you want," she says. "You know I've got you. I promise."

"Thanks," I whisper. "What I saw… was… just…"

"You don't have to talk about it," she says.

"No, I want to," I say, and I do. But not here.

But I remember a detail of the memory that *is* important. Right now. Right this minute.

"Clover and Jonah. They…" I begin, trying to figure out how to phrase this without implying anything.

They were married? Not necessarily.

Boyfriend and girlfriend?

They were lovers? Who said anything about "were"? Maybe they're still together!

"They… kissed."

Steph pulls away and raises a single eyebrow, her face full of curiosity like she's watching a juicy soap opera.

"I… saw them. They were *together*."

Her eyes go wide and she glances at the barn door and lowers her voice.

"You saw them in bed?"

"No!" I exclaim, way too fast, feeling my cheeks grow warm with embarrassment. "No, no, they were together in the yard."

I glance past her and realize—the slope of the lawn, the building behind me—I know this area of the yard. I look to where I think I might find it, and…

There it is.

The magnolia tree.

I let go of Steph's hands and approach it. It's not much taller than when I saw that memory of Clover and Jonah, and I realize Opal didn't look much younger in the memory either.

Maybe Clover and Jonah were together not *nearly* as long ago as the memory originally felt.

I look up at it, at the leaves fluttering in a breeze so subtle I almost miss it. And for me, they glisten. Almost seem to glow, humming with memories dancing on the leaves in gold, blue, red, and purple auras along the edges. I reach out and take one. It feels warm between my fingers, then freezes like ice against my skin, and then back to warmth.

"This is," I whisper to Steph, "Magnolia's tree. I saw all of them standing here. And this is where Clover and Jonah…"

"Kissed," finishes Steph, looking up at the leaves and then down to the base of the tree.

"What's this?" she asks, crouching down in the grass and inspecting a little wooden sign there. I kneel beside her, sinking to my knees on the hard, unforgiving earth, and read the inscription.

Here lies Magnolia May Biggs. We will never forget you.

"Damn," whispers Steph. "How old was she?"

"I… I don't know."

I remember what it felt like to say goodbye to my mom, knowing I would never see her again, after knowing her my whole life. I remember what it felt like to say goodbye to my dad when he walked out of our front door, not knowing if I'd ever see him again.

That was almost worse.

Believing he was somewhere out there, choosing to be dead to me and Gabe.

And I remember Gabe.

I remember standing on the mountainside with him as the rocks tumbled, catching him completely off guard. And I remember the sound of the rope between us snapping as Ryan cut it, freeing me from being dragged over the side with my brother.

Believing I could save him until the last moment.

I wonder if that's how Clover felt as she held Opal in her arms.

Or how she felt as she watched Opal on the stretcher, wheeled out to an ambulance.

"Here's your pistons." Clover's voice cuts through the silence like a knife, and I jump so hard, I turn and almost fall against the tree, but I catch myself in time. Steph pushes herself to her feet and takes the burlap bag gently, like we're museum curators, and it's a million-dollar—no—*priceless* vase.

"Thank you," offers Steph.

"You're welcome," beams Clover with—is that a hint of a smile? "Now get off my property."

I look at Steph. Steph looks at me. I can read her face like a book.

You still want to back out?

I guess it's now or never. I look down at the bag in Steph's hand, and I picture us, arm in arm, walking back to Owen's place, packing up my guitar and Steph's drum kit out of Silas's truck, maybe grabbing an extra plate of French toast for the road from the Barbazal diner, and hitting the highway.

We could be out of here forever.

We could leave behind Silas, Elias, Owen, Biggs, Jonah, Clover, and… Opal.

No.

I can't leave Opal.

Whatever is going on here in Barbazal, between the drought and the election, I just know Clover is the key to fixing this.

"Clover," I say her name before I talk myself out of it.

"Aw, hell, here we go," she grunts, turning and storming off. I hurry after her.

"I don't have any questions!"

"Uh-huh, sure. I *knew* you were paparazzi!" She's jogging now. "Leave me alone before I get my twenty-two!"

"Dude, Alex!" calls Steph, her hand on my arm, but I yank it away and hurry on after Clover.

"I just wanted you to know that we didn't know Opal had taken—" I catch myself before I reveal that I somehow know she took five milligrams of cyclobenzaprine. "—whatever she took. She offered us the Moscato, and we thought everything was fine!"

"Uh-huh, great," she spits. "Now in the warmest Barbazal way, kindly fuck off."

We're around the side of the house now and Clover begins to bound up the front steps to the porch, and I realize I have to dial this up a notch.

"What made her do it?" I holler, stopping short of the porch, and watch Clover pause at the top.

"What?" she asks.

"In the brief time I talked to Opal," I say, catching my breath, "I know she would've known what medications she was taking, and that they don't mix with alcohol. This wasn't an accident, was it?"

She looks over her shoulder at me, eyes narrowed.

Then she turns and walks back down the steps.

Fists balled.

Jaw clenched.

I'm a little girl again, standing in my childhood living room, watching my brother and father face off over nothing, and I find my hands reaching behind me for my record player. I imagine that peaches song playing as I try to drown out their yelling.

But instead, I find Steph's hand.

"You listen here, and you listen good," says Clover. "Opal is none of your concern. You don't know nothin' about us. About our family. About Barbazal or what we need. So why don't you get outta here and go home to the big city, where everything comes easy and there are no barn doors to *startle* you and you can get engine parts any ol' where."

"Because I want to help," I reply.

Clover scoffs at me, hocks a loogie, and spits it into the grass, dangerously close to my Doc Martens.

"If you want to help, vote."

I see my way in.

"For Jonah?" I ask.

The sheer mention of his *name* sends a blue spiral swirling into an aura over her head, and she blinks, giving her feelings away completely.

Jonah makes her… sad?

I didn't see that coming. Just months ago, they seemed so… happy.

How do two people go from being so close, to hearing the other's name and experiencing such deep sadness?

"I have to go," she says.

"Clover," I venture, "I'm… not paparazzi. But I do want to help Barbazal. Really. I'm supposed to play a gig tomorrow night, but I'm staying here until I can talk some sense into Jonah Macon about—"

"About this drought?" she hisses. "What do you want him to do, huh? Shoot a hole in the sky and bring rain down into the valley until the river flows through here again? Or maybe you want him to pray us all outta this?"

Bitter silence settles between the three of us, until Clover grits her teeth and says, "Ain't no talkin' sense into that man."

I look to Steph, and she seems to understand what I do. Clover's not just talking about politics here.

"Clover—"

"What makes you think I can help you anyway? What makes you think I have any influence over Jonah Macon?"

"I can hear it in the way you talk about him. It's clear you know him better than most out here. Don't you?" I ask. *Please, please, please, don't let this be too obvious of a grab.* I only know they were together because I reached into Clover's personal memories, her deepest secrets, things she's probably worked hard to repress for years, and saw them kissing under the Magnolia tree.

"I just need to talk to him," I plead. "Just for a few minutes."

"And what makes you so special?" she asks, taking another threatening step toward me. She's trying to intimidate me, but it won't work. "What makes you think he'll listen to you?"

How the hell am I going to get through such stubbornness? Clover is a rock, a fortress of resolve. She won't budge without some serious convincing. I glance back up at the magnolia tree, remembering how strong it is, and I wonder if Clover's baby sister had survived, would they be exactly alike?

"That magnolia tree. The caption. Who is Magnolia May Biggs?"

I know I can't exactly jump head first into "I know the tree is here for your sister."

Clover's face turns a shade paler, and I take a friendly step forward. "She meant a lot to you, didn't she? And what about her tree? When Barbazal dries up, how will you keep it alive?"

Clover's face goes from pale to red, but the aura over her head isn't.

It's twisty and vibrant, folding in on itself like a black hole, a confused swirl of blue and violet.

"Magnolias are some of the most drought-resistant trees in the world. She'll be *fine*. *Her memory will be fine.* Not that it's any of your business. You have your parts, now get out!"

"I won't let Barbazal die without a fight!" I holler, surprised at the emotion in my own words. "I've met so many people here who need a bug in Jonah's ear. Silas barely has enough water for himself, let alone guests. Elias can't run his shop or restore cars without water, Anita's having to ration water at the Plate and Skate, Bobby and Paisley are trying to keep the bookstore and flower shop afloat, and Magnolia—whoever she was—her tree. That caption says *we will never forget you*. But if that tree dies, doesn't her legacy die with it?"

I can't let that happen.

I won't let it happen to my mom, to my dad, or to Gabe.

Or to Magnolia May Biggs.

I expect rage from Clover. I expect an explosion. But that purple aura remains. The truth is, Clover is scared to death of letting Magnolia's legacy die. Without Magnolia, once the twelve of them are gone, Magnolia will be too.

She *has* to help me.

She narrows her eyes at me, in a way that says, *I know you're right, but I don't like it.*

"Five in the morning," she says simply.

"Huh?" asks Steph, thoroughly confused.

Clover looks at her, and then at me, like we should've understood the clue and been grateful for it.

"Jonah Macon goes for a run every day at five in the morning."

An odd fact, but I don't see how that helps us… until Clover continues.

"He takes the old path around the lake—or, what used to be a lake. Start at the tree line," she says, pointing to the far end of the property, where the grass ends and the trees begin. "Walk straight into the woods until you find the old stump. You can't miss it. Turn left until you reach the clothes line. Follow the birches until you find the lake. Turn right and follow the footpath 'til you reach the old bench. Jonah will meet you there. He'll be expecting me—"

She cuts her own sentence short. I study her as she cradles her arms around herself, turning her gaze to the grass. Clover, still taller than me by about a foot, now looks very, very small.

And I put it together.

"Clover, is Jonah Macon—"

"No questions," she snaps, shutting her eyes tight. She turns suddenly and walks off. "Take your bag and go."

I watch Clover go, and I feel Steph's fingers interlace with mine.

"Holy shit," she whispers to me. "So, Clover and Jonah are…"

"Still together."

10: Gabe

I blink my eyes awake to find that Steph has wrapped her arms around my waist in the night. I can feel her behind me, making the perfect big spoon. I feel her squeeze me gently.

"Hey," she whispers, nuzzling her face against my shoulder. "You ready to meet Mr. Big-shot politician man?"

No.

I absolutely am not.

But I have to be.

I nod.

"You can still back out any time, you know," she yawns, resting her chin against my back. "Don't think you're in too far to change your mind. You always have a choice."

"Thanks, Steph," I say, peeling the covers off and pulling myself away from her and out into the cold room. For a Colorado desert town running out of water, Barbazal can get hella freezing when the sun goes down.

"So, what do you think he'll be like?" asks Steph, swinging her legs over the side of the bed and reaching for her hat. "Especially since he's expecting Miss Magazine-ready farmer bombshell Clover and he's getting us two lugnuts?"

"Lugnuts?" I chuckle. "Speak for yourself! I'm feeling pretty magazine-ready myself after that shower last night."

"Yeah, it was about time for both of us," she smiles.

"Can't believe the convincing it took for Owen to say yes to a shower. Even in a drought, humans gotta bathe!"

I hear a *tap tap tap* from outside the window and my eyes follow the sound. Just outside, I see Owen, still in a robe and slippers, tapping his finger on a meter outside by the house.

My smile falls as I realize what I have to tell her.

"Hey, Steph? I was thinking… maybe I should go see Jonah. Like, alone."

Steph looks over her shoulder at me, eyebrows raised skeptically. "Are you crazy?"

"Yes, we've been over this," I grin. But Steph isn't smiling back. She pushes herself up from the bed and leans over it, leveling her eyes at me.

"You're asking me to let you go by yourself into the woods to meet a strange man? What if he kills you? What if he drowns you in that lake?!"

"There is no lake anymore, Steph, remember?"

"Okay, so one murder method taken care of, I guess we're good to—*hell no!*"

"Steph, I'm—" I stop myself, soften my voice, but stay firm. "I'm… not asking."

The silence that settles into the room makes me so uncomfortable, I'll say *anything* to get out of it.

"Come on, think about it. Jonah's already expecting Clover. This bench is probably their secret hideout or something. They both grew up here. Maybe they used to sneak off to that bench to make out when they were teens?"

"Uh, yeah, exactly," she says. "And if he gets irate about having his personal space invaded, you'll need someone with some city grit. *Please* let me go with you. I'll just climb a tree nearby or something and watch."

Laughter bursts forth from somewhere deep in my gut. "You want to stalk us like a panther or something?"

"No," she laughs with me, "just… I don't know. Easier than digging a hole and covering my head with leaves."

"Okay, that's probably the most city-grit thing you've *ever* said. People only do that in movies."

"Okay, maybe don't make a habit out of meeting men in the woods, and you won't *have* to know shit like that?"

We stand smiling at each other for a long, looooong time. Then she throws her arms around me in defeat.

"Be careful, okay?" she insists. "I'm serious. The last time you left to meet a man in the woods, you fell down a mine shaft."

Her voice breaks at that last word, and I shut my eyes and squeeze her tighter.

I remember when I hobbled back to the Black Lantern, all scraped up, concussed, with two broken ribs, and Steph leapt out of her chair to run to me. When I told her, when I told *all* of Haven Springs what had happened—that Jed Lucan had shot me and let me fall two hundred feet down a mine shaft—the first words out of her mouth were: *I believe you.*

And I know that whatever happens in the woods this morning, she'll believe me again.

"I will," I say. And I mean it. "Thanks, Steph."

The trek back up to Clover Biggs' house is harder than it was yesterday, and I can't decide if it's because I was with Steph yesterday, or because yesterday I didn't have soreness creeping into every muscle below my waist.

If I'm going to be standing on stage for hours at a time rockin' out on my guitar, I've gotta get better stamina than this.

Step after step, I feel the burn in my quads grow, and I wonder if I'm doing the right thing. Maybe Steph was right. Here I am, two days into my stay in a brand-new town, waltzing up to the Mayor's house, following a trail in the woods to an abandoned bench where I'm supposed to meet a stranger who's also a pretty famous candidate for the Colorado Senate seat.

Yeah, this is crazy.

I look up and see the house, larger now than when I first started my walk of course, but still far off. I take a deep breath and remember Gabe. I think of what he would say to me.

Something like, *You can't see injustice and do nothing about it.* No...

No, that's what *I'd* say to me.

Go where the wind takes you.

No, that sounds like a version of Gabe from wish.com.

I stop and sigh.

When I lost him, I swore I'd keep his memory alive, that even if it had been years since I'd last seen him, I'd never, ever, *ever* forget him. But here I am, losing his voice, losing his turns of phrase, losing his face.

I remember him less and less vividly, Gabe Chen.

"I'm sorry," I apologize into the wind.

I try to picture him standing ahead of me on the trail.

He would shrug and say something snarky, yet wise. Practical. Like, "You're really going to meet some weirdo in the woods?"

I smirk.

That's the Gabe I remember.

"He's not some weirdo," I say aloud, pressing on. "He's the answer to Barbazal's problems."

"Anyway," continues his voice in my head, "*The answer to Barbazal's problems*, huh? That's a lofty title. This guy sounds like God."

I snicker.

"Not quite," I say. "Just a guy with feelings."

"Those can be dangerous," he would say. "Did you at least bring mace?"

"Shouldn't need it," I say, feeling determination grow with each step. "He's got a lot to protect, and something tells me committing an act of violence wouldn't exactly *help* his political career. The worst that can happen is he swears at me and leaves."

I lose my footing and slip on the leaves, catching myself.

"Jesus," I exclaim.

"Not quite," Gabe would say. "Speaking of deities, though, it sounds like *you're* trying to be the answer to Barbazal's problems."

"Okay?" I say with a shrug and an implied *and?* "What if I am? What if all Jonah needs is someone to talk to? Someone to be real with?"

And if Gabe were right here, I already know what he'd say, clear as day.

"Sometimes, the fakest people are covering up a *lot* of hurt."

I guess that's true. But whatever Jonah Macon might be hiding, I'm ready to see it. It can't be worse than watching someone cradle their sister as she bleeds out on the bathroom floor, can it?

"When you see that hurt," he would say, "be ready to walk away."

That sends a chill down my spine. But I set my brows in determination. I've made up my mind. If Jonah Macon won't talk to me, then so be it. If he *will* talk to me, I'll just… toss out what he said. Dump it into the bucket of trauma I've already been through and push it down, down, *deep* in my mind until I can barely remember it.

I march forward before I can let my imagined Gabe-voice talk me out of it. Or, I guess, scare me out of it.

"I'll do what I have to do," I say. And suddenly, I can't imagine what he would say to that. Probably nothing. He'd just… let me go.

I'm fighting tears as I make my way up the hill.

I walk, and I walk, and soon, I arrive at the house.

The tree line across the lawn is calling me. Through the trees until you reach the old stump, Clover said.

The magnolia tree flickers with uncertain colors, and I get the overwhelming feeling that it's… wishing me luck?

"Well, well, well," comes a voice from *way* too close. I jump so hard I nearly fall over. But it's only Opal, lounging in a lawn chair with a glass of… something. I hope to god it isn't wine.

Especially since it's five in the morning.

I look down at her wrists, both of which have deep scars I never noticed before.

She follows my gaze to the one holding the glass.

"Stitches. Happened a while ago." She shrugs nonchalantly.

I have to ask.

"Opal, was last night an accident?"

She looks genuinely confused.

"Which part? Us meeting? Probably."

"No, you mixing alcohol and muscle relaxants."

"Oh, that."

How does she sound *so* aloof?

"I'll let you decide," she says flippantly, taking another sip.

"Is that wine?"

"You can also decide that."

I can feel my blood boiling, and it must show on my face because she rolls her eyes, sets the glass down, and pushes herself to her feet. "It's just water," she says. "But around here, it's even more valuable than wine. What are you doing back here anyway?"

Oh hell.

What do I say? *I'm here to meet your sister's secret boyfriend in the woods. But it's okay because your sister told me to. But not for kinky reasons, it's to worm my way into his deepest darkest secrets and memories and convince him to give a shit about his hometown drying up and wasting away.*

I can't say any of that.

"Wanted to make sure you were okay after yesterday."

Great, Alex, how do I get into the woods after "just checking on" Opal? She'll suspect something immediately!

"Oh," she says. She looks... surprised? Bewildered? "Well, I'm fine."

Her head erupts in blue, and I realize she's very *not* fine.

"You sure about that?" I ask.

She looks affronted.

"Why are you asking anyway? You don't have your own business to mind? Especially at such an ungodly hour?"

Oh, right.

But I don't back down.

"I'm asking because I care."

And it's true. The same reason why I'm talking to Jonah Macon.

She narrows her eyes up at me, then pushes herself out of the chair. She nearly stumbles and I go to catch her, but she knocks my hand away.

Shouldn't she be on watch after what happened yesterday?

"Opal, you have to take care of yourself," I say.

"Why?" she hisses. "What for? So I can keep living in this hellhole? The ground ain't the only thing drying up around here—look at the businesses closing up shop. When's the last time ol' Elias down at the shop had *any* cars come through there? Clover said he's so deep in shit, he doesn't even keep the store stocked. He knows he's going under. He knows this whole damn town is going under. The only reason we haven't already is because Denver has everything we need!"

I stare at Opal for a long, long time, and while I wait for that blue aura to turn red... it doesn't. It stays bright blue.

She loves Barbazal. It's clear in her voice. In her gestures. In her wide, terrified eyes.

"You... don't want to leave, do you?" I ask.

"I can't leave," she says, looking out over the lawn to that magnolia tree. "Barbazal is all I know. Daddy won't leave because Mama's here. My sisters have all left with the loves of their lives because *Daddy's* here. What am I supposed to do, go out on my own?"

Oh, man.

That's... painfully relatable.

"I did," I reply. Not flippantly, not carelessly. Determinedly. "I did," I repeat, hearing my voice crack.

Sure, it wasn't my choice. One minute, I had Mom, and Dad, and Gabe, and the next, I'd lost them all. One by one.

I was in foster care for half my childhood. I was thrown into being on my own, and then, when I got to Haven Springs and lost Gabe, Steph and I left together.

"Your sisters," I begin. "Do you ever... call them?"

"They've got preoccupations," she says, with a flippancy that's clearly masking her pain. "Babies and careers and such. No time for a single auntie."

"Do you have any friends?"

"Just you and Steph."

Holy shit, she's already calling us friends? I mean, cool! But also... has she *ever* had friends?

"Well, then you should know that friends get to demand you take care of yourself."

"Or what?" she asks, folding her arms across her cleavage, bringing her breasts together distractingly. *Don't look*, I tell myself. *This is a serious conversation!*

"Or else," I say with an eye roll. "And since Steph and I will be on the road in a couple of days, know that people outside Barbazal aren't that bad. People outside Colorado aren't that bad. And, I mean, I haven't been out of the U.S., but... I'm sure people all over the world aren't that bad. And if you're curious, I'm sure you can find someone to explore with you."

She shakes her head.

"Why are you really up here?" she asks.

My heart sinks, and I try to think of another lie.

"Clover sent you, didn't she?"

"What makes you think that?" I ask, hoping my face doesn't betray the fact that I'm sweaty as fuck trying to lie my way out of this.

"That just sounded like something she'd say, is all."

"Oh," I say.

Opal wraps her white shawl more snugly around her shoulders and shivers a little, even though it's decently hot out here.

"I'm going inside," she says, turning suddenly and heading back toward the house. Then she glances over her shoulder. "If you're going to meet Jonah in the woods, you should bring him proof that Clover sent you."

What the hell?!

"Opal, I—"

"Don't bother lyin'," she interrupts, looking me in the eyes and smiling. "I know you came to see me too."

Then she winks, slides the glass door open, and slips inside.

I stand there for a moment, watching the house.

So Opal knows about Clover and Jonah.

I get the feeling there are more secrets in this town than people are letting on.

I adjust my shoulder bag, turn my gaze to the trees, and set off toward the woods to find the stump.

11: Into the Woods

Run through the woods until you find the old stump, she said. *You can't miss it*, she said.

I've walked almost a mile, I'm sure, and I don't see a goddamn stump.

I walk on, knowing that if I try to turn around or something I'm going to end up even more lost out here. I pull out my phone to text Steph and let her know I'm alright, since I've been gone *way* longer than I expected.

5:15 am.

Shit.

It's been an hour already. I hope it takes Jonah at least fifteen minutes to run to the lake.

Aaaaand I have no cell reception. Fantastic.

Stupid cell phone, stupid stump—

"*Oof!*" My foot catches on something and I go hurtling forward, slamming into the ground so hard my glasses fly off and land in the grass. My chest feels tight, and that fall made me dizzier than I thought it could. I erupt in coughs; I've knocked the wind out of myself.

I push myself up, and my hands come away from the ground—or floor, whatever hard thing I'm standing on—sticky.

"Oh *yuck!*" I whine, wiping my hands furiously against my pants. But the stickiness only dries and gets tacky. Ugh, I need soap and water. I take a few steps back and look down, kick away some leaves, and realize…

I've found the stump.

I grab my glasses and slide them on.

And yeah, Clover was right. If there weren't so many leaves on the ground, I would have noticed. This stump is a good five feet by five feet! It's *huge*.

"Holy shit."

I wonder how old this thing is. I mean, I would count the rings if I had the time. Which I don't. So I force myself to keep walking, tear my eyes from this magical, old thing—feels like the elder of the woods, honestly—and turn left to look for the clothes line.

It's a *much* shorter walk.

There's a colorful string of flags tied about fifty feet across through the trees, and I follow it until I spot a cluster of white trees with flaky dark brown bark and branches missing all the way up and down the trunk, almond-shaped. They look like… eyes.

These must be the birch trees.

Now I'm getting somewhere!

Follow the birches until you find the lake. Turn right and follow the footpath.

The sun is just starting to rise in the distance, orange filling up the sky where blue once was, making for a kaleidoscopic sunrise of reds, purples, and blues, and I wonder to myself, is this the Earth's way of saying she's got mixed feelings about us humans? For how we've treated her?

It sounds so corny in my head, but… what if with every sunrise, the Earth is telling us that she's deeply, deeply hurt? By us?

Wish that logic would work on Jonah.

I take a deep breath and sigh as I reach the last of the birch trees and my feet find loose rocky gravel. I turn right and follow the footpath, keeping my eyes moving for the old bench where I'm supposed to meet him.

I wonder how long he's been meeting Clover out here, and

how often. Whenever he's in town, I guess. And given his job, that's probably not very often. Why keep it a secret anyway?

I hear footsteps behind me, and I whip around to see very little in the dark.

"Hello?" I ask into the early morning. "Jonah?"

More footsteps, and I gasp as a black shadow emerges from the trees, the size of a small dog, and I realize, with its feet going *thump-thump-ksh-thump-thump-ksh*, it's only a nutria.

It *thump-thump-ksh*es its way across the footpath and slips into the lake as quietly as a snake, and I smile. So there's wildlife out here after all.

But the water is a good ten feet down the embankment. Rings of dried silt line the walls, reveal the declining water level. This lake used to be twice as full of water, I realize, and my heart sinks.

I walk on.

The bench looks exactly as promised. Old. And like a bench.

It's so decrepit-looking, I'm worried if I sit down it'll disintegrate into dust under my ass. But I test it out, lowering myself as carefully as possible, and although it's been here a long while, beaten to death by the environment, much like the town of Barbazal, it's still standing.

I feel the morning breeze roll through and prickle my skin, and I look out at the lake, which is bigger than I expected for a town going through a drought. I wonder what the environmental provisions are around this water. Is it clean enough to filter and drink? Is it being used for something? Are people siphoning it off to water their crops?

Is that legal?

Will there come a time when people decide they don't care about the law if it means going without a resource so precious?

I sigh, and hope Clover was right. I hope Jonah takes his 5 am run. I look down at my phone clock. 5:25.

I hope I'm not too late.

I look around and realize just how alone I am out here, and I smile. It feels... good almost? The silence, besides the chirping of the crickets and, now that I really stop and listen, the occasional croak of frogs. This place feels more like Haven Springs than I realized, and I find myself yearning for music, my fingers itching to pick the strings of my guitar.

Something about being alone, especially by water, spurs me on to create. The ocean, a river or stream, this lake... I wonder what it's called.

Given the name of the Crown Inn and the Plate and Skate, it's probably got some cheesy name like It's a-Boat Time Lake. Or worse.

I sigh again. Maybe I don't have my guitar, but I have my voice. So I hum.

Driving to the middle of nowhere with peaches on my plate...
And I think of Steph.

And I wonder what she's doing right now. Her words flood my head until I can think of nothing else.

The last time you went to see a man in the woods, you fell down a mine shaft.

I really, *really* hope this is a good idea.

"Is that the Mooring Shores?" comes a voice from behind me, driving a spike straight through my train of thought.

I whip around so fast, my neck clicks, and I wonder if I've literally just broken it.

"Ugh," I groan, rubbing the pain out of my collarbone area and studying the source of the voice.

Jonah stands there, in electric blue basketball shorts and a gray T-shirt, hands in his pockets, fitness watch around his wrist, and a big smile on his face.

But it's not that fake smile he was wearing at the parade, the one I've seen on TV. He's smiling at me like we know each other. Like we're friends or something.

"Don't be mad," I say, but it comes out more like a question. I rise to my feet and tuck my hands behind my back, willing myself to wait until that color blooms over his head and his back is turned before I start digging into his brain. "Clover—"

"Must have sent you," He finishes the sentence for me, stepping forward and sliding onto the old bench beside where I'm standing. "So this must be important."

He smiles up at me warmly, and now that he's sitting so close to me, I can see the red flush in his cheeks.

"Oh," he says, and checks his watch like he might have forgotten something. I watch as he clicks an app, three little dots light up along the bottom, and a big green "0" pops up in the middle.

"Ah, wow," he says, looking up at me in surprise. "So you're not paparazzi?"

"How'd you know?" I ask.

"Well, for one, Clover wouldn't tell you about my secret run if you were, but for two, you don't have any recording devices going."

"Your app told you that?"

"Can't be too careful," he shrugs.

Damn. I can't imagine leading a life so public that protecting your privacy requires device-scanning apps to tell you if what you're saying is safe.

"Well then," he begins with a big sigh, clasping his hands in his lap and looking out over the lake. "Why are you here? Actually, let's start with names. I'm Jonah Macon."

He reaches out for a handshake.

I smile. This guy is actually pretty handsome when he's not all buttoned up and Ken-doll-ified for the cameras. Handsome in a real-live person kind of way.

"Alex Chen," I say, taking his hand and shaking it.

"Lovely to meet you, Alex. How can I help you?"

Oh god, where to even begin?

What the hell is up with this drought?

What the hell is up with this dam?

What the hell is up with your secret relationship with Clover?

What the hell is up with you and Elias?

What the hell is up with eating chocolate-chip pancakes and pickles in the morning?

In the end, I start at the beginning.

"My friend and I." There I go again with the word *friend*. "My… *girlfriend* and I," God, that sounds perfect. *Focus*, Alex, this isn't about you and Steph, it's about Jonah and Barbazal. "We were on our way to Fort Collins for a show tonight."

"Oh, what do you play?" he asks, intrigued.

"Guitar," I say.

"Ukulele, myself," he says with a grin. "Please, continue."

"We broke down outside of town, and ended up at Elias's shop," I explain.

And there's the first bloom.

Blue.

So, Elias and Jonah make each other soul-crushingly sad. Why? What's their history?

"Bet he wasn't in too great of a mood since I'm back in town."

"Yeah," I admit, wanting so badly to ask more. And then I decide, hell, the rest of the story can wait. "What's up with him anyway?"

"Let's just say," he says, "some people don't like change. Like, *really* don't like it."

"What kind of change?" I ask.

"The kind that helps everyone," he says, smiling at me sadly.

Oh, we're being vague now, are we?

"Like the dam?" I ask, cutting directly to the chase. Something changes in Jonah's eyes at that question, and that blue aura fades into indigo, and then into a brilliant royal purple.

The dam makes him nervous.

A wave of disorientation comes over me. The floor sways below my feet, and swirls of dizzying magenta stars float around my head, bouncing in the air, and I hear a deep, looming cackle. I know this feeling well. Jonah's not just nervous.

He has full-blown anxiety.

He's terrified.

"Um… well, yes, like the dam," he says, opening and clasping his hands earnestly. "I just… I want to do the right thing by all of Colorado, and that's hard, because technological advancements like hydropower and wind power—you know, things that will really help the environment—they make people nervous."

He's baiting me to ask the obvious question, *Why?* But I'm not going to do that. You don't get through to someone's sharpest emotions by asking the questions they expect you to ask. You get through to them by shocking them into it.

"Is Clover nervous about the dam?"

He doesn't look at me. He keeps his eyes down, glued to his own hands, which he clenchs together just a little bit tighter, and that purple glow remains.

"Clover," he begins. There's weight to her name in his mouth. I can tell she means everything to him, and I wonder what could possibly keep them apart. "Clover is… *concerned*… that if the dam remains, it will hurt Barbazal's farming community."

I cock an eyebrow, letting the silence do the talking for me. That's horse shit and Jonah knows it. Clover doesn't care about Barbazal's farming community nearly as much as Opal does. Because once the farming community goes under, Barbazal goes under, and without Barbazal, Opal doesn't know who she is.

I watch the dancing stars, that cackle welling up again in my ears.

Something else about Clover and the dam is making Jonah scared out of his mind.

"Why does Clover care about Barbazal's farming community?"

The purple aura disappears.

I fucking knew it.

His face relaxes at that question, and I realize I've asked him something easily addressed with a diplomatic tied-up-in-a-neat-little-bow answer. His specialty.

"Clover loves this place," he explains, his voice earnest. "She was born and raised here like me. We went to grade school together.

Of *course* we both care deeply about this place. She has eleven sisters who live here, and I have—" He cuts himself off, and he's quick to recover, but I catch it. "Friends. A handful of friends from my childhood."

Uh-huh.

"You don't have friends in Denver?" I ask.

Those big-wig donors who would pay anything to give him a seat at the Senate table.

"Oh, they're not the same, you know?" he says, coolly dismissing my answer. But I give him a nod, inviting him to go on.

"Clover cares about the farmers here for the same reason we all do," he says, pushing himself up off the bench and taking a step forward towards the lake. "We don't want to give up this place. *I* don't want to give up this place. This is my home. That's why I'm back fighting to keep it as great as it always was."

That purple aura is still gone, and I know exactly why. That was the most canned answer I've heard in a while. God, he's reminding me of Diane from Typhon. I'd be surprised if it wasn't written on his campaign website word for word. He's comfortable again.

"Then why are you routing water away from Barbazal?"

That aura is back, but this time it's red, blazing and angry as the sunrise.

I reach in.

And suddenly, I'm standing outside under the midday sun. It's blazing hot, hotter than it was even on that first day when Steph and I were lugging our gear miles to Barbazal. I look down, and my feet are nestled in gravel, and I hear a car engine rev somewhere behind me. I whip around to find I'm standing in front of…

…Elias's shop?

…*what?*

This is the last place I expected to end up, but then I hear my question repeated word-for-word, from a familiar voice.

"Why are you routing water away from Barbazal?" hisses Silas,

A Silas *far* different from the cheery one who met Steph and me with the most southern hospitality one can expect.

Woah, I think. I thought Silas and Jonah were cool, but I guess not as cool as I thought.

"Why do you care?" comes Jonah's voice. His *real* voice. Lower, and angry. Bitter. So, so bitter. "Another six months and you'll be out of here anyway. Off to do whatever it is they do in Minnesota."

"And? You whisked off to Denver the minute you got the chance. What's so different? At least I stayed past high school! Sellout."

"Don't you *dare* call me that!" barks Jonah. "I've worked my ass off for this place, fighting for our rights in courthouses and council meetings. You should be *grateful*—"

"Grateful!" exclaims Silas, with a sad chuckle. He steps out from inside the garage, nestling his cowboy hat snugly on top of his balding head, and walks back to his truck without another word. "When your fancy little *dam* dries this place up, you'll be fighting for the rights of a ghost town."

Jonah stands at the entrance of the garage with his arms folded defiantly over his chest. He and Silas may be around the same age, but Silas looks like he's been working out in the sun for decades, and Jonah... well, he looks like Jonah.

And I'm back at the lake.

"I'm not, uh," Jonah says to me, pausing to think through how to answer my question. "I'm not rerouting the water, per se."

"Aren't you? The dam holds up the water where the Colorado River branches off toward Barbazal, right? Doesn't that mean more water for Denver and less for Barbazal?"

"Not quite," he says. There's a bite to his voice that wasn't there twenty seconds ago, and he turns and looks at me with the same darkness in his eyes that I saw outside Elias's shop just now. Jonah's angry. *Very* angry.

I'm back in my living room, watching the silhouettes of Gabe and Dad screaming at each other, teeth bared, through the curtain on the other side of the record player. My only lifeline.

I slip a new record onto the player, rest the needle down at the perfect spot, shut my eyes and pretend to be somewhere else. Pretend like the threat of violence isn't so close I can almost see it.

But no. *Breathe, Alex. You're here. By this lake. In the woods. With this stranger.*

I take a deep breath. That helps.

"Not quite," he says again, calmer. That helps too. "I wish it were that simple: send water to Barbazal and screw Denver, or send water to Denver and screw Barbazal." He sighs. "I know how it looks to everyone. Kid who was born and raised here in a small town grows up, thinks he's better than everyone else and moves to the big city, where he doesn't have to be a big fish in a small pond—" He stops himself again. There's more he's not saying.

But to my surprise, he turns around and gives me a sad laugh. He's wound tight, and everything's complicated and compacted inside him. Anything connected to Barbazal sends him spiking off in a new direction.

"I'm working through all of that in therapy," he says. *Oof.* Congrats, I guess. Jonah didn't seem like the type who went to therapy.

"But the reality is," he continues, "I left Barbazal to *help* Barbazal. We've been facing climate-change issues for a long, long time. Electrical bills around here are two hundred and thirty percent of what they were just three years ago, which hurts a farming community just as much as a drought. The power situation is just as detrimental as the water situation, and that's what we're trying to fix with the dam."

I think for a moment. I guess I never considered the power situation.

"So the switch to hydropower would also help Barbazal?" I ask. He nods.

But then I decide to press.

"Are you sure about that?"

There it is. Purple. Jets of black ink breach a twilight core, punching through his crumbling defenses.

He turns back to the lake, his face composed, searching for words, probably looking for a way to make this look better.

I reach in.

The stars are back, dancing around me in a purple haze.

I'm sitting at a huge oval wooden table surrounded by tall office chairs, and a single person sits at the very end. An older man, balding, slightly hefty under a grey herringbone suit. He clears his throat and checks his phone just before Jonah Macon steps further into the room from behind me, sending dozens of stars flying through the air. And then I notice the ceiling. A huge thundercloud sends a flash of lightning through the room, looming over us. It feels heavy, and ominous, like it could crash down on our heads at any minute. I gulp, push down the urge to run from it, even though I know I'm the only one who can see it. It looks—feels—so real.

"Morning, Senator Brickleby, sir. You wanted to see me?" Jonah looks much, much younger, but it must have been only five years ago or so? He's the same height in this memory. Just, more vibrant. Less… I don't know, worn down?

"Yes," replies the man. "I wanted to see you."

There's a darkness to his tone, and despite the optimistic smile on Jonah's face—clearly he's eager and maybe a little bit starstruck—I know this is about to go south *real* quick.

"I want to talk about who the fuck you think I am."

Crash! The lightning flashes through the room again, making me jump.

Jonah's spirit looks absolutely crushed. He shrinks to half his size as he ventures, "Sir?"

The man—Senator Brickleby—rises to his full height and buttons one of the buttons on his suit, clears his throat again, and begins to pace.

"That stunt you pulled out there was unacceptable."

"But sir, I was—"

"Why would you ask me about the fucking dam? Of all things, why would you write a prompt question about *that*?"

"Because if I hadn't asked it neutrally, someone else would have asked you with an angle—"

"I can *handle* an angle! What I can't handle is you writing prompt questions that *invite* the angles! You saw what happened out there! You opened up a cesspool of questions about fucking Barbazal and the water, and the river, and the dam!"

Jonah looks near tears, and as silence settles into the room, I wonder what he could possibly do with that statement.

"I—" begins Jonah timidly. "I thought the dam was important."

"It *is* important, you idiot," spits the senator. "The dam might win us the goddamn election, but that doesn't mean we have to *invite* in the scrutiny on the way!"

Jonah folds his arms, and just as I think he might crumple completely, he says, "The dam will bring hydropower to small towns all throughout central Colorado—"

"The dam," the senator cuts in, "will bring *money* to small towns all throughout central Colorado."

What?

"When I hired you, Jonah, I assumed you had a basic understanding of economic principles, but—since you apparently don't even understand supply and demand—let me elucidate."

He steps forward and sets his hands on the table like he's cutting something.

"We build the dam," he explains. "We create hydropower. We power Barbazal and other small towns with clean renewable energy, right?"

The senator looks up at Jonah to make sure he's following along. Jonah nods nervously, and the senator slams both hands on the table and hollers, "*Wrong!* We sell eighty percent of that power to Denver and send that revenue to the towns."

"Oh," says Jonah. "That sounds… kinda charitable,

actually—"

"Wrong again," explains the senator. "That means more money to replace the public funding we already funnel into dead-end places like that."

Jonah narrows his eyes at him.

"So, Barbazal breaks even on funding, and… loses water."

"Listen, Jonah, it's not my first choice either, okay? But we have donors out there who will be very, let's just say, disappointed to learn that we had an opportunity to reduce their tax liability by reducing public expenditure and didn't take it."

I knew it.

All of this really *is* a cash grab for the rich! Just not in the way Steph and I thought. They're not rerouting water to Denver just to water rich people's lawns, they're selling off hydropower to reduce public funding and lower taxes for high earners!

This all makes sense now…

Little Jonah Macon from Barbazal, who came out to Denver to work in a senator's office, and—from how Senator Brickleby is talking to him, openly addressing him like he's worth little more than a gnat circling the fruit in the breakroom—tried to make a difference, tried to offer important questions as feeders on stage during what I assume was a debate or a rally, and instead of protecting Barbazal, and other towns around it, his hands are tied.

Jonah watched them build the dam. He didn't have a choice.

The woozy magenta air swells, and a wave of stuffy warmth floods me. No wonder there's so much confusion here. Every good thing in Jonah's past is all mixed up with its opposite. Even at the beginning of his career, he walked into his boss's office wanting to make a difference, and instead he got roped into *this* scheme.

And now, with calls for Jonah to tear down the dam, and restore Barbazal's water supply, what can he do but reassure his hometown that the dam is doing them good, and that the water shortage is due to climate change and not the water reroute?

If he doesn't, he'll lose his position. And without his position,

how can he represent the small towns of Colorado?

It's twisted, and I don't agree with it, but I understand now.

That thundercloud flashes a final lightning flash, sending shockwaves through my body. My hands can't stop shaking, and I feel glued to my chair. I shut my eyes against the shockwaves, which I realize are getting increasingly strong, until…

…I'm back at the lake.

And I feel *tired*, deeply, wholly. Every inch of me wants to sleep. I look over.

And that little Senate office employee, Jonah Macon, is standing before me, only years older but aged at least a decade, little purple stars dancing over his head. He looks over his shoulder at me again and smiles.

"It'll all work out," he says. "I just have to make Barbazal see it."

Pity floods me, and I sigh. Jonah really does feel stuck. And I can't tell if his fear is of being found out—he's gotten great at covering up what's really going on around here—or of something else.

"Jonah," I begin, venturing into dangerous territory. "How much hydropower does the dam generate?"

"Oh, well I'd have to look up the numbers on that one, but last time I checked, we were spittin' out enough energy to power half the state!" he says proudly.

"Does Barbazal use all of that power?"

"A farming community like us?" he asks. "Pfft, we go through power like—"

Like *water*, I'm sure he was going to say.

"Well, like air."

Safer choice.

"You…" I say, thinking, "…You didn't actually answer my question."

"How many questions do you have exactly?" he chuckles. He glances down at his watch for effect, probably to rush me. "I've gotta get some breakfast soon."

Well, Jonah, I think, *I've got all morning.*

"Just one more," I promise. I have to make this one count. Really get to the heart of his fear and turn this around.

"When Barbazal finds out what you're really up to, Jonah, what will they think of you?"

Jonah's face goes completely pale. Totally devoid of color. A long pause passes between us—so long, I wonder if Jonah's actually losing consciousness. Which would be extremely bad. I'm out here alone, with a politician, by a lake, with no cell reception. What if he has a heart attack and dies right here and everyone thinks I killed him?

No, shut up, brain, we're fine, Jonah's fine, everything's fine.

That aura over Jonah's head is a brilliant purple. The tendrils coil up, this time, like a crown of branches has taken root in his scalp. Spindly black spires that fork and breach and twist through the brilliant purple, sparkling with routes not taken. In them, I recognize the tree.

The minute he looks down at his shoes, I seize my chance. I reach in, one last time.

And I'm standing behind Jonah and Clover as they sit in front of the magnolia tree. Jonah has a sandwich in his hand with a few bites taken out, and Clover is working on a pint-sized bowl of potato salad. Peak summer.

"You're gonna let her die all over again, you know that?" she asks, her voice scathing and harried, a stark contrast to the joyful scene—the brilliant sun, the butterflies fluttering in the yard, the wildflowers dotting the grass. "You're gonna kill her memory just like you've killed the rest of this town."

"I'm working on it, alright, darling?"

"Don't you call me darling," she spits. Then she turns back to her potato salad, scooping up a spoonful, staring at it. "It's enough to make a girl lose her appetite."

"You think I'd let this place dry up? Think I'd let Magnolia's tree dry up?" he asks, his voice earnest. "I'm doing all I can in Denver to fight this, but I have to do it the right way. What do you want me to do, take a sledgehammer to the dam in the middle of the night?"

"It would be better than lettin' those pigs in Denver make all that money off what's supposed to be *ours*."

So, Clover knows the whole story.

"One hundred percent of that money should be *ours*," she continues, "on *top* of the public funding we get, which is already stripped down to the pennies and bottlecaps at the bottom of Colorado's pockets."

"I know," he says, "but how do you suggest I get my campaign off the ground if I fall out of favor with my biggest donors? I have to appease both—them *and* Barbazal."

"And it's real easy to appease Barbazal as long as they don't have a clue what's happenin'," she hisses. "You're as bad as they are."

"Darling—"

"Don't call me darling again until you grow a backbone and do something. I'm not moving. And I'm not raising this baby somewhere else just because you would let our town die."

He pauses, sets the sandwich down on the plate in his lap, leans over, takes Clover's free hand in his.

"You have my word," he says. "I'll find another source for Barbazal."

"You gonna call water down from the sky with some kind of ritual?" she mocks. "Or maybe you plan on drivin' Silas's truck up into the mountains for ice so we can bring it down and melt it here in the valley! *Anything* to appease those donors, am I right? Anything to get that Senate seat, Jonah Henry Elias Macon."

Jonah looks personally hurt by that statement. Clover rests her hand over her middle.

"I hope he's nothing like you," she mutters.

And that breaks him completely.

"Clover—"

But Clover's already on her feet, marching away, and I can see her face now, framed by those red curls, the loose ones that escaped the braid down her back falling down either side of her cheeks, and I realize… this wasn't long ago. This was recent.

Like, *this week* recent.

How often does Jonah make trips down here? Silas said it had been months, so that would mean…

Was this *yesterday*?

Is Clover pregnant *right now*?!

That explains the secret relationship. As blue as Colorado is, a baby born to unmarried parents still spells trouble for a politician, and a marriage to a politician's daughter could be seen as some kind of twisted political move…

God*damn*, is everything in Jonah's life so carefully orchestrated and over-analyzed?

I remember his secret order at the diner. Yes, it must be.

I'm back at the lake, staring up at Jonah Macon with silence settling between us like a fog, masking what either of us is really thinking. He's staring back at me with the blankest face. Even. Unwavering.

"What do you mean?" he asks, coyly. "What exactly do you think I'm 'up to'?"

But that purple glow is still over his head. He may not think I have *all* the cards, but he knows I have *some*. The question is, how much do I want to reveal that I know? I guess the answer to that question depends mostly on one ultimate question I've been tossing around in my brain like a loose marble. Am I staring into the face of a lost boy, a former intern who's still scrambling to make a difference in the world… or am I looking at a political sellout, skimming off the top of his community to appease donors? Or some twisted combination of both?

His blue eyes are flickering with something, and he must realize I'm not going to give him an answer.

"Well," he concedes, kicking his leg up onto the end of the bench, furthest from the end where I'm sitting, and re-ties his shoe. "Whatever you think I'm 'up to'," *God, he says "up to" like it's such an outlandish idea—don't protest too much, Jonah,* "I hope to win your trust as a voter this election. Whatever you believe about me personally, I hope you can get behind my cause: protecting all the communities that make Colorado beautiful, and representing all the people that make up those communities in Washington."

His foot meets the ground again, and he extends his hand to me for a parting handshake.

I glance down at it before looking back up at him, and I know I have a split-second decision to make. This might be my last chance to make things right here, to protect the water supply, and to stop Denver from pulling their "surplus" funding from Barbazal.

If I can just tap into Jonah's mind *one* more time, maybe I can find something, *anything, any* solution.

I have to try.

Before I take his hand, I give him a smile—a grin that lingers a bit too long—a knowing expression that tells him whatever I know, it's more than he wants me to know.

His smile falters just slightly, and that purple aura flares up again.

Gotcha.

I reach my hand forward for the handshake, and our fingers curve around each other's palms, and I'm in.

One. Last. Time.

What is Jonah so afraid of?

I'm standing in a dark room. A bedroom, with a bed so big it would fill Owen's entire living room. Two lumps are under the comforter, one twisting and turning frantically, whimpering in his sleep.

Is that Jonah?

He jolts upright in bed with a frantic yelp I've never heard a human make before, and the other lump jolts to meet him. Her arms encircle his torso, and she coos at him.

"Shh, shh," she says, "It was a dream, dear." I'd recognize Clover's voice anywhere, though it sounds slightly more grave than usual. Her wild red hair falls in waves over her shoulders, and she hugs him close with a chuckle. "Were you dreaming about my dad? He thinks I'm here to get supplies, remember?"

Where is here?

Denver?

Am I in Jonah's home?

Jonah, shirtless, caves in on himself, tries to slow his breathing, and looks to the window. I follow his gaze and realize I have a view like I've never seen before. The entire Denver skyline, mountains and all, lights up brilliantly against the pitch-black sky. The stars twinkle across it like I've only seen in small towns. Like Haven Springs.

Like Barbazal.

I wonder if Jonah chose this high-rise condo for that reason alone. I could see him, younger, wandering the space, unsure if he could call this home after living in Barbazal all his life, and opening the window to see the sky.

Maybe in that moment, he realized he could see himself here, in Denver, making a difference.

Then, to my shock and horror, he buries his face in his hands, and bursts into tears. Clover, somehow unfazed, turns to him, embraces him around his shoulders, runs her fingers through his hair as he embraces her back, grabbing a gentle fistful of her nightshirt like a drowning man clinging to a raft, about to be lost at sea.

He cries for what feels like forever, and I can't imagine what he dreamed about that would make him so... so... like *this*. So broken.

"Clover," he finally croaks, pulling away and dragging his wrist across his eyes. "I dreamed that—"

"Shh," she says again. "You don't have to talk about it."

Yes he fucking does, I want to scream. *He needs to get whatever this is out.* But since they couldn't hear me even if I did, I remain silent, listening.

"No, I need to talk about it," he says, pulling his legs up to sit criss-cross, and taking both her hands in his. "I dreamed that I lost... everything. I lost you. I lost the baby. I lost—"

"What do you mean 'lost'?" asks Clover, more intrigued than fearful, as if she's been through this before.

"I mean," he continues, "I was falling into a hole. An endless hole. Dark. Cold. Wet. Alone. You both," he says, glancing down at her stomach, "just... watched it happen. Didn't try to reach me. You looked... relieved. And I knew when I saw your face that I'd let you down. Both of you. And then, all of Barbazal went flying past me, all the faces I grew up with, everyone was staring at me in disappointment. Everyone was... just..." his voice threatens to break again.

I try to swallow, but my throat feels suddenly dry, remembering what it felt like to fall, endlessly, into a dark, deep hole.

"They all hated me," he practically squeaks. Clover pulls him against her again.

"No one hates you," she assures him. "But they might if you don't do something."

Damn. Clover can be direct. Kind, but direct.

He nods.

"I know."

He *knows?!* If he knows, why hasn't he done something?! Judging by this condo, Jonah Macon is secure enough—even if it's with Clover's money—and judging by his political reach, influential enough to build his entire platform on straight-up anarchy. Down with pollution, fuck the establishment and all that! Surely there would be enough people across all of Denver to get his vote. Why toe the line, when Maisie Dorsey is far right enough to have all the red votes?

I hear myself grumble, a sound I don't recognize from my own throat. Frustration.

But then I realize...

I've found my chance.

"I know," he says again with a nod. "I'm just... What if I do something and it ends up being too drastic? What if it fails?"

And then, after a long pause, so long, I wonder who's going to talk next…

"What if *I* fail?"

Oh my god. Jonah Macon? Bigshot Jonah Macon? He's not afraid of climate change or public ridicule or private ridicule for that matter.

It's much deeper than that. Jonah Macon, like me, is most afraid of failure.

Of *being* a failure.

Of people *thinking* he's a failure.

And maybe, if I can make Jonah Macon *so* afraid of failure, he'll try to succeed. Whatever it takes. Maybe he'll finally, as Clover's been begging him all this time, *do* something.

I'm getting back in that car today and driving to Fort Collins with the girl I love, and if I only have this moment to help a town of thousands preserve their livelihood then this is the moment I'll take.

Before I can talk myself out of it, I reach out to Jonah, sitting there in bed with Clover, reach into his chest and find the heart of that purple aura, twisty and sick like a snake coiling itself around a branch, crushing Jonah's heart and his resolve.

I remember Steph's words.

You're not just playing with emotions, Alex. You're playing with people's lives.

"Don't worry, Steph," I whisper to myself.

And then, with all the force of Jonah's fear in my hand, I turn my wrist, rotating my fingers like I'm holding an invisible dial, turning and turning, feeling the tingling grow and grow. My skin prickles, at first like my hand is falling asleep, then like my hand has been asleep for several minutes and someone's kicked it with a steel-toed boot, and then, like cactus spines are, one by one, digging into my flesh.

It burns.

It stings.

I feel tears bud at the corners of my eyes, and I shut them, grinding my teeth against the pain so intense it feels like it's ringing in my ears. It feels like I've reached into a jellyfish and grabbed it by its tentacles, which are slowly wrapping around my fingers, hand, and forearm.

But as the pain sears my hand, I hear Clover's voice somewhere far away.

"Jonah?" she asks, "Are you okay?"

"I, um… " he says. I hear the ruffling of bed sheets, and I force a single eye open to see what's going on out there in Jonah's memory. He goes slowly, agonizingly for me, to the huge window overlooking the city, and stands, looking, thinking.

"What if you do nothing?" I growl through gritted teeth. "What if everyone you know and love finds out you've sold them out to the state? What if they find out, Jonah Macon? What then?"

A new wave of searing hot pain envelops my arm, and I resist the urge to drop to my knees for some kind of reprieve. I keep talking as I force my hand to turn further, feeding the flames of fear I can feel growing and shifting within him.

"What about your baby? What happens when they grow up and find out their father let a dam destroy his own hometown? What happens when they find out you're a monster?"

I whimper just a little, the pain unbearable now. I know I have maybe a few words left.

"If you don't do something, Jonah Macon," I squeak out, "you *are* a failure."

Even if I could scrounge around in the strongest parts of my mind to find stamina to withstand this level of pain, I can't. If I was reaching into a jellyfish earlier, it explodes now, sending me flying backwards. My feet feel nothing below them. I'm completely airborne, falling in slow motion. I hear a scream escape my throat and I shut my eyes and brace for the impact of whatever I'm going to fly into behind me.

But I don't fly into anything.

Nothing's moving anymore.

All around me is stillness, silence so sharply deafening, it feels like all sound has been sucked into a vacuum. The smell of pond scum fills my nose, and the taste of dewy morning air tickles my mouth and throat. My forehead feels wet, the breeze cool against my cold sweat, and I look up to see my own hand outstretched, embracing the large yet smooth hand of Jonah Macon, and when I look up at his face, I'm unprepared for what I see.

Those once movie-star-like blue eyes have lost their shine. They're dull, empty, lost. His mouth is a flat line.

"Jonah?" I ask. He's totally still, staring at my face like he's gazing into a black hole. He blinks, snaps out of it, but instead of his usual smiling self, he swallows, clears his throat, takes my hand in both of his, and nods.

"Uh," he says, like he's forgotten an important meeting. "I, um… I forgot I have somewhere I have to be."

He slips his hand from mine and turns and walks—no, he *flees* back down the path, faster than he ran here.

"Jonah, are you okay?" I holler, my voice bouncing off the waters of the lake and sending a flock of Canada geese into the air a few feet from where Jonah is still running.

"I forgot I have an important meeting this morning!"

And I watch him get smaller and smaller around the lake, until he darts left into the birch trees and back through the woods.

I sit in silence for minutes and minutes, until a chorus of honks picks up in the sky and those same geese return to their home on the opposite side of the lake.

I look down at my right hand, where that searing pain ripped through my flesh. I half expect to see burns all over it, but it looks fine. Feels fine.

I sigh and look back up toward the birch trees, wondering if

I dialed up Jonah Macon's fears enough for him to do something, or if I dialed them up enough for him to do something...

...reckless.

I remember the look in his eyes when he said he had to go. Those soulless, empty, terrified eyes, and I get a sinking feeling that I've overdone it this time.

I slide my phone out of my pocket, unlock it, find Steph's number and hit dial.

No reception.

I growl, jump to my feet, and start the long walk back along the path, texting as I go.

> Steph, I think I made a mistake

I type. Send.

> Steph, I think I made a mistake

Unable to send.

"Ugh!" I grunt.

Damn small towns and their spotty cell service. Maybe if Jonah can reroute that dam money back to Barbazal, they could afford a decent cell tower.

I have to find Steph. Who knows what Jonah will do with that absolute terror I gave him? I reach up and dig my fingers into my hair, noticing my breathing is faster than usual. I shut my eyes against this. I feel my fingers, my hands, my arms, sear with that burning stinging I felt when I connected with Jonah's fears, and I wonder what the hell I've done.

Something horribly, horribly wrong.

I've created a monster.

I'm so lost in thought that I lose my footing, my shoes sliding down the gravel embankment, and I go flying.

"Ahh!" I scream as my face hits the water first. Freezing cold floods my clothes, my hair, my shoes, and I scramble for the surface as fast as I can, gasping down air when I get there.

I cough and wheeze, frantically wiping water from my eyes.

"Hey, Doctor Frankenstein," Gabe would say.

If Gabe were here, he would just stand there, arms folded, smirking down at me. I imagine his voice now, for comfort, for some semblance of stability.

"Converse? Really?" he would ask. "You couldn't have worn running shoes?"

"You suck, you know that?" I ask aloud, a surprised chuckle taking over my voice as I scramble out of the water and trudge up the rocky side. Out of breath and soaking wet, I cradle my arms around myself and step up onto the path. "And what's with the Frankenstein thing?"

Gabe would explain with something ridiculous like,

"Isn't he the most famous monster-creator of all time?"

I freeze at my own revelation, feeling my eyes narrow as the words sink in.

"I didn't technically create a monster. I just turned up the heat on what was already there."

"Would you be a different person if you were extra afraid?" he would press.

Afraid of what? I wonder.

"Well," he would ask, "were you a different person when Jed shot you?"

I stop and think about the implications of that. Was I a different person?

"I barely remember that night. But I didn't turn into a monster."

I think back to the night I lost Gabe, the memory of huddling with Ryan under the cliffside while boulders as big as cars rocketed down the mountain toward my brother, at his face, at his eyes, knowing he had no time to—

I interrupt my own thoughts.

What if I were afraid for someone else?
Someone like…
…oh my god.
Steph.

12: Not Out of the Woods Yet

I tear through the trees like my life depends on it—no, like Steph's life depends on it.

I just unleashed a highly unstable man into the town of Barbazal, where Steph is, and he's already got a significant head start. I have to make sure she's not in his line of fire, whatever that ends up looking like.

"Steph!" I holler, darting left at the clothes line and summoning more power into my feet. Why did I leave her? What's going on? If Jonah so much as laid a finger on her... And I hope, in the back of my head, in the deepest part of my heart, that Steph's okay.

I look down and try my phone again as I run—a bad idea, but what choice do I have?

The call drops.

"Dammit!" I holler, feeling my foot catch on something hard, a shelf of some kind in the ground. And I land on that same stupid tree stump with an *oof!*

"*Double* dammit!" I mutter, pushing myself to my feet, feeling my right knee searing with pain. I look down and see the bloody scrape through my jeans, and the scrapes on both my hands, and I force myself to run despite the pain.

I have to find her.

"Come on, Steph," I hiss breathlessly, lifting my phone again, gingerly this time against my stinging hands, hitting that little green phone button and running on.

Ring!

"Yes!" I scream, my feet bounding through the withered grass until I reach the end of the tree line and the fine lush green lawn. Mayor Biggs' house stands before me in all its glory, and I look around at the empty yard—empty except for that lone magnolia in the middle of the sprawling grass.

Huh. It's weird out here.

I was expecting to hear something—anything. Crickets maybe? Birds?

But no, nothing.

It's quiet.

So very, very quiet…

Too quiet.

I instinctively duck down low, slinking across the lawn like a jungle cat, the hair on the back of my neck standing on end. I feel a shiver go up my spine even though the sun, which has already risen over the horizon line, is plenty high enough to start casting its merciless heat over the valley, and over Barbazal.

And over me.

I feel the sweat beading on my forehead, and I look frantically around me as I make my way round the side of the house, between the house and the barn where they keep Biggs' classic car collection.

"Alex?" comes a voice I recognize, but one I've only come to know recently. A man's voice. Too deep to be Jonah's. Too high to be Elias's. Too smooth to be Silas's.

I turn.

Mayor Biggs stands there on the lawn, maybe twenty feet from me, casually holding a glass of water.

His face indicates he's confused.

No shit.

He told me I could come up here *yesterday*. When Clover would be home. Not today too, in the wee hours of the morning, creeping around in the woods at the back of his property, soaking wet after clearly having been in the lake.

His eyes narrow, and full-blown panic sets in. I need to think of a story, and quick.

"I-I can explain," I begin, as he steps toward me, warmly, so he can hear me better. "Clover, uh—"

Oh shit, what do I say?! *Clover gave me directions to the lake where she's been meeting her secret boyfriend?*

"Yes?" he asks, eyebrow cocked curiously. "What about Clover?"

Suddenly I hear a noise nearby—something mechanical. A door unlatching?

The sliding glass patio door leading into the living room where Steph, Opal, and I all bonded, slides open, and out steps...

"Clover?" I ask.

Her eyebrows fall at the sight of me, and she steps forward and off the patio, one hand instinctively protecting her belly before she thinks better of it and drops her hand again.

And then I realize...

...Mayor Biggs doesn't know she's pregnant.

My eyes grow wide, and Mayor Biggs leans in front of me to break my gaze at his daughter.

"What about Clover?" he asks.

"She, um," I begin. *Come on, Alex, think of something! You can't just tell him she and Jonah are together, think of something else!*

Clover's eyes are wide with desperation, and I practically hear them screaming, *Don't tell him.*

"She gave us the engine parts."

Mayor Biggs' face relaxes a bit, but his eyes trail my face, up and down, like he's reading my expression, inspecting for lies.

"Huh," he says, glancing at his daughter. "Did she?"

"They came out easy," says Clover, glancing at me. She seems to relax a little at what I've said.

"And what were you doing in the back woods on my property so early in the morning?"

"She was checking out the old stump!" offers Clover, stepping forward, fully in the conversation now. "I... told her about the old stump. You know, the one as wide as your pickup truck, Daddy."

Mayor Biggs looks between Clover and me like he's caught his daughters smoking weed at a slumber party.

"Is that true, Alex?"

"Yes," I say, *way* too fast.

Way to go, me.

"Is that *all* you were doing back there?" he asks. "Because I happened to see a certain Jonah Macon sprint out of these woods not too long ago like he had a bear chasing him."

Clover is frozen still where she stands, and I wonder if she's trying as hard as I am not to move. Not to flinch. Not to give *any* indication that we know what's going on with Jonah Macon.

"Now," he says, swirling his water and examining it like he's painting the sides of the glass with it or something, "If one of you were canoodling with that young man, I won't mind it, so long as it's you, Alex."

I gulp.

The hell do I say?

"I wasn't… We weren't…"

But then I realize, if I don't admit to "canoodling" with "this young man"—do people actually say those things? Mayor Biggs is starting to sound like a cartoon character—and I insist that Clover wasn't either, I'll have to come up with an explanation for why I'm soaking wet with lake water, and Jonah is running scared for his life through the property.

I realize anything I say right now is going to get me into trouble. I'm on Mayor Biggs' property, outside the hours he said I could be here. Clover can't exactly vouch for me any more than directing me to a huge stump in the woods. Neither of those things explains the existence of Jonah.

All I have left to tell is the truth.

I give Clover an apologetic look, and her mouth parts as if to jump in before I can say anything more.

So I say it fast.

"Mayor Biggs, there's something you should know about Jonah Macon," I begin, glancing back at Clover, and down at her belly. What I'm about to say will protect them. *Both* of them—Clover and kiddo. I hope one day she can see that, and forgive me.

"Go on?" he asks.

"That dam up the river? It's not just generating power for Barbazal. It's producing a surplus—"

"*Alex*—" Clover cuts in, but Mayor Biggs shushes her.

"Darlin', let's hear what Alex has to say. If it concerns the dam, it concerns us all."

Clover gives me one last pleading look.

But I have to do this.

"It's producing a surplus. And that surplus is going back to the city."

He pauses, staring at me like he's waiting for more. Clearly this isn't a revelation to him.

"Well yes, of course, Alex," he says finally, and chuckles. "That's how it works. We produce a surplus and bank it for future consumption. It's why Barbazal's never without power, and it's quite affordable for our residents."

"No, sir, that surplus isn't getting banked. It's being sold back to Denver, and the money's replacing a portion of the public funding you've been getting. Jonah Macon's been paying back your public funding with hydropower to appease his biggest donors. I'm—"

I feel my jaw cramping up from holding back tears.

"I'm sorry, Mayor Biggs."

I can't look at him. I certainly can't bring myself to look at Clover. What must she think of me? Revealing Jonah's biggest secret. Or… maybe second-biggest.

I stare at my shoes, expecting the inevitable questioning: *How do you know this? Do you have proof? Where is Jonah now?*

But he stays silent for so long that I wonder if he's going to say anything at all.

When I finally look back up at him, he looks from me to

Clover, and then back to me.

"You're sure of this?" he asks.

I nod, frantically, hoping, praying he'll believe me.

For his sake, not mine. Barbazal's wellbeing depends on it.

But instead of questions, instead of wanting to find out more, I feel a hand clamp around my wrist and another hand slapped over my mouth.

"Hey!" I go to scream, but it's muffled against warm fingers. Mayor Biggs is pulling me against him and starts to move. He's dragging me across the lawn.

If I can just get one good scream out...

My teeth search for his fingers, but his hand is cupped. Dammit.

"Daddy!" screams Clover.

"Shut up, Clover, and help me keep her in the house until we figure out what to do."

"Let go of me!" I holler, my voice muffled under his hand.

I look up as he pulls me along, that brilliant red aura pulsing above him, and then it sinks in. Oh my god. This is my fault.

The whole yard goes blood red, the air swirling with clots of what look like tissue, flying past my eyes. I yank and struggle in his grip, but his fingers against my arms just make them ache more.

This isn't Biggs.

This is the Biggs I created.

And if I created this in Biggs... what have I done to Jonah?

Clover steps forward and grabs at her father's arms, trying to pry them off me.

"Let her go!" she shrieks. "She's done nothing wrong!"

"Not *yet*," he hisses. "I won't hurt her, Clover, don't worry, but we have to keep her quiet."

My shoes can't find traction in the grass because Mayor Biggs keeps lifting me up so far I can barely touch the ground. My screams find no ears, I'm sure, but I release them anyway, scratching at his hands and arms as often as I can get my own hands free.

"Where the hell are you taking me?" I shriek, but it comes out like a pillowed, garbled mess under his palm.

But I get my answer.

Mayor Biggs drags me into the house, and as soon as I'm back in that living room with the leather chairs where Opal drank too much wine and nearly killed herself, he lets me go.

I drop to the floor from the force of it, and wipe the taste of his fingers away from my lips, glaring up at him.

"What the hell, man?" I spit. "I'm doing you a favor, and you're fucking kidnapping me?"

"Not kidnapping," he grins as if we're discussing a news article over a nice lunch. "I just want to talk."

Maybe I've been on the internet too much, but that *I just want to talk* is my first clue that he definitely does *not* want to talk. He won't hesitate to stop talking and start swinging if I don't do as he says.

"Daddy—" begins Clover again.

"Clover, lock the front door."

It's a command, not a question, and I half expect Clover to stand up to her father in defiance. Where is that sharp, fierce woman I met just yesterday? She melts away, and Clover obediently goes to the door and does as he says.

I wince as I hear that door clasp, sealing me in here.

"Now," he says, folding his hands together behind him and walking around me. I'm still kneeling in the living room as he does. "Alex, you told me you and your friend aren't journalists, but for a non-journalist, you seem to have uncovered some hard-hitting truths."

He won't ever know I can see into people's emotions. I wish he'd give me one. Just one aura, and I could probably get myself out of this. For a man driven by anger, he's impossibly locked down.

"The thing about commanding a small town run on love

and compassion, Alex, is the people are counting on me to keep them afloat."

What a horrific choice of words for someone steering a town through a drought.

"And if I have to do that by selling some of our excess hydropower to Denver, then that's what I have to do."

"It was *you*?" I hiss back. "You authorized the dam that's baking this town dry? Why? You need those farms to pull in revenue! What's the point? You're shooting yourself in the foot."

He chuckles condescendingly, as if he's realizing just how much dumbing-down he needs to do to get me to understand his position.

"Who said Barbazal was going to stay a farming community?" he asks. "That's no way to adapt an economy to climate change. Now, manufacturing? That's sustainable, even in a drought. But we don't have the experience. Our people know agriculture, and we know tourism. Or at least, we did, when we were the only rest stop on the 202. But we're not out of the game yet."

I cock an eyebrow, wondering how the hell he plans on bringing Barbazal back into the "tourism" game.

"A theme park would do it, wouldn't you say?" he asks, with the biggest grin on his face.

He can't be serious.

"How are you going to run a theme park with no water?"

"Well, with an economy-boosting attraction like that, Denver would be a *lot* more likely to funnel water back our way, wouldn't they? They seemed pretty keen last I talked to them. Everyone's on board but you, Alex."

I think of Silas, rationing the water bottles in his truck. I think of Anita, trying to keep the Plate and Skate alive and thriving even through these heatwaves drying up the little water they have. And I think of Clover, holding that goldfish bowl, offering it up to the magnolia, unable to care for the fish that meant so much to her in her sister's absence.

"No," I reply. "They're not."

I look up at Clover.

"Tell him," I say. "Tell him what you told me. Unless… you're in on this too?"

I feel a coldness come over Clover. An icy, cracking, stiff-as-a-glacier, blue hue settles over the room.

"I…" she begins, probably unsure of where to begin or if she should continue. She swallows. "I'm… not."

Mayor Biggs looks to his daughter in disappointment.

"You're not *what*, Clover?"

"I'm not in on this," she says, determination knitting her eyebrows together as she looks from me to her father. "Daddy, you're not seriously going to do away with the farms around here. What about the Bates'? And the mint farm we visit every year for Christmas? Opal *loves* the hayrides there—"

"This isn't about nostalgia," he growls back, "This isn't about your *feelings*, Clover. Or Opal's. Or any of you girls'."

A tiny volcano spits up a bit of lava in my stomach at the way he says *you girls* when talking about *feelings*, the irony being that we're only in this mess because of *his* feelings. The man who invited Steph and me into his home to help us get out of here.

As if even Biggs doesn't care for his own tone, he dials it back, sighs, rests the heel of his hand wearily against his forehead, and finally clasps his hands together in an earnest gesture to his oldest daughter.

"Clover, darlin', please understand," he says, "I'm not *doing away with* anyone or anything. We're building the park here in Barbazal, right by the lake. We're not mowing down anyone's farm land. But with the revenue pulled in from the park, some of them will have to make tough decisions about whether to remain an agricultural enterprise, or adapt to the times. Being a farm out here just isn't sustainable anymore, sweetie."

Clover stares at the ground, thinks long and hard about what to say and do next. Then, to my surprise, she walks to me, steps up behind me, rests her hands on my shoulders as I remain kneeling and looking up at Biggs.

"We're letting Alex go," she says. "She's done nothing wrong. Just because she knows about your little scheme—"

"Plan," he says, "not a scheme. Don't you understand? I'm doing what's best for Barbazal."

"And I'm doing what's best for my family," she says, raising a trembling hand to her stomach. She stands behind me in silence, but I look up, over my head, at Clover, and sure enough, a fire-engine red aura emanates from her, scorching the room. It bores into my skin with a fury so bright and white hot that I don't even have time to scream until it fades and soaks down deep into my bones, until all that's left is a humming warmth.

Biggs' face is aghast, his mouth parted in disbelief.

"Clover," he says, "you... you're..."

"And if you want to be in this baby's life, I suggest you do what's best for *your* family," she spits.

Holy shit.

"Who's the—" he asks.

"I don't see how that's relevant here," she continues, taking on the tone of a lawyer in a courtroom. "Your job is to look over us, to protect Barbazal, founded on pillars of love and compassion, and you're currently *unlawfully* detaining a tourist—the exact demographic of your stupid theme park—in your living room to cover up what you've done to see it through. Is that really the legacy you want to leave? Daddy?"

Mayor Biggs forms a brilliant blue aura of his own, coiled with ribbons of searing red. Tears begin to form at the corners of his eyes, and a sad smile plays at the edges of his mouth.

"Clover, please try to understand. It's what your mother would've wanted. It's what Magnolia—"

"You're *killing* Magnolia," she spits, her voice breaking. "She was only here for a short while, and the only thing we have to mark her life is *dying* because we don't have enough water to keep anything alive out here!"

Biggs' blue aura disappears, and his eyes narrow.

"Maybe you both need some time to think this over," he says.

I look up at Clover in alarm. *What the hell does he mean?* I want to scream. But Clover follows my thoughts without even looking at me.

She smiles.

"What are you going to do, tie us up and toss us in the cellar?" she sneers, arms folded.

I watch Clover, silently willing her not to taunt this man whose anger I've dialed up past overwhelming and into out-of-control territory. Everything is still pulsing red with the warmth of rage, and I can't tell whose is more intense.

Then, her smile fades. Her eyes widen in horror, and I hear a *click*.

I gasp, looking back at Biggs, who's now pointing a shiny silver revolver straight at me.

"I don't think any tying will be necessary."

13: The Cellar

The cellar isn't much like the cellars I've seen in movies. Those ones are always wet and drippy and gross, maybe a little moldy even, and you can smell the stuffiness through the TV. This one is spotless. All old wood, cedar by the smell of it. Wine bottles laid out in little U-shaped holders line the walls, displayed like trophies through the years.

From where I sit, I can see one with a label marked 2006.

"Woah," I marvel, for a moment completely distracted from the fact that I'm in a hostage situation.

I hear Clover sigh from a little further into the cellar. She sits with her legs curled up against her chest, her arms around her knees, face lowered, and I realize she's crying, softly.

"Clover," I begin, but where do I even begin? "I'm... I'm sorry."

She looks up at me, not angrily, but in surprise.

"I'm sorry I didn't leave when you said I should've," I say. "It was a mistake, staying here. I'm sorry I insisted on seeing Jonah. I'm sorry I told your father about Jonah's plan—"

"I can't believe Daddy was in on it," she grunts, smacking her lips in disgust, "At least Jonah told me about the dam. About what was really going on. But he left out the part about the theme park."

After a long, bitter silence, Clover nods.

"That must be why he was so set on our family moving to

Denver. That explains everything. He knew that the Barbazal we both grew up with," her voice crumples into a million pieces, "was going away. He… lied to me."

She buries her face in her hands and descends into sobs, deep, body-wrenching sobs.

"Clover," I say, scrambling to find some silver lining, offer some comfort, "maybe he… knew it would break your heart."

"Why do it then?!" she snaps. "To think I wasted so much time on that man, building a life in Denver, building a *family*. And for what?"

She drags her arm across her eyes and rests her chin on her knees.

Her face, it breaks me.

But…

We have to get out of here.

Mayor Biggs didn't take my phone off me. Didn't even ask if I had one.

When I pull it out and look at the screen, I remember why. *No signal.*

But I also see that I have a missed text.

From Steph!

> STEPH: Hey, you okay? Either your conversation with Jonah is going super well, or you're locked up in a basement somewhere…

Holy shit, Steph, I want to scream, *you have no idea!*

I let out a deep sigh.

"Hey," I say. "I'm sorry. I really, really am, Clover. I can't imagine what you're going through."

Even though I literally can. I feel that same icy coldness envelop me from earlier, a welcome release from this inferno that's been buzzing on my skin from Clover's wrath.

My words, somehow, have replaced it with despair.

"But," I continue, "I might have a way out of this. I can text my friend Steph, but I need reception."

"Pfft," she scoffs, glancing past me. "Good luck. Daddy had this cellar signal-blocked because his poker friends used to be on their phones instead of talking."

I turn and look to where she glanced, and see, all the way down the hall, a huge geometric table with a green top. Must be a poker table.

"Is there *any* way to get signal down here? Come on, Clover, think."

To my dismay, she turns completely away from me, curls her legs up again, and wilts against the wall, blue aura still glowing overhead.

Fine.

I feel annoyance welling up. But then I remember, Clover doesn't really have anything to escape from down here. She's in her own house. *I'm* the only prisoner.

I push myself to my feet, determined to get the fuck out of here. Steph is out there somewhere, definitely wondering what's taking me so long, and definitely a sitting duck if Mayor Biggs went to find her...

So help me god, if he so much as touches her...

I charge deeper into the wine cellar, past bottle rack after bottle rack, until I find the far wall with the tiniest window I've ever seen, high up near the ceiling.

"Clover, where's the ladder?" I know there has to be one somewhere in here. No way anyone could reach those bottles up there near the top. It's at least ten feet up.

"They're sliding ladders," comes Clover's voice, weak, defeated. "Good luck pulling them loose."

We'll see about that.

I look down the hall and find a wooden ladder fixed to the shelf, from the floor to the top of the rack, and I make for it. I reach out for it, try to wiggle it. It won't budge.

Clover's right. This thing is practically fused unless I slide it—yup, it'll move from side to side.

Until I see a sledgehammer in the corner, between the rack and the wall.

"Yes!" I whisper, grabbing it and lifting it high above my head.

"Hey, what are you—?" comes Clover's voice.

I don't wait.

Wham!

The wood is unmoving.

Wham!

"Hey!" she calls. I can hear her scrambling to her feet. "Stop! Daddy'll kill me—"

"If I stop"—*Wham!*—"he might kill *both* of us."

Wham!

The top of the ladder comes free, hanging off the rack. One more blow to the bottom and...

I feel the hammer catch over my head, and I look up to find Clover's hands clamped around it. She yanks it from me, and I stare at her blankly for a moment.

Am I really about to wrestle a hammer out of a pregnant woman's hands?

I stop, holding out my hand as if I'm keeping a snarling dog at bay.

"Clover, please," I offer, "I don't want to fight you. But I have to get out of here. Please understand—"

"I won't let you destroy anything else here," she says, and I know she's not talking about the ladder anymore. She's talking about everything. Since I got here, Opal was sent back to the hospital, Clover found out her father was in on a plan to strip Barbazal of its lifeblood, *and* build a theme park in place of all of her childhood nostalgia. And finally, the love of her life—or at least the man she thought was the love of her life—was orchestrating the whole plan.

"If you help me leave," I say, "I'll never bother you again."

I feel tears welling in my eyes, realizing I couldn't help.

Couldn't help Barbazal. Couldn't help Jonah. Or Opal. Or Clover.

All I've done by staying is make things worse.

Steph was right.

We should've just left.

"Alex?" I hear a sharp whisper ring out from somewhere nearby.

I know that voice anywhere. And suddenly, I don't care how menacingly Clover's holding that hammer. I turn around toward where I heard the voice, and up there—*way* up there, near the ceiling, on the other side of that little window I was trying to reach earlier—is the face of the girl I love.

"Steph!" I whisper back, my voice almost breaking into an elated scream. "How'd you find me?" But I already know. She knew to meet me at dawn… but then how did she know to go snooping around basement windows?

"I could hear that hammering from across the yard," she says, her voice urgent. "More important question: how did you get down there?!" She looks around to make sure the coast is still clear, and then lowers her voice even further. "Who put you down there?"

"Biggs," I say without hesitation. "Clover's down here too."

Clover comes up behind me, gingerly, as if apprehensive about letting Steph help us. What the hell?

"Can you lower a rope or something to us?"

"You think I just have rope lying around?" asks Steph. She turns away from the window and I hear shuffling.

"There's a rope hanging on the side of the barn," offers Clover suddenly.

"Thanks," I smile at Clover. That aura of hers is purple swirls of writhing vines, and I wonder if… Wait, it clicks.

"Your father can't legally keep you in here either, you know," I say. "This isn't right, what he's doing to you."

"He knows I'll talk," she says, cradling her arms around herself.

"Will you?" I ask, knowing what it would mean for Jonah if she did.

After a long moment, she nods.

Thlip!

I look behind me where I find a ten-foot rope hanging from the window, where a smiling Steph greets me. I smile back.

I climb, promising myself I'll get back in the gym and do some more lifting so this isn't such hard work. I reach the top and turn to help Clover climb. But it turns out, even while pregnant, Clover's more in shape than I am.

She's right behind me.

"Up we go," I say, pulling her through the rest of the way.

And we're free…

14. The Lawn

...or at least I thought so.

Until I turn and find myself staring down the barrel of a gun.

It startles me so bad, I stumble backward and nearly fall against Clover and Steph. I stretch out my arms instinctively to shield them behind me, although I really have no idea what the hell I'm doing.

I've been here before, on the business end of a silver revolver.

That same sick feeling coils up into my throat and sends my heart rate into hyperspeed.

Biggs is looking over the sight at me with narrowed eyes and a cunning smile.

"Alex," he sighs, "I had so hoped I wouldn't have to do this, you know."

"You can't shoot us," Steph barks. Alarm bells ring out through my head.

"Steph," I whisper over my shoulder, hoping she fills in the rest. *Not a good idea to challenge the guy with the gun.*

"Everyone in the town will hear you," Steph explains, clearly *not* filling in the rest.

She has a point, right?

...I hope?

Mayor Biggs begins his answer by cocking the gun. *Click!*

"That's a fabulous point," he explains, and when the three of us remain silent, he waves the gun toward the tree line before yanking it back in our direction. "It's the start of hunting season. If I, as a law-abidin' citizen, went for a stroll in the woods back here on *my* property, and I heard a noise, I'd be well within my right to deploy my firearm to bring down a deer or a rabbit. Or even in good old-fashioned self-defense."

Shit, he's right.

But I know not to say anything. Apparently Steph and Clover do too.

"*Especially* after finding two reprobates sneaking around my homestead."

"Daddy—" comes Clover's voice.

"And *you*," he snaps, his grip on the gun tightening. He thinks he's going to scare me with that? To be fair, he's right: I'm fucking terrified. I can feel my fingers shaking even as I continue holding them out on either side of me. And then, that red aura blooms over Mayor Biggs' head, warming us all again with brilliant heat, and…

…I'm the only one who can get us out of this.

I have to talk him down.

"Clover, move outta the way," he says. I look up at him, studying his face, his eyes wide and wild, his hands trembling ever so slightly.

"She's not going anywhere," I say, my voice shaky and, I'm sure, unconvincing, but I'm sticking to it.

"Alex, what are you doing?" whispers Steph from behind me.

"It's okay, Steph," I say, lowering my hands to either side of my body and stepping forward.

All at once, Clover and Steph gasp, and Mayor Biggs flinches, but he takes half a step back anyway, red aura twisting in on itself like a smoke cloud forcing itself into an origami shape in the sky, geometric outlines turning over each and folding into magenta, and I realize… he might be bluffing.

"This isn't the man you are, Griffin Biggs," I say. "You love your daughters more than anything, all thirteen of them." His eyes grow even wider as it sinks in that I know more about him than he realized.

"So you've done some googling," he spits.

"No," I say, "I've *studied*. I know you're a broken man, and your life has been full of the greatest joys anyone can know." I glance over my shoulder at Clover with a smile, then turn back to Biggs, pointing at the magnolia across the yard. "And the greatest sorrows."

He doesn't follow my finger. He doesn't need to. Blue explodes all around us, suffocating and heavy. I look down at the grass as it withers rapidly beneath my feet, the plants in the yard, the trees, all of them bending and convulsing as the life is sucked from them. They brown and shrivel, and lastly, so does the magnolia.

Everything around us, everything Biggs has cultivated here, is dying.

I turn back to him and reach my hand out to him, acting like I'm trying to keep him at bay.

But I'm in.

I'm standing in a hospital room, and I immediately remember standing beside my mom as she squeezes my hand as hard as she can—I barely feel it—but no, this isn't my memory. It's the memory of Griffin Biggs. And there he sits, cradling a tiny, tiny bundle wrapped in pink. He's facing away from me, shoulders trembling as he rocks back and forth.

"Griffy," comes a voice from nearby. A gentle voice, much like Clover's, but slightly older, smoother. I look to the hospital bed, where I find a woman in her forties with messy dark waves of hair falling over her shoulder. She opens her eyes groggily and moves her hands to sit up.

"How is she?" she asks him. He sits, frozen, staring back at her. "How's our little girl?"

My heart is thundering in the silence, so hard that it feels like the loudest thing in the room.

Wisteria's eyes wander from Biggs to the bundle, and then back up. Her smile falls.

"Honey?" she asks.

And I'm back.

I feel my cheeks wet with tears, and I look up at the gun pointed at my face, at the man holding it, at that blue aura around his head.

"The greatest," I repeat, searching for words, "the greatest sorrows. But, Mayor Biggs, you have *twelve* of life's greatest joys, don't you? And thirteen reasons to put the gun down, and do the right thing."

Biggs' eyes dart from me to Clover behind me, and then back to my eyes, his wild and crazy.

"Fourteen," thunders Clover from behind me, hand over her middle. She steps out from behind me, behind my wall of protection, and in front of me and Steph, staring down her own father.

"Clover—" I say.

"It's okay, Alex, I know what I'm doing," she assures me, glancing over her shoulder with a faint smile, weary and sad.

"Look around you, Daddy," Clover says. "We grew up here. This is our *home*. You taught us to fight for what matters. For what we believe in. Well, I believe in Barbazal."

I feel Steph reach forward and grab my hand, squeezing tightly, her fingers trembling in mine. I turn and pull her close against me, both of us still behind Clover.

"Alex," Steph says, and she doesn't have to say more. I understand. There are so many things I could say to her right now—I love you? I'm scared too? I'm sorry?

"I know," I say, burying my face in her neck as I hear Clover continue.

"You can't just uproot us all," she hisses, "some of us literally."

I hear a movement of fabric and realize she's probably gesturing to the magnolia.

"Now," she says, defiantly. I feel her hand rest on my shoulder. "You're going to put the gun down, and you're going to let these two lovely ladies go on to Fort Collins, where they can play their music and change the world for the better."

I feel a gentle squeeze on my shoulder.

"They've already changed Barbazal's."

I look up at Clover in absolute shock.

What?

In a single day, I sent her little sister to the hospital, outed her boyfriend-baby-daddy as a low-life politician-ass-kissing sellout, *and* provoked her father to commit at least one felony.

Well, I guess that last one's still unproven in court. Still, the first two would be offense enough to shoot me herself.

But I study her smile and realize something.

I guess Clover really does value the truth above all else. *All* else.

"Hrgh!" growls Mayor Biggs, shaking the gun at the three of us.

Clover spreads her arms to shield me and Steph and whispers… "Stay behind me."

Slowly, Clover begins to walk backwards, and we move with her.

"Clover!" exclaims Biggs, his voice gruff and unrecognizable as the buttery-voiced, warm-smiling man who told Steph and me all about Augustus Jeremiah Oscar Rhett Barbazal, II, back at the statue. "Just where the hell do you think you're going?"

"I'm leaving, Daddy," she says, her once strong voice now soft, yet sure.

We look ridiculous, I'm sure, like something out of a silent film, Steph and I huddled behind Clover, who walks backwards, shielding us as we make our way to the other side of the backyard, around the side of the house, and to the front yard.

We continue our shuffle across the circular front driveway and down the hill until…

Mayor Biggs, now maybe thirty feet away from us, standing up on his front porch, gun at his side, studies us.

"You're not going anywhere easily," he growls. I can hear the shaking in his voice.

It sends a chill through me. The hell is he doing? What does he know that he's not saying?

And then I look behind us at the tree line, and I remember that it's at least a mile walk downhill into town.

"Clover," whispers Steph when we reach the steps leading down from the property and stop. "What does he mean?"

I glance over at the trees again, knowing what comes next.

"Run," whispers Clover to us, and suddenly we're all bounding down the hill, dodging trees and roots and sticks, rocketing through the forest like our lives depend on it.

Bang!

Bang!

Bang!

Ffft, crunches an explosion of leaves to my right, and the realization sinks in.

These aren't warning shots.

15. Biggs

Purple explodes through the air, emanating from all three of us, hot and scathing like a nuclear blast. Violet knives rain from the sky, searing through my flesh as every ounce of adrenaline in my body surges forth.

"Holy shit, holy shit, holy shit!" screams Steph. "Is he really trying to fucking kill us?!"

Bang!

Bark splinters away from a tree to my left, sending shards of wood cascading over my head.

I scream, startled, and trip, my hands finding jagged earth. Steph is under my arm in seconds, hauling me to my feet. We run on.

Bang!

"Is he planning on chasing us all the way into town?!" I scream.

"Just to the end of the property line!" hollers Clover. I hear the implied *I hope* at the end of that sentence, but I shake my head and run on. There's an *I hope* thundering through my chest right now too.

I force whatever power I have left in my body into my legs. I run for Steph. I run for me. I run for Barbazal. I run for the car, and my guitar, and Steph's drum kit, and our gig tonight. We can make it. We can *all* make it.

We just have to show the world the truth.

The end of the tree line glows with brilliant midday sunlight, and I sprint for the finish line. Steph and Clover bolt into the open field past the trees, and I follow, my fingers grazing the last tree when…

Bang!

The force hits me first. Like a wayward branch snapping free from a tree and knocking me forward.

"Alex!" I hear Steph scream from somewhere that feels far away. So far away. I see her turn, and everything fades into slow motion. "Alex, oh my god!"

I hit the ground so hard and fast, I don't have time to think.

Pain explodes through my right calf, and I wonder, through the foggy haze clouding my mind, whether my leg is gone entirely. I blink my eyes open, my eyelashes crunching against the leaves. And suddenly, my arms are lifted, and then the rest of me.

"Dammit, Clover, move out of the way!"

"I won't, Daddy! I'm leaving and there's nothing you can do about it!"

"You're…"

His voice is softer somewhere behind me now. Sadder. Heavier. I can put weight on my left leg. I test the ground with it, hard and sturdy and water-deprived. I test my right leg.

Nope.

I go down.

Or at least, I would have, if Steph and Clover hadn't been under each arm to stabilize me.

"It's her calf," comes Steph's voice. "We have to get her to a hospital."

"Closest one's in Strathmaugh."

"How far is that?" asks Steph.

"Twenty minutes."

"I hope you know how to make a tourniquet," says Steph, as she and Clover hobble me forward.

"I didn't join JROTC to stare out a window," smiles Clover.

I look over my shoulder at Mayor Biggs one last time, a blue aura christening his head, thin and fragile, falling in streams around him and running down my arms and legs like water. His arms go limp at his side, and he drops the gun at his feet. It tumbles over itself down the hill until it comes to rest in the grass under some leaves. His face is tear-stained, his eyes wincing in what looks like physical pain.

I know that look. I remember that look from when Dad got the phone call from the hospital. The last one we'd ever get, about Mom. I remember that look from the mirror, after Gabe died.

Clover lets go of my arm and scrambles to grab the gun. At first, I think she might fire it right back at her dad, but to my relief, she clicks the safety on and shoves the gun into the back of her jeans.

"Clover," he whimpers, "please. Where are you going?"

I expect Clover to tell him to fuck off, or tell him she's going to Denver to start a new life with Jonah, or with herself, or whomever. But she doesn't say any of that.

She doesn't say anything.

"Clover!" he now hollers. And then...

...he lunges at us.

"*Alex!*" he grunts as he bounds down the hill.

"Holy shit, *run!*" hollers Steph. But of course, between Steph and Clover holding me up, and me without the use of my—holy shit, now that I notice it, my whole calf and foot feel wet, I hope that isn't—a strong pair of arms grips my leg, and I go down.

"*Please,*" he cries.

"Get off me!" I holler, kicking my good leg wildly under his grip. I shuffle backward through the leaves and sticks and grass.

"*Please, you have to listen!*" he cries. I stop.

His teeth are gritted, his eyes clamped shut. He's breathing like he's just run a marathon when *I'm* the one that's been shot.

I'm about to start kicking at him again, but then I notice his aura.

It's no longer blue. It's… purple. Brilliant, sharp purple, sharp as swords, growing up from the ground, unavoidable and deadly.

Mayor Biggs is scared to death of something he can't outrun. Of what? Losing Clover? Probably.

My safety? Not likely. He's the one who fucking shot me, after all.

"You can't tell anyone about this," he says, lowering his voice to almost a whisper.

"Oh yes she fucking can," spits Steph, squatting and scooping my arm into hers. I look up at her with a look that I hope is apologetic and also pleading.

"Wait, Steph," I say.

I look back to Biggs, whose face by now is twisted into a grimace of despair.

He hesitantly peels his fingers away from my good leg, and for the very first time, I get a good look at my bad leg. It's *soaked* red. Blood has seeped through my jeans, my socks, my shoes.

I feel the blood rushing away from my head, and everything starts rotating. Suddenly Steph's arms are under both of mine, and she kneels beside me, cradling me against her.

"I'm good," I say. "Just a little dizzy."

It's not a lie—I *am* good—but I'm also grateful I can't see the back of my own calf from this angle. I don't want to know what it looks like.

Clover doesn't waste a second. She shoots her father a scathing glance and kneels beside me, untying the sweater from around her waist and tying the sleeves around my leg, just above the knee. She picks up a nearby branch, cracks it across her knee, and slips one half under the tie, twisting and twisting.

"*Hey!*" I call out. "Does it have to be that tight?!"

"If you don't want to bleed out," says Steph.

"It's not *that* serious," analyzes Clover. "Looks like it went clean through. Most of the bleeding has stopped. But we can't be too careful until we can get you to a hospital."

She glares at her father again, who's now kneeling and staring down at his own hands, open, palms up, shoulders trembling as he cries.

"You'd better get to talkin'," hisses Clover. "Thanks to you, Alex doesn't have all day."

He sniffs, drags his arm across his eyes and nose, and looks up at me like a child begging forgiveness for breaking their parent's favorite vase.

"Alex," he says, "you have to understand. This job… the title of *mayor*," his voice practically *sings* the word, "is more than a job to me."

He takes so long to continue, at first I wonder if he's waiting for me to respond. He clenches his fist, that purple aura as vibrant as ever.

"That all you had to say?" asks Clover, cold as ice.

But I stare at that aura, and I know, beyond anything, there's more he wishes he could say. And why can't he?

I reach out, and I'm in.

I'm standing again, which is strange, both legs perfectly intact. I'm back in that living room with the green chairs, the TV on across the room, with the ferns and the vines and the foliage sprouting from baseboards and windows and couches, flowers now blooming from every piece of greenery in the room. Garlands of pink and purple blooms burst from every inch of the vines now. Petals rain down from the ceiling, and everywhere, people cheer, throwing hats in the air and popping champagne. A dozen little girls chase each other around with red, white and blue party poppers, and a couple squarely in front of the TV share an embrace and a warm kiss, smiles tugging at their lips, each of their heads encircled with a daisy chain. A few vines creep up from the floor and wrap tenderly around their feet and ankles, knitting them together. She rests her hand against his cheek before pulling away and beaming up at him.

"You did it, Griffy," she laughs, a huge yellow lily tucked behind her ear. "You're the mayor of Barbazal."

He takes her hands warmly in his, and it's then that I notice the single joyful tear rolling down his cheek.

"*We* did it, Wisteria."

And then, royal purple explodes through the room, whipping right through me like a winter chill as every flower, every vine, every leaf, curls up on itself and withers away into brown, mangled death. Biggs' eyes tear away from his wife as he looks around.

"No," he pleads.

The girls, one by one, sink into chairs, collapse onto the floor, exhausted, eyes fluttering as they're overcome with sudden fatigue. They are literally wilting.

"Daddy?" asks one of the youngest.

"What's happening?" asks another.

Biggs watches helplessly as his precious daughters wilt around him, and then, finally, Wisteria's eyes flutter shut. She collapses forward into his arms, and he scrambles to cradle her.

"Darling?! Darling, no!"

My fingertips freeze, and then my hands, and my arms follow, as the world around me rushes past in a vortex until…

…I'm sitting on the rock-hard ground among the leaves and the sticks, my tourniqueted leg pulsing with pain, and in front of me, a heartbroken shell of a man—Mayor Biggs—kneels, tears dripping from his chin.

"It's all I have left," he says. "Please, you have to understand."

Clover stands, arms folded, dead silent as her father pours his heart out to me.

"You can't take that away from me," he says with a sniff. "Please."

"She didn't," says Steph. "You took it away from yourself when you threatened us, and when you shot Alex!"

"I know," he whimpers. "I know, and you'd be well within your right to go straight to the authorities, but I… I have to ask… your mercy."

"You want us to keep quiet?" asks Clover. "After all of this? Daddy, you need *help*."

"What do you expect, huh?" he asks, raising his hands to gesture all around us. "When my girls all left home, and the two left despise me."

"Daddy, I don't—" says Clover, softening, but she straightens again suddenly. "Don't make yourself the victim here. This isn't about you or your job or how you pushed your own family away after Mama died."

Damn.

That would be a knife in the heart of any family man. But Mayor Biggs' aura stays purple.

And that tells me all I need to know.

"Mayor Biggs," I begin, and all eyes turn to me, the center of this discussion. I guess since I'm the one who took the bullet, I'm the one who gets to decide whether to report the injury. "I've met people like you before. People who choose their career over their families."

I remember Dad, dragging himself through the front door after a long day at his dead-end job, too tired to even eat, let alone prepare something for Gabe and me. And certainly not the way Mom did. She used to make fried rice and lo mein, if only I'd have the rice ready by the time she got home from work. Mom wasn't living at home anymore by then, at the hospital for days, weeks, months, and finally, we learned, forever. But I kept making the rice, hoping she'd walk through that door until that last call from the hospital.

And once she was gone, most nights, the rice was all we had for dinner.

And then all we had in the house.

Gabe was furious.

"She's a kid! How the hell is she supposed to build a body and grow up strong if she doesn't have food, Dad?"

"You watch your tone! Don't you think I'm doing everything I can? Working extra hours? Working faster? Leaving before you're even up, back after you're supposed to be in bed?"

And finally, when he realized he couldn't do it anymore,

"*Someone will come. That woman from CPS. Someone. I'm sorry.*"

He left.

Even if it was in self-preservation it didn't hurt any less.

As I stare at Mayor Biggs, I feel tears burn my eyes.

"People who throw themselves into something, anything else, to cover up the pain of their past. Even if it means neglecting the ones they love, abandoning what was once the most important thing to them."

A whimper escapes his lips, and I lean in closer, until pain shoots up my thigh and I wince.

"Alex, we need to get you to a hospital before this gets worse," urges Clover, reaching down and gripping my arm to support me to stand, but I don't. I stay right here.

And I realize *this* is what I had hoped to see from Jonah Macon. This kind of remorse, this clear turning point, a moment that might mean the future of Barbazal. And I have a second chance right here, right now, with Mayor Biggs.

"You have a choice," I continue. "You can continue to run from your pain. You can keep covering it up…"

He winces and sniffs again.

"…or you can reach out to your daughters. Hold them close. Put away this idea of paving over your family's history with a theme park. Stop trying to bury what you're feeling, under the guise of doing what's best for Barbazal tomorrow. Because the Barbazal of *today* needs you. They need water. And they trust you to lead them to greener pastures."

He's solemn, and painfully quiet, digging his thumbnails into his nailbeds and peeling away a hangnail, fraught with nerves.

It's time to put him out of his misery.

"I won't report this," I say. He looks up at me with wide, unbelieving eyes.

"You won't?" he croaks.

"Why would I?" I ask. "It won't help anything. You'll just be a sad, lonely man... in *prison*. And Barbazal will move on with that theme park with or without you, burying the history of all the hard-working farmers and diner-owners and mechanics who have called this place home since they were born."

Biggs blinks once or twice in disbelief, and I squeeze Clover's hand, indicating I'm ready to go. My leg is still screaming, and I grimace against the pain as she and Steph help me to my feet—or my one good foot.

"I won't report you, Mayor Biggs, because I think you and I both know," I say, as I hobble to turn around, draping my arms over Steph and Clover's shoulders, "you have work to do."

He nods frantically, and even after I turn my head and focus on balancing my weight between Clover and Steph as they help me across the field to the town square, I know he's sincere.

I've had days, weeks to dwell on what happened to Jed. Righteous flares of anger turning to disgust and then sadness, then the recognition that only letters of contrition are left to him now. Biggs' bullet has pierced me deeper than Jed's, but that doesn't mean a cell for him is the best way to help *this* town.

I hear him shuffle his fingers in the sticks and leaves and grunt as he stands to his feet.

"Yes," he says behind me. "Yes, I do, Alex."

He's silent for a long while, and I wonder if he's just going to... let us go? Take my words to heart? Save the whole city? Is this the part where Steph, Clover, and I walk off into the sunset? Or, I guess, to the car? So we can replace these pistons and get me to somewhere with some serious pain meds?

"Clover?" he asks, his footsteps getting louder in my ears.

I look to Clover for direction, but she marches on, her eyes fixed directly ahead. She's not going to stop for him.

I look to my left where I find Steph's face, so close to me. I look into her eyes. Hers glance back at Biggs, and I hope she understands, in the silence between us, that the choice is up to him.

We can only hope he makes the right one.

"I want to be in this baby's life," he says.

Warmth floods me, and relief.

Clover freezes, and I hear a soft grunt escape her throat.

"I want," he continues. "Well, I guess I've been doin' a lot of talkin' 'bout what *I* want. Whatever you want, Clover, I want to support you. Promise you that. Just… don't shut me out? Not totally?" His voice cracks. "Please?"

Silence passes, and I wonder if Clover is going to say anything this time.

"Okay," she whispers.

"What?" he asks, clearly making sure he heard her right.

"I said okay," she says, looking at me for permission. I nod and slip my own arm from her shoulder.

"I never wanted to shut you out," she sighs. "But I don't know how I can have you in my life *and* the Barbazal I know and love."

He shrugs.

"I'm… sorry, Clover. I'm afraid Barbazal has already signed a contract with the Water Republic of Denver. I can't reverse it. There's… there's nothing I can do—"

"I know," she says, turning and supporting my arm again, spurring us forward. "That's why I'm going to."

Alarm bells ring through my head.

Steph looks at me and asks a single question, "Alex?"

She asks the same thing I'm thinking.

Clover, what are you planning?

16: The Car

The car is exactly where we left it, parked safely at Elias's shop, tucked away in the garage. With each step—or, for me, hobble—I wince more and more.

Jesus *fuck* this burns!

I keep my eyes on that burgundy wonder that got us from Haven Springs to… well, *almost* to here.

Steph lets out a relieved sigh and steps forward, resting her hands on the trunk.

"Missed you, girl," she says.

Clover grunts, "You talk to this car like you're talkin' to a horse."

"About… *six* horsepower if you count the one on the dash," says Steph, swinging the back door open and scooping her arms underneath my good leg. "Now help me get *this* one out to pasture."

Steph and Clover gently lift me between them and help me into the back seat. *Fuck fuck fuck it hurts.*

I yelp in pain as my hurt leg *whacks* the center console.

"Fuck!" I scream.

"Ooh, sorry, I'm so sorry!" cries Steph, cupping her hands over her mouth, as frantically as if she'd been the one to whack her shot leg on something. "Are you okay?"

"Yeah," I grimace, gripping the seat and scootching my way deeper into the car until my head clears the door.

Steph leans forward into the car and asks, "Need anything? Before we go, I mean?"

"Got any whiskey?" I ask.

"Wow, it *is* bad," she says, smiling. "That's not even your drink of choice."

"Better than a shot of Bedazzled Kiwi Schnapps." I try to smile up at her, but a wince takes over as another splintering pain rips through my leg.

"Now, I'm happy to help y'all on your way," Clover says, "but I need a question answered first."

"What's that?" asks Steph.

"I need to know who Jonah made the deal with about this dam power siphoning."

She wants me to out a politician on intel that I gathered with my powers? Absolutely no way am I telling her that. What if it gets back to me? To Steph? I glance at her, and her face tells me all I need to know. This isn't my choice to make. It's both of ours.

"I-I don't know," I say.

Silence hangs in the air between the two of us.

"You're a godawful liar," says Clover, stepping up to the car and leaning against the driver-side door. Red radiates from her, filling the room with a shower of sparks, spraying in all directions. I flinch, and the quick jerk sends another shockwave of pain through my leg.

"We're not going anywhere until you prove to me you haven't been lying this whole time. If you learned something from Jonah," she says, resting a hand over her stomach, "it's my right to know."

"You're really going to do this *now*?" hisses Steph, motioning to me. "While my girlfriend is in excruciating pain from a gunshot wound?"

"Steph, don't—" and then the word *girlfriend* sinks in. My eyes find hers, and I can't help but smile weakly, though this pain is searing hot.

Clover remains immovable, and I quickly realize there's no other way out of this. Luckily, Steph and I think alike.

"Tell her, Alex," she says. "It's the only way to get you help."

I sigh, knowing she's right.

I level my eyes at Clover and say the name so sharply I hope it hurts her.

"Brickleby," I admit. "It was Senator Brickleby. Happy?"

"Quite," she says, grinning cunningly before stepping around to the passenger side and swinging the door open.

The engine hums to life—a sound I've waited for for what feels like weeks—we back out of Elias's shop, and I look around as we peel out of the driveway and down the highway, hoping to catch a glimpse of anyone...

Elias. Silas. Owen. Anita.

...Opal.

We didn't say goodbye to any of them.

And I guess I didn't help them either. Unless Mayor Biggs decides to do something about it. And who knows how genuine those tears were? Anyone will cry at the thought of losing family, no matter how distant.

I push myself to sitting with a weary groan, and I see Steph's judging eyes in the rearview mirror.

"Alex, please, sit still."

"I'm just putting on my seatbelt," I protest. "Bleeding or not, I'm more likely to die in an accident if you're gonna drive this fast."

"I'm doing eighty, it's not a big deal," she says.

"In a fifty-five?" asks Clover. "Darius'll have your neck."

"What, is Darius the *one* cop in Barbazal?"

After a moment, Clover nods.

"Actually, yeah."

Steph and Clover look at each other, and I see something I never thought I'd see five minutes ago.

They... *smile* at each other.

"Hey," says Clover, "I'm... sorry. I just knew I wouldn't get that information outta Jonah, and... I just had to know. How am I supposed to fix this problem if I can't find the root of it?"

"I don't know," replies Steph. "All I know is Alex and I have a gig to play in nine hours, with a six-hour drive ahead of us, and a fucking bullet wound to address first."

Steph sighs in exhaustion.

"Sorry, Alex," she says, "your leg is the priority. I just…"

Her voice cracks.

"I *so* wanted to make it to Fort Collins."

My heart shatters into a million pieces for her. Steph, who only wanted the open road and the wind in her hair, who wanted that, with *me*.

Because of *me*, our car broke down.

Because of *me*, we took our sweet time stuck in Barbazal, and *now* we're going to miss Fort Collins by mere hours because of *my* gunshot wound?

I look down at my leg. The pain's subsided a bit. I can't tell if that's a good thing or a bad thing. I guess I'll find out. I turn my knee. From the tourniquet down, my leg is bright red, and I wonder if Clover tied it too tight. Am I at risk of a blood clot with this thing being wound so many times? A wave of nausea washes over me.

I quickly force my eyes away, focusing on the trees flying past us out the window instead.

Breathe, Alex.

I let my mind meander. How long could I sit here in this car with this bullet in my—

"And before you even *think* about it, Alex, we are *not* driving to Fort Collins until you've been given the all-clear at the hospital."

"Y'all won't make it to Fort Collins in time, then."

The silence settles into the car like a thick, stuffy cloud that we all struggle to breathe through. The truth settles with it.

We're not making it to Fort Collins.

At least not tonight.

"Hope you plan on spending the night with us at the hospital then," says Steph, "because we are *not* pushing ourselves past our limit anymore. We're *tired*. We're *hungry*. One of us has been *shot*, thanks to your dad."

More silence, before Steph sighs.

"Anyway, apology accepted."

"Really?"

"The hell else am I going to do?" asks Steph. "Carry a grudge forever?"

I can't help but smile. She's so quick to forgive. That's my Steph. Tough outer shell. Soft and gooey inside.

"Besides," she says, shifting her weight in the driver's seat. I turn my gaze back to the window, where I find a gap in the trees and see a *huge* gray wall in the distance, maybe a hundred yards from the road, rising up to the sky. "Without help from an army, you're not going to take down the dam by yourself."

And then I notice the crowd gathered around the bottom, on either side of a ten-feet-wide river of water, more like a creek really.

And they're all staring, hands up to shield their eyes from the late-morning sun, at the very tip top. And who stands on the very tip top of the dam?

A man in electric-blue shorts and a gray shirt.

"One person can't take down a dam," says Steph, still waxing poetic to Clover.

But he's going to fucking try, I realize.

"Stop the car," I demand.

17: The Dam

The minute the car screeches to a halt, my seatbelt is off. "Alex, what the hell are you doing?!" screams Steph as I lean my body out of the back seat and *mean* for my good leg to find the ground, but it catches on the edge and I spill onto the pavement along the shoulder of the highway.

"Making things right," I groan, pushing myself to my feet, slowly, painfully.

Clover's out of the car too and around the side to help me up. Steph joins eventually, after getting over how stunned she is, I'm sure.

"Are you trying to *die* out here?" she thunders. "Forget what I said about Fort Collins. I just want you to be okay. *Please* get back in the car!"

"You don't get it, Steph!" I blurt out, even as she helps me forward. My good leg finds dry withered grassy patch after dried withered grassy patch as I explain, "When I met Jonah up there at the house, past the woods, by the lake, I talked to him. But I didn't tell you how it went."

"Oh no, Alex. You didn't."

"Didn't *what*?" asks Clover.

I glance at Steph, who returns my gaze with her own. *What the hell do we tell Clover?* That I wormed my way into her boyfriend's memories and sent him running off into the woods, terrified of his greatest fears realized, afraid to lose her *and* lose Barbazal? Even more afraid than losing the election?

"Alex has a… way with words," explains Steph. "She probably just told Jonah how dire the situation with the dam is, and he… didn't take it well."

"What?" asks Clover, who only now notices the enormous crowd gathering at the base of the dam up ahead.

"Holy shit," she says, turning her gaze slightly upward. "Oh my god! Is that—?"

"Jonah Macon," Steph and I say in unison.

"What the hell did you say to him?!" cries Clover. "What if he jumps?!"

"He won't," I say.

"You seem damn sure for someone who met him yesterday."

"I told you, Alex has a way with words. She *knows* people. And if she says Jonah won't jump, then I believe her."

"Well," says Clover, gently stepping out from under my arm as Steph takes all my weight upon her, "my baby's father's *life* depends on her bein' right."

She jogs ahead, cupping her hands around her mouth and hollering, "Jonah Macon, you get your ass down from there *right* this minute!"

I can't help but note Clover's tone. She's taken on the sharpness of a Southern grandmother hollering at her grandkids to come home from the creek 'cause it's getting dark out. Even though he's probably too high up to hear any of us from way back here.

Jonah Macon, atop the dam, takes a seat. He swings his legs over the edge, and I gasp, along with everyone else in the crowd. I was so confident before that he wouldn't jump, but now, with him sitting up there, and his legs swinging like that…

We join the spectators at the back, and I hear their whispers now.

"Is that little Jonie Macon? Is this some kinda demonstration?"

"He better not jump or his daddy will be heartbroken."

And then I hear two voices I recognize.

"His daddy's the one person here who *wouldn't* be heartbroken," says Bobby, from Bobby's Books.

"He'd better get down from there before the news gets wind of this," replies Paisley.

"Alex, what do we do?" whispers Steph.

"I-I don't know," I say.

I truly don't.

Do I just march forward—hobble forward—and demand to talk to him? Talking to him got us *into* this mess! This is all my fault—I crept into his memories, his sadness, his fears, and made them more intense just to further my own agenda.

My chest sinks with the weight of the question: *Am I no better than Senator Brickleby?*

I can't leave things like this. I have to do something.

"Can't you talk to him?" asks Steph.

"I couldn't get up there on top of the dam if I wanted to," I say. "Besides, I think if he saw me again he'd just panic and be even more afraid."

"Why?"

"I, um…"

It's time to confess.

"I kind of… grabbed ahold of his fears and… dialed them up a bit?"

"Yeah, we talked about that. His fears about the environment going to shit?" she asks, before she sees my face and realizes this was something far, far less ethical. "Alex? What fears did you dial up?"

I sigh, shame washing over me like a freezing-cold wave.

"Jonah Macon isn't afraid of the environment wasting away. What he's most afraid of… is failure. He's afraid of everyone he knows and loves thinking he's an utter waste of oxygen. Especially—"

I glance up ahead to where I see Clover worming her way through the crowd.

"Especially Clover," I say, and I lower my voice. "Especially their child."

Steph gasps.

"You… told Jonah they… think he's a failure?"

"Well, no, not… *exactly?*" I offer, looking at her. But her eyes narrow at me, glance at me up and down like she doesn't recognize me.

Tears prick my eyes. I'd give anything to never have to see her look at me like that, ever again.

A red aura springs to life around her head.

…Dammit.

"You said you were going to be careful!" she snaps. "I told you playing with people's emotions was dangerous, and now look what you've done!"

"Steph… I-I'm sorry—"

"Don't apologize to *me*," she hisses, "apologize to Jonah! He's up there all by himself thinking his friends and family think he's a failure! What do you think he's thinking up there, inches from death? *Talk* to him, Alex, you have to!"

I look up at him, leaning his elbows on his knees, resting his face in his hands, sitting atop the thing siphoning power back to Denver that he helped build.

The sky darkens, darkens like a bruise, purple and angry, rain falling in purple tears around us, and I look to Steph.

"You lied to me," she says, her red aura growing, bleeding into the purple air around us like watercolor.

"No," I shake my head. "No, I did my best—!"

But I don't get a chance to finish.

Lightning flashes around us, yanking me back to Jonah, and now, when I look up at him, I see what he sees. All around, there's not a human to be seen. Just huge, purple blotches so dark they look almost black. Glowing white teeth and eyes face Jonah, mouths hissing hungrily as if they might climb the dam and eat him alive.

"I have to get up there," I say, mostly to myself, but Steph hears me.

"*What?!*" she cries, pulling at my arm. "You are absolutely not going up there. Can't you yell at him from here? Or call him?"

"Steph, if I don't go up there," I say, "Jonah may not make it down."

"But if you go up there, you might *scare* him down," she says, glancing back up at him.

I follow her gaze, remembering how Jonah and I ended our conversation, with him making up the quickest excuse—*any* excuse—to get the hell away from me.

A thought strikes me like a sack of bricks.

What if by dialing up Jonah's fear of failure, I also made Jonah afraid of the thing that made him afraid?

What if Jonah is afraid of *me*?

What if he's afraid of what I'll do if he doesn't do something about the dam? About the environment? About Barbazal's future?

Steph is right, I realize. I can't go up there. And I can't be the one to talk to him.

"Jonah Macon, I know you can hear me!" hollers Clover's bullhorn-like voice from among the crowd, her own red filling the air around us, battling his purple with glowing fury. "Come down from there right now and let's talk about this!"

Her accent is coming in strong now that she's angry.

"Whatever the hell kinda notions you've got in that head of yours, you need to talk to someone. Just talk to me!"

I look back up to Jonah. He's painfully still. Unmoving. Unwavering. He says nothing.

Clover's shoulders slump in defeat, but she's not giving up quite yet.

"I know you've been overwhelmed with the election and… everything," she says. I remember the baby they're about to bring into the world together, and it strikes a bolt of pain through my chest at the thought that this child could grow up without a father if I don't do something. *Quick.*

I can hear the tears in Clover's voice as she continues.

"But like you said, we're gonna make it, right?" She turns to the crowd around her, the purple monsters, some with cameras now, all eyes on her now. "We've *got* to make it."

Affirmative *yeahs* and *mhmms* and even a *preach!* from the crowd indicate she has their ears.

"Jonah Macon will bring home the bacon!" she yells to everyone who will listen. "Jonah Macon will bring home the bacon!"

With each repetition, more voices join the chorus.

Jonah Macon will bring home the bacon!
Jonah Macon will bring home the bacon!
Jonah Macon will bring home the bacon!

Jonah pushes himself to his feet.

The chanting crowd of blotchy gremlins clips into a series of gasps and shrieks.

"He's gonna jump!" cries a nearby elderly woman frantically.

But he doesn't.

He stands there. And he yells.

"Clover!" he calls, his voice echoing across the vast fields now that the crowd is dead silent. "Thank you. For your kind words, and your kindness. But I have thought about this for a long time, and I've made my decision."

This unwavering purple storm begins to swirl in the sky like someone is stirring the clouds with a giant spoon.

"No," I hear Clover's voice bark, her red cloud flaring against his, beating the darkness back.

"I'm not going to jump," he assures the crowd. Everyone, including me, breathes a huge sigh of relief. Thank *god*. "But I am going to keep my promise. I have something to admit to you all."

Wait, what?

He's not going to—?

"I've been keeping something secret from you for a long, long time—"

Wee-oo-wee-oo.

A police siren wails right behind me, and I turn to see the flashing blue and red lights and a short man climb out of the driver's seat holding an *actual* bullhorn. His badge number says 001, next to the name, Darius.

I roll my eyes.

Of course.

The *one* cop in Barbazal.

How's he going to help this situation?

Darius lifts the bullhorn to his lips.

"Jonah Macon, this is Officer Darius. I'm gonna need you to come down from there immediately."

"I need to borrow that," hollers Clover, marching her way back through the crowd, past me and Steph until she reaches Officer Darius.

"Hey—"

"Jonah Henry Elias Macon, you have until the count of three to get yourself down from there and start talkin' some sense. *One!*"

Officer Darius snatches it back before she can continue.

"Miss Biggs, I can't let you do that," he says.

"You don't understand!"

And they go back and forth like that while I look at Steph, and I'm pretty sure she's thinking what I'm thinking. Clover is *not* the person to talk some sense into Jonah Macon. She's too close to him, too involved. It's like a therapist who's already best friends with their client – it's definitely not going to work. But who then?

I can't be the one—I'm the *amplifier* of his trauma.

I think back to Mayor Biggs, who's in his own horrific mental state after today. No, no, no.

Steph doesn't know the details of the situation. She doesn't know Jonah like I do. Like Clover does.

Clover's voice pierces my brain, ringing out what she said crystal clearly.

Jonah Henry Elias Macon...!

Elias?

Wait, *that* Elias?

Is…

I rewind my brain, way, way, way back. All the way back to that first memory I saw here in Barbazal. The flashy red classic car with the whitewall tires. The million-dollar smile from Mr. Jonah Macon, a far cry from the tortured, confused man sitting atop the Barbazal Dam about to admit something to everyone he's ever known and loved. He's waving to his followers, his supporters, his local donors, his voters, looking effortlessly carefree, and happy.

And then there's Elias.

Standing in front of Elias's Shop. Hands in his pockets. Scowl on his face. Jonah's mouth flattens ever so slightly, so slightly in fact, that I almost miss it.

No way…

"I've been lying to you all," comes Jonah's voice, breaking me from my spell. "About everything. About who I am. About what I've done."

His voice is falling apart up there as he says,

"This dam isn't making Barbazal more money."

A series of gasps ripples through the crowd, and Steph turns to me.

"Alex, what do I do? I'm freaking out here. What if he does something crazy?" she cries. "This sounds like some kind of final statement or something. What if everything's about to go sideways?"

"This dam is producing enough hydropower to power Barbazal, and even some of Denver. *And* with the money it makes selling power *back* to Denver, it costs the state of Colorado less in public funding."

"What's he saying?" asks an older gentleman from a few rows up.

"He's saying the dam is costing us funding!" comes the voice of the woman beside him.

"Damn these city-slickers comin' in here, damming up our

river, taking our money!" another voice from deeper into the crowd calls out. "Makin' money off our backs!"

"They're taking away our water to pay Denver?!" cries someone else.

The whole crowd of hissing monsters growls and snarls up at him, feral and vengeful.

Goddammit, this is getting so out of hand *so* fast. What do I do, what do I do, what do I do…?

I reach into my back pocket and find my phone.

"What are you doing?" asks Steph, clearly losing it. "Calling Ethan?"

I shake my head, finding Elias's Shop on Maps and click the phone number, then dial.

Ring.

Oh thank god, I've finally got a signal out here.

"Who?"

"Elias."

Ring.

"What? Why?"

Jonah raises his hand, like a true politician, for silence. It doesn't work. With each passing moment, there are more *what the hell is he doing…* and *I can't believe, all this time…*

Ring.

"I'm sorry!" he calls out to the crowd. "From the bottom of my heart of hearts, I'm sorry. To my friends, and my family. To Clover."

Ring.

I freeze, feeling a shock zip up my body. I find Clover in the crowd, looking pale, still as a tree, unmoving, clearly not knowing what the hell he's thinking, telling everyone in Barbazal that they're together.

"Let me make things right!" he pleads.

Ring.

Then, Jonah disappears over the other side of the dam.

"What the hell?!" asks Steph.

"Where is he?" asks someone in the crowd.

"What's he doing?!" screams another.

Ring.

He re-emerges, sending a surge of chatter through the audience, which is maybe four hundred people strong now. He lifts something over his head. Looks like a long stick. A broom?

No.

It's a sledgehammer.

Wham!

It comes down hard enough against the wall to send a loud *clang* through the air.

Metal on metal.

"Oh my god, Alex!" cries Steph. "He's trying to bring down the whole dam!!"

"And if that thing comes down, he's going with it," I whisper, the full realization sinking in.

"Can he bring down a whole dam by himself?" she asks.

Wham! A spark sizzles out of the wall to his left, some kind of control panel.

"He doesn't need to break down the whole dam," I manage, my voice shaky. "He just needs to get into that control box. He's going to overload it!"

"Does he know what happens when a dam breaks?!" Steph asks urgently, squeezing my wrist and taking a step back.

"Y'all might want to *move!*" he hollers as he brings down the sledgehammer again.

Wham!

I shake my head, totally unable to think. My chest feels tight, and my skin crawls with what feel like little bugs. This is *way* too much. All of it is just so *much*.

"Hello?" comes the aggravated voice on the other end of the receiver.

I'm so startled, I falter, and my leg gives out underneath me.

Steph isn't quick enough to catch me, and I fall to the ground, dropping the phone from my hands.

Searing pain rips through my leg, but I scramble to pick the phone back up.

"Alex!" cries Steph. "Are you okay?"

I don't have time to answer her.

"Hellooo?" comes the voice on the other end.

"Hello?" I call out, wincing as I adjust into a sitting position that doesn't send more pain coursing through my lower half. "Hello, Elias?"

"Yes, who is this?" He sounds suspicious as hell, already having forgotten my voice since we only just met the other day.

"I-I'm Alex. Steph and I visited your shop the other day?"

"Yes," he says with a sigh. "What can I do for you?"

"I need you to get to the dam." I say, "I can explain when you get here."

"Now just a minute, miss," he says, clearly affronted. "I don't know how you do it in the city, but out here we don't just go callin' up folks and tellin' 'em what to do with their time—"

"It's about your *son*."

Silence.

Wham!

I wince at the sound booming through the air. That one sounded particularly impactful.

"Somebody stop him!" cries Clover. That red aura radiating from her now fades into a violet to blend with Jonah's, droning and heavy. I hear the jingling of chains among the clouds, but I can't see them. There are tears streaming down Clover's face.

And then, finally, I hear Elias's voice through the phone.

"I don't have a son."

Click!

"No!" I holler, scrambling to re-dial. *Please, please, please.*

Ring.

Wham!

Ring.
Ring.
…Beeeeeeep.

"No," I whisper, looking down at the phone in disbelief. I look to Steph.

"He…" I say, tears scrambling my words. "He… hung up."

Why didn't I just explain what was going on? Of course he has no idea this could mean his son's *life.*

I send a text, although there's no way to know if Elias's number is textable, or if it's a landline. Knowing Elias, it could be either.

And because of me, Jonah Macon might die, and Elias will find out he might've been able to save him.

> Jonah is in grave danger
> trying to destroy the dam.

"So, what do we do?" asks Steph, but there's already defeat in her voice. She knows as well as I there's nothing we can do from down here. A blue aura forms around her head, and she lowers herself from a crouch to a kneel. "Alex?" she whimpers, letting a sob escape.

My phone buzzes with a text back.

> This number cannot receive text messages.

I reach for her, taking her in my arms, squeezing her tight.

A tear rolls down my cheek and disappears against Steph's shoulder, and I shut my eyes harder and squeeze her tighter.

Wham!

"I'm out of ideas," I say, "and Jonah's going to die because of me."

We *all* might, if I can't stop this.

"No," snaps Steph, pulling away and cupping my face in her hands. She leans in, presses her forehead to mine. "Jonah is a grown man making his own choices. His mental health is his responsibility. Don't you *dare* take the fall for that. You did nothing wrong, Alex. You tried to help hundreds of people through a drought."

Wham!

Every time he swings that hammer, it feels like it's twisting a knife in my heart.

I think back to how Elias looked, staring up at Jonah as he rode through town, just wanting to make a difference.

I don't have a son.

What could Jonah have done to warrant that kind of hatred from his own father?

I think back to how Jonah's smile fell, even as he rode in that flashy red car and—

My eyes go wide.

I gasp.

"Steph," I say, grabbing her gently by the shoulders. "I need my guitar."

"But—"

"I'll explain later, I promise. It'll all make sense. Hurry!"

Steph pushes herself to her feet and darts for the car without further question.

I look up at Jonah, where I see...

A huge, looming blotch monster, rising up behind him, claws extended overhead, towering over him from behind with hungry teeth as he flips the switch and steps back.

BOOM!!!!

It sounds like a glacier cracking. Something rumbles through the air, a sound like a crackling bowl of cereal. The ground trembles under my feet. After looking to Steph, who looks just as confused as I am, I look back up and...

Oh my god, there's a crack in the dam wall.

A small one, maybe five feet down from where Jonah stands. A chunk of rock the size of a loaf of bread breaks away and falls, tumbling down the side until it plunges into the dark river water below.

"He's really gonna break the dam!" shrieks a teenage girl just a few dozen feet ahead of us.

"He thinks he's taking on his fears," I whisper to myself as that colossal beast behind him grows larger still, teeth dripping with purple drool as it leans even more closely over Jonah.

But this isn't the way. As it fully sinks in that Jonah is going to bring this thing down, I do the only thing I can think to do to get everybody to safety.

"Everybody, run!" I holler.

"Get in your cars!" Steph follows.

And suddenly, from where I sit in the grass, hundreds of people turn, and run at me.

"No, no, no," I mutter to myself, scrambling to push myself to my feet before I get trampled to death. I turn away from the crowd, raising my good leg up until my foot finds the earth.

Oof!

Someone hits me square in the shoulder, knocking me forward.

I turn to look up, but someone else's foot swipes my chin. Pain explodes through my face, and I'm down again.

I blink my eyes open, and everything seems blurry except for a neon-purple glow zipping across the sky. All I can see, all around me as people run overhead, is fear. I do the only thing I can do: I curl up into the tiniest ball I can curl into, and I listen to the thundering footsteps around me as everyone sprints back to their cars before this whole place takes on *way* more water than anyone dreamed of.

Yes, Barbazal will have water, but at what cost?

When the footsteps fade in my ears, and I can hear Jonah again...

Wham!

...I look up to the top of the dam, where Jonah's monster

is still hovering. He's taking the sledgehammer to the concrete now.

"I got you," comes Steph's voice. And suddenly, before me, she holds out my guitar.

I smile, finding new strength, and she helps me to my feet.

"What are you planning, Alex?"

"I'll show you," I croak, my voice hoarse and weathered from… well, everything.

I lift my guitar over my head and lower it until the strap settles over my left shoulder.

My fingers find their home—their familiar place along the fret and—

Steph reaches into her pocket and pulls out a pick.

"Thought you might need it," she grins.

No way. How does Steph think of these things?

I give her a grateful smile, take the pick and find the note I want.

"You know me too well," I say.

"I kinda like you," she says again, stepping back with a gesture that says, *Well?*

I pick softly at first, gingerly testing out the tune. It's only Steph and me out here now, besides the occasional—

Wham!

I pluck string after string, and when my eyes find Steph's, hers are huge.

"Why does that sound familiar?" she asks. "I know I've heard that tune. Like, *recently*."

I keep picking, a steady handle on the tune now.

"Music box," I say, playing the tune like I've known it all my life. Bless my ability to play by ear.

"Oh yeahhhhh," she marvels. "Wow, you picked that up fast. Why are you—"

I study her as she connects the dots.

"Are you going to play that for Jonah?"

"Maybe if that song meant something to Elias, it'll mean something to Jonah," I sigh. "If I can't get Jonah to come down, maybe I can bring Elias... *up*."

I keep playing, my fingers finding their rhythm and memorizing where to fall over the strings, feeling little notes of joy *plink-plink-plink*ing from the strings. An A chord releases a bright red burst of vapor, and a D releases yellow to follow, a purple G, and then an F launches a blast of blue into the air. Finally, I land back at a D chord, which raises up a golden yellow cloud all around me. The tune sinks into my hands and into my blood as I let my fingers play among the strings.

And then, I step forward.

"No, Alex," whispers Steph, cradling my arm. "Let me help you."

"I can't play if you're holding me, Steph. I... I really do have to do this one alone."

She looks at me with huge searching eyes, looking for some kind of excuse, a reason to keep me from walking on my leg like I'm about to.

Wham!

But she understands the stakes as well as I do, and hesitantly, sadly, she clasps her hands together and takes a step back.

"I'll be right behind you," she says with a nod, her eyes brimming with tears.

I give her a grateful smile.

I love you, I want to say. It feels so *right* to say it.

But I don't.

I back out, like a coward.

"I know," I say. *Goddammit*, that's not quite what I meant but there's no time to make it right. "I...have to do this."

I grip my guitar and drag my bad leg along, my fingers moving over the strings, plucking hard enough that the music seems to vibrate in my ears, humming over the grass as I walk-drag-walk-drag-walk-drag across the open field.

"Jonah!" I holler up to him. God, he's so high up. Maybe fifty feet. I wonder if he can even hear me from down here. "Jonah Elias Macon!"

The sledgehammer swings up over his head again, and it freezes. He stares down at me.

"What do you want?" he asks, his voice faltering now. He lowers the sledgehammer and lets the handle drop at his side. "I've done what you've asked. Are you happy? It's all coming down, Alex!"

There are so many things I want to fire back at him. How *dare* he insinuate taking down the dam was *my* idea? I dialed up his fear, unfairly, arguably unethically... but... I didn't *tell* him to go climb up the dam and take a sledgehammer to the hundred-foot wall beneath him!

But I shut my eyes tight, blocking out his accusation, and focus on making my fingers move, sending a rainbow of colors into the air, soothing the angry purple clouds above.

A long moment passes. Moment after moment, and I don't hear another *wham*. Instead, I hear Jonah's voice again.

"That tune..." he says, so softly I almost miss it. "How... how do you know it?"

I look up at him, eyes narrowed, playing even harder, letting the chords answer for me.

He stands staring at me, mouth agape.

"You've... been to see my father?" he asks.

"No one thinks you're a failure, Jonah," I say, which isn't a lie. "I've talked to so many people in Barbazal the last few days. Even knowing what you had to do in Denver to get the platform you have, you've made such a huge impact on this place. Look at you. You're willing to do anything to give Barbazal your best. Even if it means giving up your *life*."

I keep playing, and as I stare up at him, I see that monster look down at me and send an angry *HISSSS* in my direction.

"I don't need your patronizing!" he hollers. Thunder crashes overhead, and the clouds deepen into an even richer purple, glowing neon in the sky. It's just him and me out here, alone, in this field by this river that could surge with water from behind the dam at any moment. That five-foot crack from earlier has grown another two feet, and I take a deep breath, steadying myself. I know that if I can't talk Jonah down from there…

…I'm gone.

"Steph," I whisper behind me. "Go to the car."

"Alex—"

"*Now*," I hiss bitterly, knowing this might go south. "If something happens to me out here, I'll know I did my best for this place. If something happens to you, I'll never forgive myself."

She steps forward, a tear rolling down her cheek. She rests her hand on my lower back and slides it around my hip, leaning in and kissing my shoulder.

"Then let me forgive you for you," she says softly. "But I'm not leaving. Because if something happens to you out here, and I left, *I'd* never forgive myself."

I sigh because I know she's right. The only scenario worse than both of us getting killed out here is me going on living without Steph.

I can at least grant her that.

I give her a nod before turning back to Jonah. He hollers down at me again.

"You made yourself very fucking clear, Alex!" Past the diplomacy and platitudes, there's a real live man under there. And here he is. "Unless I do something about this dam, I'm a failure, and everyone knows it."

"That's not what I said!" I yell. "Jonah, I'm sorry I made you feel like you're a failure. Like anyone in your life might think you're a failure unless…"

I confront the root of the problem, stare it in the face holding a can of gasoline, drizzle it all over the top, and light it on fire.

"…unless you did what I wanted."

Crack!

… What the hell was that?

Jonah's let go of the sledgehammer, and there's nobody else out here. Most of the spectators watch silently from their cars parked along the side of the highway. I turn to look at Steph, whose eyes are huge and scared like I'm sure mine are.

We're out of time.

"Jonah, get down from there!" I holler, my fingers still playing despite everything. "Please, if this dam comes down, you're—"

"Going where I can be most useful!" he hollers, his voice shattering.

Suddenly I hear another voice behind me, this one warm and rich and raspy. Familiar.

"You're most useful in Denver!"

I turn so fast I almost fall over, but Steph is there to catch me under my arm. But it breaks my playing. And my guitar is replaced by the droning, soulful wail of a harmonica.

And there, Elias Macon steps forward, cradling the instrument against his mouth and playing with all his heart—the same song from the music box. A far cry from the Elias who just hung up on me.

Relief sinks into my chest like a cooling salve, and I let out a sigh. I stare at him, and finally, he looks from Jonah to me. His eyes are even, his cheeks full of air, his mouth preoccupied with playing. I give him a nod, and force a smile. Whatever he said to me on the phone, about not having a son, the point at the end of it all is…

…he came after all.

I look back up to Jonah, who's gone completely silent, his mouth hanging open in shock.

"Dad?" he calls.

He asks it with a tone that says both *I can't believe you're here*, and *I kind of wish you weren't.*

But Elias doesn't stop playing. He marches forward, past me, past Steph, across the open field. I keep my guitar going, matching Elias's notes but staying where I am. This conversation is between Elias and Jonah.

Working man and politician.

Father and son.

Elias plays on. Jonah sits down, legs swinging, even with that ten-foot crack splitting the dam down the middle. Wait, it's ten feet now?

And getting... longer?

"Alex," says Steph, gripping my arm.

And then I realize. That's not a crack in the rock. That's... a water trickle.

"Alex, we have to go," she urges, pulling me.

"Steph," I say, squeezing her hand. "Go."

She stares at me for a long moment, her face a few shades paler. "*What?*"

"Go meet Harson. Play your drums. Rock the place. I know you can."

"Alex, what the hell am I supposed to do without a vocalist and a guitarist and—"

Crack!

A force rattles the ground beneath us, and Steph gasps. We look at each other. Then we look up at the dam.

That seven-foot crack is now fifteen feet tall, and that trickle is now a spout.

"The dam's gonna go!" hollers one of the remaining spectators from their car.

I squeeze Steph's hand.

"I'll be okay," I say.

She furrows her brow. "What the hell am I supposed to do without my girlfriend?" she asks, getting to the root of it all. "I'm not going without you. Stop asking me to."

"I want you to live the life you want—"

"And I want you to stop living your life for other people!" she

219

screams. "You tried to do it for Gabe, and Ryan had to save you. And if I have to drag you away from this dam to keep you from doing the same thing for Jonah Macon, then so help me, I will!"

"Jonah!" calls Elias's voice, *finally*. But it's not the voice of an angry man, or an enraged father—I know that voice—it's that of a desperate man. "Quit playin' around and get your hoity-toity ass down from there!"

Okay, *now* he's angry.

But just as the warm moment sinks in,

Crack!

Whoosh!

That spout is now a slightly bigger spout, oozing over the side of the dam wall.

"I'm doing it, Dad!" comes Jonah's voice as he lifts the sledgehammer over his head. "I'm doing what's right for Barbazal!"

Wham!

My gasp catches in my throat as the hammer comes down right where that crack meets Jonah's feet, wondering how many more *whacks* before the whole thing comes down, and Jonah with it.

I pluck on, as Elias pockets the harmonica and cups his hands around his mouth.

"I don't give a damn what's right for Barbazal if…" He hesitates. "… if… it takes away my only son."

I didn't even believe the tone of that, and I'm new to both Elias and Jonah.

Jonah lets out a mocking, "*Ha!!!*" and wipes his forehead. "You want me dead! You all do! Don't lie to me!"

He raises the sledgehammer again.

Whack!

"I *don't!*" hollers Elias. "I know I've said some things in the past."

Whack!

"I know I've made mistakes. I know I've hurt you. Real bad."

Whack!

Elias's tone dials up to eleven, and a huge purple aura around his head flares into a blue supernova, radiating in all directions, fizzy almost like soda, nostalgic.

"But do you really want to die on me?!" he screams, his voice echoing through this vast, flat land. "Please, Jonah, come down and let's talk about this! I'll do whatever you want—" his voice crumples into sobs. "I'll do whatever you want, I'll say whatever you want! Don't take my boy away from me! I'm sorry!"

Jonah, sledgehammer raised above his head, stops.

The whole world seems to stand still. And slowly, surely, as the water hisses through the wall of the dam, Jonah Macon lowers his sledgehammer to his side.

"You… what?" he asks.

"I'm sorry, Jonie!" calls Elias. *Little Jonie Macon.* "I'm sorry for it all. I'm just… I'm sorry."

That huge monster over Jonah recoils in pain, shrinking just a bit like a slug under a blanket of salt.

Tears prick my eyes, and I shut them against the memories surging up in me.

My own father, slamming the bedroom door in Gabe's face. Throwing a ceramic cup against the kitchen cabinet and shattering it into a million pieces. Throwing his sweater down angrily on the sofa and his shoes down the hallway.

And then I try to imagine his face looking down at me. Maybe his eyebrows are relaxed this time, his eyes soft, his smile slight but there.

Saying…

I'm sorry.

And I open my eyes, because I can't picture it.

But I imagine, as he was down there in the mine, pinned behind a mountain of rubble, clinging to the necklace Mom gave me, the one he took with him when he left us for good, that maybe, just maybe…

…he said it.

"I'm sorry!" calls Elias again. "Now, please come down!"

That monster over Jonah shrinks just a bit more, writhing now, withering under Elias's words, until it vanishes in a puff of purple smoke.

And just like that, Jonah—little Jonie Macon—steps to the side, takes hold of the safety rail along the steps downward, and disappears behind the dam wall.

"Oh my god!" exclaims Steph.

"Is he coming down?" I ask, to Steph, to myself, to no one.

And then, out from the other side of the dam, emerges Jonah Macon, dragging the sledgehammer behind him.

"Dad," says Jonah flatly.

Elias says nothing, but I can see his hunched shoulders trembling. He pushes himself forward, looking like he might collapse at any moment, until he meets Jonah and embraces his son so tightly, it's like everything between them has been forgotten.

"I know I've been a shitty son," says Jonah, burying his face in his father's shoulder. "I... abandoned Barbazal when it needed me most. I disappointed you, and Mom—"

"I may have been disappointed," interrupts Elias, "but don't you *ever* think your mama was disappointed in you. She's lookin' down on you even now, hear? And as for me... I should've been more understanding."

A long silence passes, until Jonah pulls away and stares down at his father in disbelief.

Elias sighs as he continues, "I should've... realized how bad you were hurtin'. I shoulda seen it. Shoulda recognized it. Cuz I've been feelin' the same hurt."

"Aw, Dad—" Jonah cuts his own sentence short. But he's said all he really needs to in those two words.

He throws his arms around his father's shoulders, and a golden burst of light glows from both of them, melting the purple haze all around us, both of their heads glowing like the sun with joy. The lightning stops, the clouds dissolve, and the blue sky returns.

"There's a lot you don't know about me, Dad," explains Jonah. "I'm in a lot of pain, but—"

"You wear it well," says Elias. "Or… you hide it well. For the cameras."

"Barbazal doesn't want a leader who can't acknowledge his own feelings."

"But Barbazal—hell, Colorado—*needs… you.*"

I hear Steph gasp softly beside me. "Aww," she says.

Jonah smiles like I've never seen him smile. Not here in Barbazal, not in that memory of him riding through the town square grinning down at his supporters, not when he spoke to me by the lake…

It's a smile of sheer gratitude.

"So," he says, chuckling, "does this mean I have your vote?"

Elias extends a hand for a firm handshake.

"It means we have a lot to talk about."

I smile along with them.

Crack!

All of us turn back to the dam, where that steady flow of water has progressed into a whitewater surge, bursting from the crack down the side.

"Um, guys?" asks Steph, ushering me back.

"Let's go," says Jonah, hand in the middle of his dad's back as they run to us. I turn as fast as I can and move, the ache in my leg unbearable. Steph, without a word, darts under my arm and heaves me forward across the unforgiving ground. I yelp in pain.

"Steph, my leg!"

"I know, Alex, I'm sorry! We have to go—"

Crack!

Crack-crack-crack-boom-boom-boom!

"Oh my god!" Steph and I scream at once. Elias and Jonah climb into Silas's truck up ahead, and I look back, even as I hobble as fast as I can.

The whole dam wall, once solid concrete, disintegrates before my eyes, melting into nothing as the water explodes through the rock. The sound. The *sound*. It booms in my ears like thunder.

My heart races.

Our car is a good hundred feet down the highway. We'll never make it!

"Steph, the truck!" I scream.

Silas is closer. *Way* closer. He leans out the window of the truck, arm extended.

"Alex! Steph! Get in!" he calls.

I glance over my shoulder again. The water, a monster behind me, surges forward with such force into the river, spilling over the banks.

I feel Steph let go. She leaps up into the truck as fast as a tree frog and immediately starts grabbing for me, tearing at my clothes and limbs to haul me into the truck bed. I don't feel my leg anymore – I don't have time to. I collapse into the truck bed with a *thud*. I hear tires squeal.

I'm propelled to the wall of the truck bed so hard my head spins. Everything goes fuzzy, and Steph's voice turns to jello in my ears.

"Alex?" she calls from far away.

"Alex, can you hear me?"

But I can't hear her anymore. I can't hear anything. Everything goes black.

18: The Hospital

Mom looks beautiful, I'm sure, under that lid.

Under the flowers arranged in a bright red bouquet on top. Under the harsh fluorescent lights she was way too familiar with toward the end of her life. She should've been home, with us. Doing what she loved. Cooking, reading, laughing with Gabe and me, keeping the family glued together.

"My strong girl... your brother, your father, they're going to need you. You have to be strong," she'd said to me, caressing my cheek. I reach up and clutch the necklace, feeling the wetness on my cheeks as I grit my teeth against the pain.

I force my eyes open, and there she is again, lying in her hospital bed, frail, her wrists bony, her limbs graying and skeletal.

"Mom," I whimper, collapsing to my knees and burying my face in her side. "I can't do it," I sob, gripping her hospital gown like everything depends on it. If Dad were here, he would tell me to stop crying. Stop bothering her, he'd say. Can't you see she's going through enough?

I feel her fingers in my hair, running them through it gently.

"I remember when you were born," she says. "You were bald."

Even through the tears, I have to smile at that.

"Was I?" I ask, my voice still fragile. I wipe away my tears as she continues.

"Yes," she affirms, "you were my bald, happy girl, Alex."

"I wish I could be happy now," I whimper.

"I know you do," she says. "And I wish so too. But you will be."

"How are you so sure?" I ask, looking up at her. "I've been tossed from foster home to foster home, and then Haven Springs and… I lost Gabe. And now I might lose Steph." I crumple into sobs once more, and I feel my mom's touch against my shoulder.

"Steph? What proof do you have that you've lost her?"

"It's my fault we're even here!" I practically scream. "It's all my fault."

"Because of you, Barbazal might be able to save its own farming community," she says soothingly. It's enough to quell my crying enough to listen to her. "Because of you, Ethan has somewhere to stay when he visits his uncle. Somewhere familiar. Somewhere he calls home. You gave up the concert of a lifetime to save a city," she says with a smile and a nod down at me. "And I believe it's going to pay off."

"Pay off?" I ask, but when I look up, she's gone. The blanket she was under falls limp in my arms, and I shut my eyes tight.

"Alex?" comes Steph's voice. My eyes shoot open again, and suddenly I'm the one lying in a hospital bed, looking over at her. She has her hand on my thigh, slides it to my fingers, and squeezes them with a hesitant smile. "How're you feeling?" she asks.

"I'm…" I begin, the memory of everything sinking in— Barbazal, Mayor Biggs, Clover, Opal, Jonah, Elias… *Oh my god, the dam!* "Holy shit!" I exclaim.

"Yup, she's back," smirks Steph, glancing across the room at Clover, who's sitting comfortably in an armchair with her arms folded.

"I'll say," she shoots back.

"Steph," I say, "what happened? Is everyone okay? Where's Jonah? And Elias? And—?"

"Everyone's okay," she says.

I stare at her in disbelief, remembering the surge of water barreling toward us as we hauled ourselves into the back of Silas's truck. *No way.*

"Everyone?" I ask.

"Yes," she says, but her eyes drift away to Clover for a split second. There's something she's not telling me.

"Steph, just say it. What is it? I won't be mad, promise."

What the hell would I have a right to be mad about here anyway? Mad that *I* forgot to refill the oil? Mad that *I* decided to stay an extra night in Barbazal so I could talk to Jonah Macon? Mad that *I* chose to manipulate him into believing everyone around him would think he was a failure unless he did as I said?

Holy shit, I really am a monster.

So no, I'm not mad. Whatever Steph has to tell me, I'm ready.

I nod at her, and she gives Clover one last glance for confirmation before she takes a deep breath and squeezes my hands.

"Alex," she says, unable to look at me anymore. She stares down at the folds of my hospital blanket. "We… lost the car."

It sinks in in waves.

And then in literal waves. Huge blue fabric swathes the room, malleable and evolving, cool on my face, dissolving into a fine mist around us, hard to explain and impossible to define.

"What?"

"We lost the car," she says again, louder this time, looking up at me now as I take it in. "The dam flooded the valley. Everything flooded, the whole town. We made it to Silas's truck—" she shakes her head, "—but our car… was parked too close."

The pain of losing the car hits me square in the chest, as it was new to us, and now we'll have to—*I'll* have to—buy a new one somehow. With what money, I have no idea.

And then, I realize something else. Something far more painful. My entire world shatters, and I muster two words I hope to never say again.

"My… guitar?"

Steph goes quiet, staring at the blanket again.

"Oh my god, your drum kit, Steph!"

She shuts her eyes as I say it, as if the mere words declaring it hurt her all over again.

"I knew we had to climb into Silas's truck," she says, her voice shaky. "But… I also knew what we were giving up."

She sniffs and lets the silence sink into this room.

I feel determination well up in my throat.

"Steph, maybe the venue has guitars and drums, you know? Maybe Harson has—"

"Our show was nine hours ago, Alex," she cuts in before I can dream further and inflict more pain. "We missed it. Completely. But your surgery went well, and that's all that matters. Really. They even said since the bullet missed tendons and shit. You should only need a few weeks of physical therapy."

This girl really is incredible.

I feel tears begin to well up in my eyes and my jaw stings from holding them back.

"I'm sorry, Steph," I plead for her not to be mad at me. "I'm sorry for everything. I really am—"

"Don't be," she says, pushing herself to her feet. "Really, Alex. It's okay. If a whole town gets their livelihood back, then hell yeah I'd give up my drums for that. I can't think of anything more punk rock."

"Steph," I offer one final time, my voice a squeak, "we can't just give up. Okay? I won't give up! I can't just… leave this here."

"Too late," she says, gesturing to my leg, which I now notice is elevated in a huge white cast in a sling hanging from the ceiling. "You're in post-op recovery, darlin'."

"Don't tell me you've already picked up a Barbazalian accent," I say with an eye roll.

"Barbazalese," corrects Clover.

"Really?" Steph and I ask in unison.

Clover shrugs.

"Sounds better, doesn't it?"

"No," say Steph and I.

"Y'all an old married couple and didn't tell me?" she asks with a grin. I *refuse* to look Steph in the eye in this moment, or I might blush so hard my cheeks will fly into space.

Knock-knock-knock.

I look to the door. Then I look to Steph. Then to Clover. We're all equally confused about who it could be, but just as Clover sets her phone down and begins to push herself to her feet, the door squeaks open, and in steps…

"Oh my land," Clover gasps. "Jonah? Wh-what are you—?"

He steps into the room gingerly, respectfully, nodding at me before closing the door behind him. His hair is slightly messier than usual—frizzy, like that of someone who went for a run and then spent several minutes swinging a sledgehammer over his head. But this time, instead of a sledgehammer, his hand is wrapped gently around a *huge* bouquet of flowers. Purple and gold lilies bursting with color.

Fear and joy.

Clover's eyes go huge, and she looks like she wants to run, hide, and slap Jonah all at the same time.

"Miss Chen," he says and nods at me, "How are you feeling?"

"Great," I say, and I mean it. My leg aches a little in this cast, but I'm sure they've got me so numbed up that I won't feel any *real* pain for a long time.

With the pleasantries out of the way, Clover dives into a question she's clearly been wanting to blurt out since Jonah walked in.

"What the hell are you doin' here?"

"Clover," he says, stepping forward, letting the door shut behind him and taking her hand in one of his. He pulls it up to his face and kisses it. "I'm sorry."

She rolls her eyes and yanks her hand away.

"No, really, I am."

"For the spectacle that you pulled? For the hell you raised today? For embarrassing our family the way you did?" she thunders. "You've got a lotta nerve showin' your face around here, Jonah."

She folds her arms and turns her back to him to stare out the window. She huffs out a deep sigh and shakes her head, fury flashing in her eyes. A red bloom envelops the room and freezes around everything, slowing it down to an unnatural speed, like artificially turning down the speed on a record player. It's stifling, stubborn, firmly immovable, the air thick like smoke.

"Clover," continues Jonah, "I'm sorry for *everything*. For lying to you. For keeping the truth about the dam from you. For trying to fix what I did to Barbazal by… doing what I did today."

"Yeah, speaking of," interjects Steph, "shouldn't you be, like, in jail? For destroying public property?"

Jonah clears his throat sheepishly.

"There's a squad car outside for me right now," he admits.

"Oh," says Steph, glancing at me. "Great. I mean… sorry."

"It's only fair," he smiles sadly, turning back to Clover, who hasn't moved from the window. "Anyway, I came to apologize. And I know you don't owe me forgiveness. You can hate me for the rest of your life if you want. But…" His voice is pained. Even, but pained. The aura over his head blooms bright purple. "If you'll have me…" And then, amidst mine and Steph's gasps of absolute *what-the-fuck-is-he-doings*, he lowers himself to one knee and goes fishing around in his pocket.

"Clover!" I whisper.

"What?" she fires back at me, glaring at me with fire in her eyes. I nod at Jonah, and she rolls her eyes and turns around, and the rage melts from her face. That red aura remains, but her hands fly to her mouth in shock.

"Jonah Macon, you get up from the floor right now," she whispers, shaking her head frantically.

"Clover Wisteria Biggs," he says, setting the flowers on the hospital floor next to him. Steph takes my hand in hers, and we both exchange a glance like *I don't know what to think of this but holy shit this is wild*. Jonah takes the box in his hands and pulls the lid up to reveal the shiniest diamond ring I've ever seen. It sparkles even in the fluorescent light, and I just *know* it was worth a fortune.

"I love you, Clover," he says, his voice shaky and unsure—as it *should* be, given how he lied to her about a massive scheme to send the town of their childhood's entire economy careening into a valley-wide drought in favor of appeasing Denver to keep his political platform—but he continues, "I know… I haven't been honest with you. I was so afraid to lose you. I was afraid of what you'd think if you knew."

"Well," she says, tightening her folded arms even more, "now you know."

He sighs, staring at the ground between them, and nods. "I know. And… I don't know if you can ever forgive me. But there's never been a right time to ask, with how much I've been on the road, and now that everything I've ever known is uncertain, I realize there's only one thing I do know, Clover Biggs, and that's…" He pauses, looks up at her, and I realize there are tears in his eyes. "…that I want to spend the rest of my life with you."

A long, painful silence begins, and I watch Clover's fingers tighten around her forearms, and her lips purse, and her eyes narrow.

"You tried to kill yourself earlier today, Jonah Macon," she says, "and you could've killed four hundred more. Explain that."

"I know," he offers with a hefty sigh. "I, um…" A tear falls loose and rolls down his cheek. He's still holding up the box with the ring, but he lowers it just a bit, resting it on his knee. "I thought you would be better off without me. Both of you."

His eyes dart from Clover's face to her middle, and her eyes soften at that, and when she wipes at her eyes I see she's been holding back tears too.

"We both need you, Jonah," she says, her voice softer than I've ever heard it. "But I can't be with you."

I suppress a gasp, and I feel Steph squeeze my hand silently. I feel her flinch, and I wonder who she's rooting for here. I wonder who *I'm* rooting for here. Jonah made some… decisions today, sure, but were they *all* his? If Clover knew the extent of the hand I had in this, maybe…

It turns out I don't have to worry about that.

"I can't be with you like this," she finishes, her voice rattling into weeping. "You… you need help."

"I'm going to get help," he promises, nodding. He shuffles forward on his knees, reaching out his hands to hers, taking them and kissing her fingers. "I'm *getting* help. My assistant sent me a list of therapists. I'm going to pick one tonight, make an appointment for as soon as they'll let me, and I'll be there." Clover stares down at him, pity in her eyes, silent. "And even," he continues, "even if the answer today is… no…" his voice is breaking, "I'll prove it to you. That you can be with me. That you're *safe* with me. That you can trust me. I'll do anything to get that back."

"Jonah—"

"Don't give up on me, Clover," he urges. "Please."

Clover glances at me, and then at Steph, and we both stare back blankly. The hell do I say here? A purple aura over Jonah's head. A purple aura over Clover's. I look between them, searching for words, and a single squeeze on my arm from Steph and one look into her eyes tells me everything I should've realized before.

Nothing.

That's what I say here.

This is their conversation. Clover and Jonah. They both have a lot to work through, and that work should start today.

"The answer *today*," she says with a shake of her head, "is no."

Steph and I let out twin sighs. I don't know about Steph's, but mine is of sheer relief that a decision was made here.

Jonah's shoulders fall, and his hands drop. The box gets closed and slid back into his pocket. He sniffs.

"I understand," he admits, true to his word.

"But," says Clover, "I will give you another chance, Jonah Macon. *If* you get out there on that stand and apologize for what you've done."

"Done," he says without hesitation.

"*And* take your father to at least one therapy session with you."

After a long moment, Jonah nods and sighs. "Done."

"*And,*" continues Clover.

Damn, she isn't done! How many demands can she think of to —

She nods at us.

"Charter these two a car."

"What?" asks Steph, letting go of my hand to cup her own cheeks.

"For real?" I ask, shifting my weight in the bed before remembering my leg. I wince against the pain shooting up into my hip.

"Oh, and one more thing," continues Clover. "Cover Alex's medical bill, please. Poor girl wouldn't be here this long if it weren't for your dam."

Jonah looks up at me, pushes himself to his feet, and nods, determinedly. "Send me whatever bills you receive for your surgery from Strathmaugh Good Samaritan, Alex, and I'll cover the cost. You have my word. And, I'll have Daphne send a car tonight."

Steph and I exchange a glance, at first out of sheer glee that we're finally fucking getting out of here, but then I follow Steph's gaze to the clock on the wall, which reads 6:05, and my heart sinks.

"Our show started hours ago."

"Your show?" asks Jonah.

"They're musicians," explains Clover, "*and* they lost their instruments in the flood."

Jonah looks from Clover to me, and his face turns a shade whiter.

"I'm… I'm so sorry, Alex."

"It's okay," I say, but I'm surprised by the shakiness of my own voice. *Do not cry, Alex, this isn't about you.*

"If there's anyone who deserves an apology, it's Steph," I say. Steph looks to me in surprise.

"What?"

"I'm *so* sorry about your drum kit, Steph," I say, squeezing her hand. "It was selfish of me to make you stay in Barbazal when we had a show to do. I wanted to go on tour with you, I really did, and—"

"Alex," she interrupts, leaning down and pressing her forehead against mine, giving my hand a squeeze. "I'm glad we did this."

"*Really?!*" I can't contain my confusion. "You're glad we missed the show?! What if we never meet Harson again?"

"I'm glad," interrupts Steph, "that if I was going to miss the show of a lifetime, it was to spend time with my… girlfriend… in the middle of nowhere."

I shut my eyes and breathe in, enjoying the scent of her for a moment. And a flood of gratitude overwhelms me. I want to hold her and kiss her. Tell her she's mine.

Best friend? Nah.

"Y'all must really love each other to help each other through all this," marvels Clover.

I open my eyes to find Steph staring back at me. I search her eyes for some kind of confirmation. An okay. A *yes*. She smiles. Might as well be just us two in the room, as we reply in unison, defiantly,

"*Yes.*"

We both laugh, and she throws her arms around my shoulders.

"I… I love you, Steph."

She pulls away, and her eyes are wide with awe, her cheeks red.

"For real?" she asks, her voice shaky. "I mean… like… those are *big* words, Alex."

Her hand comes up, tucks her hair behind her ear and shakes her head.

"I," she says, staring at the ground. I know how important those words are to her. I take her hands in mine, lean in, and hope my face shows just how *much* I feel this.

"I *love* you, Steph Gingrich."

She smiles, her eyes glassy, and something in my chest swells, and I feel like I could fly.

She reaches out, cups my face, and pulls me in for a kiss. I drink in the warmth of her, wanting her to know just how much I care about her, how much I want to make her smile.

"I love you too," she says once the kiss is broken. She presses her forehead against mine and shakes her head. "Best friend."

"Stop," I laugh.

"More than friends then?" she asks. But she says it like a statement. I grin, basking in how *right* this feels.

"More than friends."

She's warm against me, and I don't want this moment to end, but Jonah clears his throat.

"You mentioned a… Harson?"

"Yeah," replies Steph, pulling away to look up at him. "Bigshot producer who was going to be at the show tonight. We were supposed to play for him, but… no instruments? No car? No way to rewind time?"

"*Isaac* Harson?" asks Jonah, stepping forward. "I went to grad school with him. We go way back."

"What?!" come Steph and I's voices together.

He pulls out his phone.

"I'll give him a ring. See if he's free to talk."

He raises the phone to click through it, and I cannot believe this. All this time, Jonah and Harson have *known* each other?! What are the chances??

"Oh," he says. "Oh shit."

Clover's eyebrows knit together in concern.

"It's nothing," assures Jonah, looking at Steph and me sheepishly. "It's just… he called me eight times already."

He clears his throat and raises the phone to his ear, but he quickly yanks it away.

"Jonah Elias Macon, what the absolute fuck!!!!!"

My eyes fly open, and Steph and I exchange a glance full of stifled giggles.

"Hey, Isaac," drones Jonah. "Listen—"

"No, *you* listen!" hollers Isaac. Jonah rolls his eyes and clicks the speaker button, projecting Isaac's *loud*-ass voice through this tiny hospital room, because *might as well*. "I been tryin' to call your ass for the past twelve hours after I heard your ass was standin' on top of the Barbazal dam, what the *hell* were you thinking, coulda got yerself kilt, I never heard such a crazy-ass idea, what the hell were you doin'—"

"Mental breakdown, Isaac," cuts in Jonah. To my surprise, silence comes through the phone.

"You alright now?" asks Isaac, his voice instantly even and full of concern. He sounds like a totally different person with the single revelation that his friend needs help.

Jonah nods, then seemingly realizes that Isaac can't hear him through the phone.

"Yeah, yeah, I'm okay now, but, um... weren't you supposed to be at a show tonight?"

"How'd you—Oh the Fireworks concert?" he asks. "I couldn't make it knowing some crazy shit was going on with you and Barbazal and that dam... Jonah, what the hell were you thinking? Your daddy coulda had a heart attack out there worrying about you—"

"I know," Jonah says. "I apologized to him already."

"You... wait, you did?" asks Isaac.

"Yes. I'll explain later. Promise. But I heard two musicians were supposed to be joining you tonight?"

All I can hear in the silence in this room is the sound of my own heart thundering in my chest.

Harson sighs.

I look at Steph. Steph looks at me.

"Yes," admits Harson. "I saw a video of them playing at a festival over in Haven Springs and I knew I *had* to hear 'em in person. Tried gettin' ahold of 'em, but they went dark. When they didn't show for sound check, I figured they no-showed."

"Well," Jonah smiles, glancing up at me, "I have good news. They didn't no-show. They were late. Because they were busy saving my life."

"What?" asks Harson.

"You heard me," smiles Jonah. "Alex talked me down from that dam. Well," he corrects himself, "she *played* me down, really, 'longside Daddy's harmonica. She's... she and Steph are the reason we're speakin' again."

Harson's voice is low and awed. "Well, I'll be damned. Where are they now? So I can personally thank them?"

Jonah lowers the phone to his chest and raises his eyebrows at me to ask if I want to talk to him, and Steph and I can't nod fast enough.

The phone is unsteady in my trembling hands.

"Hello?"

"Alex? Or Steph?"

"It's Alex," I say, my voice all over the place. "Alex Chen, Mr. Harson, sir."

"You can call me Isaac. What kinda man would I be if I didn't grant you first-name basis after you saved my good friend's life?"

"Thank you," I offer, unsure of what the hell else to say. "And I'm sorry we missed the Lamplighter Festival."

"Miss, you coulda missed my wedding day and I'd be glad you did if it meant saving Jonah Macon's life. You and your friend are goddamn heroes in my book."

At the mention of that word again—*friend*—I glance up at Steph before clearing my throat and correcting what I didn't correct earlier.

"Girlfriend," I say.

"Oh!" he exclaims. "Girlfriend! Two heroes together. Love to see it."

I look up at Steph, who's smiling the biggest smile I've ever seen. It almost makes up for how she looked at me yesterday.

"Thanks, sir," I smile.

"So, Alex, would you and your *girlfriend* like to get coffee this week in Barbazal? I'll be in town in a few days and we can talk about your career in music, and maybe even get you some new instruments."

I look to Steph for approval—how could we say no to this? A chance to meet Harson in person? About our music careers? And maybe even new instruments? But Steph's face tells a different story. Her smile has fallen just a little, and her eyes wander down to the phone to avoid mine.

And then it sinks in—what's really wrong here.

"Sir?" I ask. "That's a super kind offer, but we've gotta get back on the road. I've kept Steph in Barbazal long enough."

After a long pause, and a shallow sigh from Harson, I hear the *best* thing I could've hoped to hear in a million years.

"How 'bout we rent us a tour bus and y'all can show me your talents on the road?"

I gasp, giving away how fucking *perfect* I think that would be, but if that didn't lay all our cards on the table, Steph's squeal definitely does.

"I'll take that as a yes!" he says, chuckling through the phone.

Steph reaches forward, wiggling her fingers to ask for the phone. I offer it willingly, and she grips it like her life depends on it.

"Just say you can accommodate a recovering gunshot wound victim on the road, and you've got yourself a deal, sir."

"A *gunshot wound*?!"

"It's a long story," comes my voice, Steph's, Jonah's, and even Clover's.

We all exchange glances, and I smile at Steph and mouth the words, *thank you*.

19: The Road

Turns out the bullet went straight through my calf muscle and out the other side, not even making it to the bone, so my recovery is supposed to be quick. Relatively. As quick as a gunshot wound can be, I guess. That first one in Haven Springs was a graze, so it took days.

This makes the second time inside of six months getting shot in Colorado, after living in Portland for twenty-one years. My trust issues are going to have trust issues, but at least the recovery is shorter than I thought it'd be.

I'll be on these crutches for four to six weeks, I'm told.

Good thing I can play the guitar sitting down.

I ease into the plush chair in the far corner of the bus and lean my head back.

"Water," commands Steph, thrusting a bottle at me. I roll my eyes and take it.

"Jesus Christ, Steph, I just drank a whole one."

"I'll keep refilling it until you hit your daily one hundred twenty-seven ounces. I'm keeping count, since I know you'll round down."

"Thanks, Mom," I say with an eye roll.

"How are you planning on healing those muscles if you aren't lubricated?"

"Um, ew." I wince, re-capping the bottle. "There has to be a better way to say that."

"It's the body! It's not gross."

"The body is hella gross," I argue.

Steph smirks and folds her arms across her chest in defiance, saying *try me* with her eyebrows. I breathe out, and snort in, pretending to hock up a *fat* loogie.

"Okay, okay, shit," says Steph, holding out her hands for me to stop. "Gross or not, *your* body has some repairs to do. So get to it."

She gives me a wink and turns to look at the rest of this place.

"Can you believe this is our new hotel on wheels for a while?" she asks.

"Not much more than I can believe you're my girlfriend."

Her cheeks bloom with red, and a gold aura flares above her head.

"I can't believe it either," she says, turning and picking up her drumsticks from the nearby window sill. "And I can't believe these babies are mine. Or that that baby's yours."

She turns and nods to my guitar beside me, leaning against the wall.

My heart skips.

"Steph, how did you—"

"I've got connections," she shrugs.

"What kind of connections?"

"Okay, fine, looking cool and aloof was fun while it lasted," she concedes. "It was a little banged up at the dam site, but Harson knows some repair guys out here who fixed it up for you. My idea."

I look down, pick it up, feeling its familiar weight in my hands.

"Good as new," I marvel, feeling tears spring to my eyes.

I take the strings in my fingers and begin to pluck, shutting my eyes and letting the hum of the notes seep into my skin, my bones, the whole instrument fresh under my fingers now that the head's been repaired, the strings replaced. I sink into the moment, playing away, letting the notes carry me off into a reprise of the peaches song.

I'm going to Fort Collins.

With the love of my life.

And a flashy new-ish guitar.

And Isaac Harson's eyes on my talents.

So… what's missing?

I let out a sigh, and I hear Steph's voice in the darkness.

"Oh, that reminds me," she says. "I… kinda got you something."

"Kinda?" I ask, opening my eyes to find Steph standing and rummaging through her backpack.

"Harson helped," she says, pulling out something that fits in the palm of her hand and turning back to me. "Close your eyes."

I raise an eyebrow.

"Just do it, okay?" she says and laughs. "Promise, it'll be worth it."

I do as I'm asked and hold out my hands. She places what feels like a deck of cards in my palm, and I feel their edges, all different sizes and shapes.

"Steph, what—"

"Okay, open 'em."

I look down to find… stickers?

The top one is…

"Peaches?" The logo of The Weirdest Gears is intertwined with a peach sliced in half, like a clockwork peach. It even has the little "1985" guitar logo at the bottom. I haven't seen this logo since…

"Steph," I say, my cheeks flushing hot, "did you save this from my guitar case?"

"I wish," she says, folding her arms. "That guitar case was totally gone. But *some* guy in Atlanta, Georgia, happened to be selling a Weirdest Gears sticker from their concert in 1985, so I had it overnighted."

My eyes well up, and I'm instantly back in my room, listening to "Peaches," drowning in the music while my family drowned in their own rage next door.

"Thank you, Steph," I say.

And then I remember there's more. I look through the stack. Every. Single. Sticker. Is there.

The Toils.

Gastrowhale.

Wooden Arthropods.

Questions and Her.

"Steph, how did you *find* all of these?" I ask, in total awe.

"Harson helped," she says, shrugging.

"But… you had to *remember* my case. You had to remember every single sticker on there! How did you…?"

"I kinda like you," she says and shrugs again.

I push myself to my feet, despite her protests, and throw my arms around her.

"Thank you," I croak.

She embraces me back, and then she pulls away, takes my face in hers, and leans in.

The kiss lingers, and I never want this moment to end. I want to stand here forever with her, right here in the middle of this tour bus, just outside Barbazal. I squeeze her tight, basking in the feeling of her lips against mine, and I wonder where this might lead until—

"Ahem," comes a voice from the door.

Steph and I both jump and look over to see Clover leaning against the door frame.

"Don't mean to interrupt," she says, smirking with a raised eyebrow. "Just wanted to say goodbye before y'all set off into the sunset. And also apologize for… you know… misjudging you at first."

Steph and I exchange a grin, mutually agreeing here.

"I'd say helping us escape a massive flooding incident makes up for it," says Steph. "Maybe just don't do it again."

"Deal," says Clover.

"So," continues Steph, "what's your plan, Clover?"

"Not sure yet," she sighs. "Jonah and I are stickin' together.

For now. 'Til he gets some help. We'll probably settle down in Denver for a while. Maybe I'll see y'all around. If... you know... if you wanna, like... hang out?"

"Sounds like a plan," says Steph.

Relief washes over Clover's face at that. She looks at me.

"You've been out for a while. Did you hear Maisie won the election?"

I shouldn't be this disappointed. If you're going to destroy public property with a sledgehammer while trying to win an election, I figure you know what you're throwing away.

"No, I didn't," I say, truthfully. I haven't had time to think about it. Clover shrugs, and then a laugh escapes her.

"Guess Crazy Maisie didn't end up being the crazy one after all," she continues, her smile fading to make way for a blank stare, lost deep in thought. "For the best, I guess. Jonah... he needs help."

Silence hangs in the room, because what do Steph and I say to that? She's absolutely right that Jonah needs help, but it's definitely not for the best.

I don't want to think about all the legislation that might pass, thanks to her. All the bad healthcare, all the lack of healthcare, the straight-up attacks on women's rights. Has it all been worth it to save Barbazal? I guess that's a battle we can keep fighting. I would do it all again.

Maisie is tomorrow's battle.

"So..." she continues, before she can reveal *too* much emotion, "Y'all heading straight to Fort Collins, or are you going to stop anywhere on the way?"

"Is there... *stuff* to do on the way?" I ask. I honestly have no idea what's out there, but I don't particularly care. I squeeze Steph's hand.

"Sure," shrugs Clover. "Millersborough's about an hour north of here."

"You know," I say, turning to Steph again, "Millersborough would be a great town name for a LARP."

I look up at Steph, and her smile curves to match the smile in her eyes.

"What's a LARP?" asks Clover.

Steph grins at me before turning to Clover.

"Keep hanging with us, and you'll find out!"

"I would, but I've got…" she reaches up to rest a hand over her belly, "preoccupations."

Yeah, she's right. I smile. Steph nods. Clover turns to leave. Once she's shut the door behind her, Steph and I both breathe a sigh.

"Looks like it's just us," Steph says, nudging me. "Again."

I reach over, take her hand in mine, and draw her to me. I look into her eyes, deeply, gazing at who she really is.

"I love you, Steph Gingrich," I say.

She leans in and kisses me.

When she pulls away, she presses her forehead to mine.

"I'll go anywhere with you."

"Road-trip pals for life?" I ask.

She nods.

"And all their associated benefits."

Acknowledgments

Before I got my start in game development, I dreamed of telling a Life is Strange story.

It was a pipedream to return to the world of Max, Chloe, Sean, Daniel, Alex, Steph, and Ryan, not as a player, but as a writer. And with Heatwaves, I got to do that! So first and foremost, thank you to Life is Strange fans everywhere for making this fan community as colorful and passionate as you have. Thank you for your choices, your theories, and your hottest takes. I hope I've done right by you with this next installment of the Alex and Steph saga.

Thank you Quressa and The Folio team for putting this book in great hands, and for cheering me on from page one.

To the lovely folks at Titan Books—especially my editors Daquan Cadogan, Michael Beale, and George Sandison—thank you for helping to shape this book into something beautiful. And to Andrew James and the wonderful folks at Square Enix who generously left Alex and Steph's story in my hands for awhile, thank you for your trust and your faith.

Thank you to my closest friends — Laurie Halse Anderson, Ari Bloom, Becca Boddy, Roseanne Brown, Sydney Clark, Damian DiFrancesco, Alexandra Keister, Jackie Mak, Christopher Mikkelson, Anastasia Nuñez, Aaron Oaks, Luka Quay, Eric Smith, James Stoner, Grayson Toliver, and Molly Vaughn. I love you all to bits.

Thank you to my son, my adventurer, who keeps showing me new ways to look at things. I hope to create worlds you'll enjoy playing in one day. That includes the real one.

About the Author

Brittney Morris is the bestselling author of *The Jump*, *SLAY*, *The Cost of Knowing*, and *Marvel's Spider-Man: Miles Morales - Wings of Fury*. She is an NAACP Image Award nominee, and ALA Black Caucus Youth Literary Award winner, and an Ignite Award finalist. She holds a BA in Economics from Boston University, and she lives in Philadelphia. You can find her online at AuthorBrittneyMorris.com and on Twitter and Instagram @BrittneyMMorris.

LIFE IS STRANGE
Steph's Story

ROSIEE THOR

"So, what kind of lesbian are you?"
"The kind that... likes... girls?"
"Same."

Steph Gingrich has finally run out of couches to surf. Now she's back at her dad's place in Seattle to figure out what she wants to do with the rest of her life.

Steph fills her time working at the local gamer café during the day and running RPG sessions at night, that is until Izzie whirls into Steph's existence clutching a crumpled stack of band posters. Izzie is electric: a punk, a girl who likes girls, and a hella good guitarist. Turns out the punk life is exactly what Steph needs. She loves the music, the art, and the fashion, but most of all she likes the girl. Entranced, she offers to drum for Izzie, forming the band Drugstore Makeup.

A hit in more ways than one, Drugstore Makeup compete in a battle of the bands before deciding to tour the offbeat punk venues of America. But Steph and Izzie soon find themselves on different wavelengths, unable to communicate, and needing different things.

TITANBOOKS.COM

LIFE IS STRANGE

FROM THE WORLD OF THE
LIFE IS STRANGE: TRUE COLORS **GAME**

For more fantastic fiction, author events,
exclusive excerpts, competitions, limited editions and more

VISIT OUR WEBSITE
titanbooks.com

LIKE US ON FACEBOOK
facebook.com/titanbooks

FOLLOW US ON TWITTER AND INSTAGRAM
@TitanBooks

EMAIL US
readerfeedback@titanemail.com